THE
SPANISH RELATION

THE LUKE TREMAYNE ADVENTURES

(In chronological order of the events portrayed)

1648-9	The Irish Fiasco
1650	Chesapeake Chaos
1651	The Black Thistle
1652	The Angelic Assassin
1653	The Frown of Fortune
1654-5	The Spanish Relation
1656	The Dark Corners
1657	The Garden of Deceit
1657	Lady Mary's Revenge
1657-8	Murder In the Maghreb
1658	A Queen Besieged
1659	The Dale of Despair

A LUKE TREMAYNE ADVENTURE

THE
SPANISH RELATION

MURDER IN CROMWELLIAN ENGLAND

GEOFF QUAIFE

Author ReputationPress
Creativity & Branding

Copyright © 2019 by Geoff Quaife.

All rights reserved. No part of this publication may be reproduced, distributed, or transmitted in any form or by any means, including photocopying, recording, or other electronic or mechanical methods, without the prior written permission of the publisher, except in the case of brief quotations embodied in critical reviews and certain other noncommercial uses permitted by copyright law. For permission requests, write to the publisher, addressed "Attention: Permissions Coordinator," at the address below.

Author Reputation Press LLC
45 Dan Road Suite 36
Canton MA 02021
www.authorreputationpress.com
Hotline: 1(800) 220-7660
Fax: 1(855) 752-6001

Ordering Information:
Quantity sales. Special discounts are available on quantity purchases by corporations, associations, and others. For details, contact the publisher at the address above.

Printed in the United States of America.

ISBN-13: Softcover   978-1-970081-80-0
          eBook   978-1-970081-81-7

SOME LEADING CHARACTERS

The Army
Luke Tremayne	Cromwell's Man
Roger Pennock	Tremayne's Deputy
Andrew Ford	Tremayne's sergeant
Thomas Baxter	Local military commander

The Royalists
Anthony Noakes	Murdered local squire
Nicholas Noakes	Anthony's son
Robert Noakes	Anthony's younger son
Elizabeth Noakes	Anthony's second wife
Lydia	Elizabeth and Anthony's daughter
Toby Noakes	Anthony's cousin
James Clark	Anthony's steward
Stephen Basset	Former rector, now chaplain to Anthony
Katherine Basset	His daughter
Richard Pelway, Lord Lidford	Wealthy peer

The Parliamentarians
Edward Lampard	Senior magistrate and Somerset's political boss
William Rutter	High Constable and business man
Walter Weston	Constable and large landowning Puritan
Hugh Weston	His son and lawyer
Henry Gibbs	The Puritan rector

The Village
William Pyke	Landlord of the Black Swan
Eleanor	His wife

Daniel	His son
Tamsin	His daughter and Elizabeth's maid
Mary Miller	A wench at the Black Swan
Martha Rodd	A wench at the Black Swan
Susannah Thorne	A wench at the Black Swan

Troublemakers?

Giles Yalden	Leader of Royalist clandestine militia
Thomas Hastings	Murdering thug
Amos Hogg	Religious enthusiast
Mother Sparrow	A witch
Aunty Jane	A witch
Rebecca	A young witch

1

It was late afternoon on his last day in London when there was a loud rap on the door. Colonel Luke Tremayne was preparing to spend several weeks on his family estates in Cornwall while awaiting re-assignment to active duty against Spain, hopefully in the Americas. His regiment had just been stood down after five months of garrison duty at Whitehall and Luke was delighted to relinquish responsibility for the safety of England's ruler, Oliver Cromwell. He approached the door reluctantly and found a cornet, a lieutenant of horse, from the regiment that had relieved his own standing to attention. 'Sir, my Colonel requests your presence in his quarters, now. He said that you should see this as a necessary request and not as an inappropriate demand.'

Luke sensed some sort of coded warning in his successor's hint that this was not an occasion to stand on protocol. He followed the cornet to the quarters of his successor who greeted him at the door. 'Apologies, but if you step inside you will understand.' Luke entered the chamber and immediately recognised the man standing at the window. 'My Lord Protector, I thought I had seen the last of you when I handed over to my colleague here.'

'Good heavens Tremayne at least you could have greeted me with one of the boring proverbs you were so fond of spouting, which I have not missed over the last few days.'

'Sir, a good maxim is never out of season but as I do not know the reason for this meeting I won't risk an inappropriate comment. Is this visit social or political?'

'Social as far as Whitehall is concerned. An old soldier farewelling the colonel of the retiring regiment and welcoming the commander of the new—three soldiers relaxing. In addition, the old general's health needs the brisk walk from his chambers to the army barracks.'

Cromwell's ruddy complexion was more flushed than usual and his continual pacing reflected considerable agitation.

'Gentlemen, as Lord Protector I must walk a fine line between granting maximum clemency and leniency to our former enemies while protecting my government against continued treason. God gave us victory against Royalists, Parliamentarians, republicans and dissident elements in the army but now the Lord God requires me to reconcile the nation. If I can bring these various groups together in my Council to work toward healing the nation's wounds, then I may be able to do it for the country as a whole. This does not mean that I countenance treason. Since you have been at Whitehall, Luke, I have dismissed a Parliament, cashiered several senior officers and put down a Royalist uprising. But I fear there is trouble brewing in Somerset. I want you to investigate the recent murder of Sir Anthony Noakes, a local royalist squire.'

'Why does the murder of a West Country squire concern the Lord Protector?'

'It may be central to the reconciliation of the nation, or completely unimportant. I will know the answer when you tell me who murdered him and why? But there is more.'

Luke could see that the old general was deeply concerned. Cromwell continued. 'For some months regular unauthorised dispatches from within Whitehall are taken by professional messenger to somewhere west of Taunton in Somerset. Charlton Noakes, the home of Sir Anthony, is west of Taunton.'

'Surely your household intelligence has isolated the source?'

'No, it goes through so many hands that its author within my Council is unknown. Every second Monday at dawn it is collected at the gates of Whitehall. Twice the messenger has been followed. He doesn't seem to care until he reaches Somerset. When he enters Taunton he disappears.'

Luke anticipated what was to follow, 'As I am heading to the West Country, originally to visit my relatives, but now to investigate a murder, you want me to track the messenger to his destination. Have you any idea who are involved in this enterprise?'

'No. Any faction in the Council may be responsible. They may be contacting supporters or dealing with their enemies. The destination could be the royalist Sealed Knot, the military command in Taunton or the Parliamentary magistrates who misgovern the county. I do not know whether this correspondence is a danger to me or not but with the murder of Sir Anthony Noakes I am nervous.' Luke silently recalled the axiom that much power makes many enemies as Cromwell handed him a sealed letter. 'Colonel this authorizes you in my name to take any steps that you feel necessary, and commands all jurisdictions to obey your instructions. The messenger leaves at dawn tomorrow.'

Luke dressed in civilian attire was mounted just within the entrance of Whitehall as dawn broke. He noticed, as expected, a horseman waiting patiently against a tree a little beyond the gate. Within a few minutes a young boy approached the horseman, gave him something and disappeared into the receding gloom. Just as Luke was about to follow the messenger at a discreet distance he heard his name. 'Colonel Tremayne, you are taking to heart your change of duties. I hardly recognised you in such shabby attire.'

It was the cornet of the previous day dressed in full military apparel about to undertake his turn on duty. The two men rode through the gates of Whitehall together. Without warning a continuous volley of musket fire began. Luke was deafened by the noise and choked by the smoke. Several men were firing from close quarters. He flung himself along the opposite side of the horse from the source of the shots. The flashes and the smoke temporarily blinded him. He felt warm blood coursing down his face. As his horse carried him forward the shooting continued, but it was not at him. Slowly he realised he was not harmed. The assailants had not fired on him but on the young cornet who could not have survived the concentrated fire, and whose blood and brains were scattered widely including over Luke's face. Luke quickly regained the saddle and saw he was not followed—and his quarry was still in sight. The messenger must have stopped to witness the outcome of the assault.

Luke settled in for a long journey but his peace of mind did not return. Someone knew that he was leaving at dawn on a special mission and was determined that it would not even begin. In the gloom the attackers saw a well-dressed officer leave Whitehall on schedule. The cornet had been mistaken for him. A civilian groom had been easily overlooked. But why the murderous assault? Was it to stop him following the messenger, or to prevent his investigation into the murder of Sir Anthony Noakes? And why was the Lord Protector so concerned with a parochial murder?

Neither quarry nor follower made much attempt to disguise their roles. On the third night out they reached the Golden Acorn, a small inn on the Wiltshire border with Somerset. This third day out of London had been unseasonably warm. Luke settled into a corner of the tavern and enthusiastically consumed the local brew. Luke was a hard drinking, whoring professional soldier with two political obsessions—absolute loyalty to Cromwell and the army, and hatred of Catholicism. He had seen service in Europe and Ireland as well as in England. He enlisted as a seventeen year old, some eighteen years earlier to help the Dutch fight the Spaniards and had spent five years in Ireland, experiences that confirmed his anti-Catholic prejudices and fuelled his desire for active service.

As the evening progressed he vaguely remembered seeing his quarry in deep conversation with the landlord, and later an unsolicited flagon arrived with a large breasted, big-lipped barmaid who made her intentions clear. Luke was in the mood and the two of them, and the flagon made their way to the garret, which was Luke's abode for the night. She was an active wench and after Luke and she lay exhausted on the bed he picked up the flagon and drained its contents in one swig.

Luke did not wake until the sun was well up. He quickly realized that his drink had been laced with a sleeping powder. He ran through the inn and found that his quarry had long since departed. He had been a fool. He assumed that the messenger would not take any diversionary measures until he had reached Taunton. Luke had his horse saddled and returned inside to pay the landlord. He was turning to leave when the landlord stopped him.

'Not so fast sirrah, trying to pay me with fake coins?'

Before Luke could respond two burly ruffians appeared behind him with daggers drawn while the landlord was suddenly in possession of a large butcher's knife. Luke drew his heavy cavalry sword, which was difficult to wield in the limited space of the inn's entry. Luke was holding his own until yet another of the inn's servants appeared on the scene and dispatched a small but heavy barrel into Luke's neck. He fell to the floor completely disoriented. The rogues moved in and while one cut Luke's money purse from his belt the other removed the sword from his numbed hand. He saw the landlord gesture with his thumb pointed to the ground. Luke passed out.

He awoke to a bucket of cold water thrown in his face and the fulsome breasts of his companion of the previous night swaying before his eyes as she leaned over him with genuine concern. There was no sign of the landlord or his cronies.

'Leave quickly, sir, before my master returns. I don't know where your friend has gone.'

'My friend? I have no friend here.'

'Well you were lucky sir that a complete stranger came to your aid and sent my master and workmates scurrying away from his flashing blade. He was a real gentleman with a magnificent golden cape.' Luke was perplexed. Two attempts to kill him and then a stranger saves his life. The Protector had dropped him into a web of intrigue. There was much more to this mission than Cromwell had implied.

Luke caught up to the messenger by late afternoon of the fourth day on the outskirts of Taunton. Luke was tense and concentrated on his quarry's every movement. The messenger rode straight to the cattle market where he was intermittently obscured by cattle pounds, moving cattle and excited buyers and sellers. All at once a tall person with a long black cape rode past the messenger, and the intruder and the messenger suddenly accelerated away in opposite directions.

'Zounds,' Luke muttered aloud, 'Do I follow the newcomer or the messenger?'

He followed the intruder who led him out of town in a westerly direction. Luke was most impressed with the steed of his new quarry. It was a large black Friesian, a breed that captivated him during his service in the Netherlands. He spent much time since at horse sales trying to purchase any Friesians that came on the market. He found several in Ireland but this was the first he had seen in England. Luke was determined not to repeat the experience of previous agents. He would not lose his new quarry. The Protector was right. The horseman was heading in the direction of Charlton

Noakes. Luke could see the famous Gap that provided an outlet for the river and an entry for the road, loom up ahead of him. Just before the Gap the horseman left the road and headed for a coppice.

Luke dismounted and rested behind a boulder and waited for the horseman to re-emerge. He had probably left the road to relieve himself or rest in the shade of the trees. The minutes multiplied. Luke was increasingly agitated. After half an hour Luke remounted and approached the coppice. Once among the brambles and trees vision was reasonable. After twenty minutes of searching Luke could not believe his eyes. There was no one there.

2

Luke quickly discovered what he needed to know about Charlton Noakes. It was, despite the exception of a few wealthy Puritan farmers, a Royalist village stoically awaiting the return of the King. The village supported two inns and an illegal alehouse that reflected divisions within the parish. The Three Keys was the meeting place of the more respectable farmers, the God-fearing minority of hard working labourers, and the few who had supported Parliament during the recent conflict. Visiting magistrates and respectable travellers made it their base. The Black Swan, formerly the Crown and Sceptre but prudently renamed, attracted on the one hand the struggling small farmers, the landless labourers, and criminals of varying degrees of deviancy; and on the other, those of vastly differing status who had maintained their loyalty to the King, and to their squire Sir Anthony Noakes. Four fifths of the villagers drank at the Black Swan. Vagrants, and the destitute drank at an illegal alehouse, which a poor widow had created in her hovel on the wastelands.

Will Pyke, host of the Black Swan was the village leader and determined to find the murderer of his patron under whom he had served in the War. He was very unhappy with events since the murder. He rejected outright the conclusions of the village constable, the Puritan, Walter Weston that a gang of cutthroats murdered Sir Anthony. But Will did not expect justice from men who had been the squire's political and religious enemies for four decades. Will was also concerned by the sudden increase in visitors to the village. Some were expected. The local gentry had paid their respects to the widowed Lady Elizabeth, as had the new military jurisdiction, which sent its local commander, Colonel Thomas Baxter, to express sympathy and at the same time make clear to the county elite that the army would play a major role in maintaining security and morality.

Of more interest to Will were two strangers with the bearing of regular soldiers. Both frequented his establishment. The leaner of the two stayed at the Black Swan where he befriended Will's son, Daniel. His activities during the day remained a mystery. Was he one of the cutthroats who had murdered Sir Anthony? According to Daniel he was Cuthbert Mowle, a Royalist prisoner of war recently returned from Barbados, who scraped a living together taking day labour in distant parishes. Will was not fooled. The soft hands, and white skin beneath the dirt, indicated that this man was no labourer, and had not been, at least recently, in the West Indies.

The second man, tall and well built with sparkling blue eyes, claimed he was Luke Tremayne, a recently disengaged soldier, and now a bailiff acting for a Taunton merchant who had an interest in the estate of the late Sir Anthony and that of his neighbours. Perhaps this explained the stranger's keen desire for details of the murder, and of the social and political relationships within the village. It might also explain why having taken up lodgings at the Three Keys, he spent considerable time at the Black Swan. This man openly sought information. Will was not fooled by this deception either. He noted the expensive cavalry boots that the inquisitive stranger wore and the cavalry gait of his horse and concluded that Tremayne had not been long out of the army, if at all.

The tall stranger's serenity and dignity impressed Will, as did his appetite for beer and meat. To an innkeeper Luke's enthusiasm for the local ales suggested a profitable acquaintance. Luke was a man who elicited trust. He was a great listener whose normal public pose, when he was not downing expensive ale, was to suck gently on an often unlit pipe. Will decided to cultivate the tall stranger. It didn't hurt to appear helpful to an impressive looking visitor; especially one who may be able to help Will deal with his local enemies. Luke, for his part, had quickly established that Will also enjoyed his food and drink and recalled the old Roman adage that 'to like and dislike the same things is the basis of true friendship.' More importantly Will was a font of knowledge about the village, and exerted considerable influence on its attitudes and activities. Luke knew he had impressed the landlord but realized that a Royalist village would not confide in or assist the most hated of its enemies—a Cromwellian trooper.

This realistic assessment was changed by a fatal but fortuitous incident. Luke decided to revisit the coppice to search for hidden caves or tunnels which might explain the horseman's mysterious disappearance. As he rode through the Gap beside the fast running Charlton as it plunged down into the Vale of Taunton he saw two armed horsemen attempting to rob a group of villagers returning from the market. A woman was struck to the ground and when one of her companions appeared to remonstrate he was shot. Luke accelerated and the two rogues initially happy to confront a lone horseman turned to face the intruder. Luke was soon upon them. They quickly realised that he was a professional, well versed in horsemanship and swordplay, and with a quick gesture to each other they headed off down the Taunton Road. Luke was not to be outdone. The horseman who had discharged his pistol fell behind his compatriot and Luke was soon upon him. Dislodging the fugitive from his horse with a stiff arm Luke quickly dismounted and had his pistol to the man's head. Two of the attacked villagers reached the scene and took charge of the soon heavily roped robber.

'Any of you hurt?' Luke asked as he returned to the scene of the attack.

'Yes, Goodwife Pyke was knocked to the ground when she refused to hand over her purse and finds it difficult to walk, and old Jake is dead.'

Luke put Will's wife upon his horse and led most of the grateful group back into the village. Before they reached the High Street mounted men led by Will Pyke, alerted by a passer by, met them. It was decided, after discussion with Luke, not to follow the escaped robber but they took charge of the prisoner and placed him in the pillory on the village green. Others rode out to retrieve the body of old Jake. Luke's exploits were soon all over the village and his prowess increased with the telling. Will was particularly impressed. The man had saved his wife, and his military bearing and ability confirmed Will's suspicion that this stranger was not whom he claimed to be. Will invited Luke to drink with him in his private parlour—an invitation which Luke readily accepted.

Once his pint mug was filled Luke did not waste words nor hide his inquisitive intentions. Immediately he asked Will to relate to him the circumstances of Sir Anthony's murder. Will did so and expressed his serious misgivings with the official verdict that thieves disturbed by the squire's unexpected return home had bludgeoned him to death. Luke downed most of his first pint and asked, 'What's wrong with that version of events?'

Will had his maid refill their mugs and responded with passion. 'Every puking pottle-deep pignut knew that Sir Anthony had lost everything in his support of the King. Noakes Hall provided poor pickings. Fore God, why did Sir Anthony return home so suddenly? Why was the library ransacked? Why, unless the thieves were local and recognizable, was it necessary to kill the squire? If they were local lumpish louts they would have certainly known of squire's cursed poverty, and robbery could not have been a motive. The churlish claybrained constables got it wrong.'

'Well what do you think happened, Will?'

'Zooks my friend, I know you fought for that poxy hedgeborn Parliament and I for the King. God rest his soul. The King lost and with the rise of Cromwell and the Army that dissembling traitorous Parliament has also lost. We live in changing times. Those who supported the Parliament are as unsure of the future as are we Royalists. That roguish swag bellied Lampard, who since the King's defeat has striven to replace the squire's local influence, needed some act to endear him to the Protector. His fawning foot lickers killed Sir Anthony. With his death the Noakes influence ends. Jesu, his rightful heir Nicholas is missing, believed dead and his second son, that mammering milk-livered minnow now claiming to be Sir Robert Noakes, is an ill-favoured goose. He is an untrustworthy trimmer and probably a paid agent of the Government. The Devil take him. Enough talk, lets settle down to my best ale.'

Many pints later Luke vaguely remembers asking Will to tell him about Nicholas. Will answered, 'God's mercy, man, you ask a lot. Bodikins, there is still plenty of ale and the night is young so what the harm if I tell all.'

A very relaxed Will, interrupted by several long draughts from his mug, recounted that, 'When Nicholas was nine, about a quarter of a century ago his father sent him as a page to Lord Rimington who soon after embarked as English envoy to Spain. The boy grew up at the Spanish court and revealed a clear military bent. He joined an English company within the Spanish army and fought throughout Europe in the Catholic cause. He did not return home to fight in the Civil War. Some five years ago Captain Nicholas Noakes led an assault on a Dutch city but did not return from the mission, or that is what his father wanted the world to believe. Nicholas probably came to an untimely end years ago and that it was either imprudent, or too painful, for the squire to admit it. Robert has behaved for years as if he were the heir. Who knows? I just hope for the sake of the village and the King's cause that Nicholas is alive. It will save us from his motley minded unworthy brother.'

'Will, you have been honest. I know you see through my pretence as a bailiff. You're right. I am Luke Tremayne, special envoy of the Lord Protector, sent here to investigate the murder of Sir Anthony. Despite our differences, and my initial subterfuge, I hope we can work together.'

Will was not surprised by the revelation and affirmed to himself that Luke would be an even more useful ally and together they would find squire's killer. Luke also was anxious to take advantage of the mutual goodwill.

'Will, who else should I talk to about the secrets of this village?'

'Giles Yalden,' was the slurred reply.

3

But Giles would not talk to Luke. Too much had happened in the past month, most of which he did not understand. He would pass no information to an enemy colonel.

Giles Yalden was a tall man in his mid forties whose hair retained its distinguishing auburn red. He wore it long in the Cavalier style determined to protest against the cropped hair of the Roundheads which had become prudent fashion. He leased a couple of enclosed fields a few miles up the valley of the Charlton. However Giles farmed little. He was a soldier who had joined every Royalist rising over the past decade. Alone among the villagers of Charlton Noakes, and against the advice of the squire, he had fought a month earlier in the abortive Royalist revolt led by Penruddock. Giles, while effective in avoiding arrest, did not hide his loyalties. He flaunted the sky blue coat of his old Royalist regiment whenever he could, and in the village of Charlton Noakes wore it as a badge of honour.

Giles led a band of former Royalist soldiers who faded back into normal activity for most of the year but could be rallied to carry out appropriate missions. They had lost much because they were on the losing side yet they were confident that the tide would turn. They would then return to the more prominent places in society from which they had been tumbled. When on a mission they proudly wore the semblance of a uniform—some part of their clothing or equipment was in the sky blue colours of their leader. Giles regularly acted for the Sealed Knot which co-ordinated Royalist resistance to Parliament and Protectorate. He knew that Sir Anthony and

Lady Elizabeth Noakes were the local leaders but he had met neither. He took his instructions from Will Pyke. For the moment Giles was lying low. In the aftermath of Penruddock's Rising Colonel Thomas Baxter had orders to patrol the woods and hills to seek out and eliminate Yalden's men as a dangerous Royalist militia.

Just before the death of the squire, Will and Giles were shaken by the orders from the Sealed Knot. Will informed his friend, 'God's Blood, Giles, there is a tottering toad-spotted traitor amongst our leaders. The treacherous turncoat has been tried and sentenced to death by the King. You will execute this ill nurtured inhabitant of Noakes Hall at once.'

There were tears in Will's eyes as he handed Giles the coded letter. Giles was astounded. His men had dispatched many a traitor but the prominence and the previous extreme Royalist sympathies of the designated victim disconcerted him, but he would do his duty. He met two of his men in the woods that backed on to Noakes Hall. He had decided not to reveal the specific target. They would follow Sir Anthony, his wife Elizabeth, his son Robert, his steward and his chaplain for three or four days to establish their habits, and then determine the most convenient time and place for the execution.

Giles postponed his plan when he discovered that the household was still in Devon. Before heading home he went to the Black Swan and was surprised to find a message from his nephew. Giles had moved into the valley of the Charlton because his sister, now deceased, had married James Clark, Sir Anthony's steward. The only child of this marriage, and Giles's only living relative, was a tenant of the squire, obtaining the very lease that Tom Hastings, the notorious brigand had relinquished years earlier. As a tenant, Matthew Clark had a house in the village and use of its common lands.

The death of the boy's mother, his sister Jane, continued to trouble Giles. She had been found raped and murdered in the ditch that divided the manor from the village. Parliamentary troopers were blamed and as it took place during the war no thorough investigation was ever carried out. This event heightened his hatred of Parliamentary cavalry now represented in the village by Colonel Tremayne. He had also heard the village gossip that hinted that locals might have been responsible, but for the sake of his young nephew and his own sensitivities, he had previously refused to concentrate his energies on this still painful incident.

Giles realized as he approached his nephew's house that Matthew was distressed. A glazier and carpenter were repairing damaged doors and windows. and Matthew was running towards him shouting, 'Thank God you're here.'

After mutual vigorous hugging and back slapping Matthew outlined his days of strife, 'For a week my house and person have been harassed. On Monday I found the windows shattered, the front door twisted off its hinges and great holes gouged out of the walls. I went to the Black Swan to drown my sorrows and on returning I was set upon by two men with long staves who threatened me with worse if I did not give up my lease and return to the Hall. Yesterday the excrement of the whole village was piled up against my new door. Last night a mob threw rocks at the house, shouting "out, out, out" and threatening to burn it to the ground.'

'Why? People here have known you all your life and have readily accepted you into their midst. Your father, despite being the squire's steward, is popular, and I have very many friends here.'

'I have no idea. I have farmed the land associated with the lease for years but it is only recently that I have taken possession of the house. Sir Anthony allowed old Mrs Hastings to stay here until her death and there was plenty of room for me with father up at the Hall. Perhaps her son is to blame?'

'No, the move to get you out of the house is too clever for that beef witted murderer. Hastings would just kill you. Did you recognize any of the trouble makers?'

'Yes, but it doesn't help. They were the urchins from the hovels on the wastelands. They refuse to talk. This is why I need your help.'

Giles, in addition to leading the clandestine Royalist militia unit was the enforcer of village morality. The pro-Government constable, the wealthy Walter Weston, formally administered the law at the local level. However the Royalist common folk maintained their own value system with William Pyke providing leadership, and Giles Yalden enforcement,—but Giles had little desire at this stage to bully destitute urchins from the wastelands.

'Nephew, I will stay here for the next few days and see if we can catch the perpetrators in the act. They won't leave it all to the children. Your staff wielding jackanapes will return.'

Giles spent two nights with his nephew. On the first night nothing happened. On the second night apart from four horsemen galloping through the town and the constant giggles and cries of anguish and exertion from the lovers concealed in the doorways little was heard other than the revelry from the Black Swan. This proved too much for Giles who went there leaving his nephew alone for almost two hours. He returned just after midnight and had hardly closed the door when they heard loud knocking. He grabbed for his sword but relaxed when he heard the voice of his brother in law, James Clark.

'Son, is Giles there? I need to speak to him urgently.'

'I am here James. What do you want at this ungodly hour?'

'Get dressed. I will explain as we ride. Matt you know nothing. Should you be asked, deny that I ever came here, and that your uncle ever left.'

On the way back to the Hall James Clark told Giles that the squire had been murdered. 'Unfortunately Giles that is not the end of the trouble. There are three corpses at the Hall not one. Two senior servants have also been killed—a deputy steward and Robert Noakes's personal groom. I want you to dispose of the servants. This is in the interests of the Sealed Knot. It does not want the investigation of the squire's murder to be confused by the other deaths.'

Giles completed the task for his brother-in-law and was cantering slowly back to the village, amazed at the turn of events, when he saw fire flaming into the sky above one of the houses. His nephew's roof was ablaze. The whole village appeared to have been mobilized and were passing leather buckets of water in a chain that began at the well. More effective were men up ladders quickly raking down the burning thatch. Just as the fire appeared contained there were cries of alarm from further down the High Street. Two other houses were alight. It took most of the night to contain the fires which were restricted to the easily replaceable thatch roofing. Giles was privately alarmed. A projected execution, three murders and an attempt to burn down the village. What a night! What a mess!

Giles and Matthew spent what remained of the night at the Black Swan. If Giles expected any respite he was to be disappointed. Next morning Will confronted him with what clearly troubled the menfolk of the village. Something had to be done to rescue their womenfolk from the clutches of a religious fanatic, Amos Hogg, who had elevated random sex to the level of a sacrament. The drinkers at the Black Swan wanted Giles to deal with Hogg. Giles was not amused, 'I am not going to get involved. Good God, my friend there are far more serious problems than a little religious lunacy. The women feel sorry for Amos. He is a local boy who is a little demented. They know he is not John the Baptist.'

'But Giles, that beslubbering beetle headed cocklorel is still disrupting a lot of households,' Will uttered crossly. He was convinced that the bachelor Giles did not appreciate the gravity of the situation. Giles also responded angrily, 'Fathers and husbands must control their women not us. Besides there is a greater threat to our women than Hogg. Why do so many young girls disappear without trace? Over the years one or two might be so fed up with life here that they just run off to London and are never heard of again. Three or four a year is not normal. Ever since my sister's murder I have felt there is an evil out there. Another girl went missing last week. I raised it with the old Constable who being born in the village could add to my list of potential victims. The situation seems to have started ten or so years ago.'

'Codso, what's happening to the girls?' asked Will.

'They are abducted for the bawdy houses of London or even the Americas, or they are the victims of a foul fiend who lures them away, defiles and then kills them. There is a monster out there preying on our women.'

'Jesu, let's hope not,' replied the more optimistic Will. Giles silently disagreed. Perhaps it was time to investigate his sister's rape and murder, and the fate of the village girls. But first he must execute a traitor.

4

Will, disappointed by Giles's refusal to help Luke, was even more determined to show his good faith in the mutual effort to find Sir Anthony's killer. And Luke assured Will that even though a cornet and sergeant would join him in the investigation he would still have a major role to play. 'Will, I know that you have little time for the official report that Sir Anthony was killed by brigands but given your wife's recent experience this area is overrun by such ruffians. The rogue we arrested belongs to a particularly nasty group whose leader has hated the squire for decades.'

'Yes, the gooseturds are brazen faced ruffians led by our own, villainous half faced hedge pig, Tom Hastings.'

'What a name!'

'They call themselves the Green Glove. It gives them a sense of achievement to leave a green glove at the scene of their exploits. Unfortunately the greyish green dye they used reminded people of goose turds.'

Luke suddenly became animated, 'Let's question the prisoner.'

'I'll get the Constable,' replied Will, 'I'm a deputy for detaining suspects and dealing with the drunken troublemaker but the questioning of prisoners is for the Constable alone.'

'No, the prisoner in the pillory is under my military jurisdiction and will be questioned only by the Protector's personal representative.'

'You can interrogate the ill nurtured varlet in my storage room.'

'No, I'll take our friend out to the coppice beyond the Gap, and test his courage.'

The prisoner having suffered several days of public insult and assault by various degrading potions and substances, and kept light on rations and water was at first relieved to be taken into the Black Swan. His fear grew when he realized that the landlord was the husband of the woman he had struck to the ground, and he became mute with terror when he realised the Colonel was taking him to the coppice. Luke led his prisoner, roped around the neck, out of the village followed by a jeering crowd who stopped at the Gap although Luke could still hear their raucous yahooing as he entered the coppice. He untied his prisoner and with his fists systematically beat the rogue into a whimpering, bloody mess. Luke tied the limp body to a tree and began quietly to question the gooseturd.

'Tell me what I want to know or you will die a slow and painful death. My five-year service in Ireland fighting those Papist barbarians taught me some useful techniques. Every time you give me the wrong answer I will prick your body in vital parts so that ultimately you will slowly bleed to death from countless small cuts. Did Hastings kill the squire?'

The man did not answer. Luke inserted his dagger some distance into the prisoner's wrist. Blood began to ooze over his already bruised and battered hand. Gradually after a few more refusals and subsequent discrete cuts the prisoner realized his predicament. Fear of a slow painful death overcame fear of his leader but given his parlous condition words came slowly with long pauses as he struggled to remain articulate and conscious.

'We went to kill him, but he was already dead.'

'Rubbish, tell me the full story and I might believe you.'

'We rob people near markets and great houses. A few weeks ago we were in Dorset—near the home of a wealthy royalist, Lord Lidford. A courier left Lidford House and headed in our direction. A rope attached to a tree on each side of the path, drawn up suddenly, brought down horse and rider breaking the neck of the messenger. Tom could hardly conceal his delight on reading the courier's letter. It was addressed to Sir Anthony Noakes .Tom crowed that he had intercepted a valuable letter between Royalist leaders.'

'You are a gang of cut throats. Why was Hastings so interested in politics?'

'He wasn't. It was money.'

'What did the letter say?'

'Heirlooms, Thursday night, Fourth Hour.'

'What did it mean?'

'Obvious. The Noakes family fortune was arriving somewhere the following Thursday around midnight. Tom ranted and raved that Sir Anthony was a cheating knave. Somerset's senior magistrate and politician before the civil war, Noakes claimed that during that conflict he spent his total fortune for the King. All the time it was safely hidden. Now it was being returned, and we would take it.'

'What did you do next?'

'I replaced the courier and delivered the letter to Noakes at his Devon estate while Tom and a few others followed me. On reading the letter Sir Anthony saddled his horse, quickly farewelled his wife and headed for Charlton Noakes. Tom was convinced he was heading home to collect his treasure.'

'Why was Tom so obsessed with the squire?'

'Twenty years ago he had been a tenant of the squire and betrothed to Agnes, his mother's dairymaid. Sir Anthony lusted after her, as he did with most of the village wenches, especially those who had not yet known a man. This goatish bed swerver forced her to be his servant and for almost a year he was naught with her day and night. As soon as she was with child he discharged her. She returned to the village and Tom immediately married her so that the child would be no bastard, and he could claim to be the father. Agnes died in giving birth to a girl which Sir Anthony immediately removed. Tom never saw the child.'

'That explains Hasting's hatred of Noakes but how did he become your leader?'

'After the death of Agnes he was distracted with drink and neglected his work. He became a work-shy axwaddle and tosspot. When he accused Sir Anthony of murdering his wife his neighbours concluded that he was deranged. They did nothing when the squire threw him off his land and made sure that he would never work again. He had no option but to join us. His obsessive hatred gave him the drive to become a ruthless leader.'

'So you were following Noakes to steal his treasure, and for Hastings to exact his revenge?'

'Yes.'

'What happened when you reached Charlton Noakes?'

'The squire confused Tom. Instead of going to Noakes Hall he turned into the village High Street and did not return back through the village but continued beyond the village and a mile or so on entered Winslade Wood, an extensive forest some of which formed part of his estate. Sir Anthony's decision to take such a long way home worried Tom. Why go miles out of your way when you are in a hurry to get home and receive the treasure? I suggested that maybe the exchange would be made in the woods which seemed to improve Tom's mood. This notion was immediately quashed as the squire having crossed the woods headed straight for his manor house.'

'Was he welcomed home by his servants with lanterns lit?'

'No, he headed neither for the front porch nor for the servants' entrance at the back of the house. He approached his own house as a thief.'

'Did you follow him into the house?'

'Not at first, we fell behind Tom and when we reached the house we could see no lights and did not know where Noakes or Tom had gone. After some time we found the door of the library slightly ajar and could hear Tom raging inside. We found him towering over the seated body of Sir Anthony. The identification was guesswork as the skull of the victim had been so heavily crushed that recognition was difficult. A heavy rounded object and a sharper edged instrument must have simultaneously been used to attack the head. Bits of brain and bone splattered the table. Blood continued to drain from a multitude of stab wounds. Tom was ranting and raving in such a frenzied manner we never doubted for one minute that he had finally taken his revenge.'

'But you said earlier that he did not kill the squire, did you lie?'

'No, we eventually realized that Tom's rage was, because as he said, he was twice undone. He did not kill squire, and he missed the treasure. He explained that as he followed Noakes through the library door he was hit on the head. When he regained his senses the room was empty. He had only discovered Noakes's body as we came in.'

'Don't expect me to believe such nonsense. A vicious killer who hates Sir Anthony follows him home alone, and the squire's body, brutally bashed is found by his would be killer who nevertheless claims to be innocent?'

'At first we didn't believe it either. But Tom Hastings was not pretending. Someone else killed the squire before Tom could get to him.'

Luke turned away, primed his pistol and placing it behind the left ear of his prisoner squeezed the trigger. 'That's for old Jake.'

5

Luke's proposed visit had caused disquiet among the county's ruling clique. Sir Edward Lampard was worried. He had controlled the county since 1645, having been elected to the various Parliaments along with five or six of his cronies. As the senior magistrate he represented the face of the central government to the people, and the face of the people to the central government. He was the local law. But his position was threatened. Parliament had been dissolved three months earlier and was not likely to be recalled for two years. The government had imposed military jurisdiction on his county which could undermine his authority. If the Protector proclaimed a new list of magistrates that did not include him his power would be eliminated over night. A potential threat had been removed with the timely death of his long time rival, Sir Anthony Noakes. But it was Noakes's death that provided an immediate worry.

Lampard now wished that he had been more involved personally in the inquiry but his investigating constable, Weston, was a substantial and honest man who on the evidence had reached a sensible conclusion. A gang of robbers who had been disturbed by Noakes's unexpected return home had murdered him. Yet if it was that simple why had Major General Desborough immediately demanded that he reinvestigate the murder, and within days this was countermanded by a direct order of the Lord Protector that he was to co-operate with a special envoy sent to examine the case on the Protector's behalf. He could see no reason why Cromwell would be interested in Sir Anthony. This was not a simple murder investigation.

Lampard was convinced that it was an unofficial enquiry into how the county was progressing under his stewardship, perhaps a precursor to his non-reappointment as a magistrate.

He must be careful and well prepared for Cromwell's agent.

Lampard met with the constables Walter Weston and William Rutter, and the rector, Henry Gibbs, in a back room of the Three Keys a few days before Luke arrived. To the villagers these men were flint-hearted, sanctimonious traitors. Weston was the exception and alone was acceptable. He was village constable because it was the turn of a property he owned to provide a man to that position. Although his status and wealth allowed him to name another less important person to carry out the actual duties, Weston insisted on doing it himself, as his forbears had done for over a century. Rutter, an outsider of dubious reputation, had none of the expected qualifications for a High Constable. He owed his position entirely to Lampard. Gibbs, another outsider had been imposed on the village by a parliamentary committee at Westminster after it evicted his popular predecessor, Stephen Basset.

Lampard went straight to the point. 'In a few days a special envoy from the Protector will be poking into our affairs and those of the village. Sir Anthony's death is an excuse for a bit of prying, but we must ensure that we did everything we could have done in that investigation, and if we didn't, to cover our tracks. We must also make certain that any of our past activities, which might arouse suspicion, are not uncovered. Is there anything I should know?'

Henry Gibbs, an austere, intolerant puritan responded. 'I have nothing to hide. My past is on record. For decades I have fought for a free Parliament and a united national Church in which all people follow God's way, which we clearly set out for them. I have opposed corrupt, interfering Bishops on the one hand, and the license to believe anything you like on the other. I have never supported this usurping army or its toleration of Baptists, Quakers and the likes of Amos Hogg. I will not modify the position which I enunciate each week from the pulpit just because the usurping Protector is sending a lackey amongst us.'

'Is it not true preacher that you exclude most of the village from communion, that you corrupted the last election of church warden, and that you have received from the village double the tithes collected by your predecessor?'

Lampard's allegations stunned the group except for Gibbs who responded with conviction. 'I do not admit sinners to communion. Charlton Noakes is a sinful village. I will not allow sinners to stand for office within the Church. It is better that some of the wealth of the village is directed to God's cause rather than drunk away or squandered in lechery at the Black Swan, or even worse fill the pockets of equally depraved gentry.'

Lampard silently resented Gibbs's general intolerance and his jibe at the gentry. This fanaticism could be a problem in dealing with Cromwell's man. Old Basset would have been less trouble. Coming back to reality Lampard turned to the others, 'You have all done very well in the last ten years—acreage doubled, wages reduced, and the sick, poor, and elderly moved to neighbouring parishes allowing you to abolish the poor rate, although the recent invasion of the waste lands by the needy must be addressed. As your wealth has increased, how have you treated the needy soldier? I am sure Cromwell's special envoy, a soldier, will be interested in your known lack of charity to veterans. Rutter, you have been engaged in a long dispute with the late Sir Anthony over portions of his lands and your alleged rights over them. Rumour has it that once Sir Anthony was dead, Robert Noakes, for a price would give what you wanted. An ignorant, honest soldier might think this good enough reason for murder. By heaven, your business dealings are shoddy.'

Weston was about to come to the defence of the group but Lampard cut him off. 'No explanations. Save them for Cromwell's man. But I do want to hear again your account of Sir Anthony's murder.'

Walter Weston recalled the events. 'I had been abed for several hours and was awoken by a servant sent from the Hall. He reported that his master was dead, apparently murdered. I immediately sent men to inform you and the High Constable. I summoned the watch and went to the Hall where Clark led us to the library. Sir Anthony lay across his desk with his head shattered. Clark did not know that Sir Anthony had returned and was engaged in his final check of the house before retiring. He was surprised when entering the library from the adjoining parlour to be met by a stiff breeze alerting him that the door from the library into the garden was wide open. It was then that he noticed the body of his master. With first light I returned to the Hall, noted the situation in the library, questioned Clark more fully, and reached the conclusions I sent to Rutter and yourself.'

Lampard interrupted, 'Has time for reflection led you to alter that assessment?'

'No, the evidence suggests that Sir Anthony interrupted thieves and was brutally beaten and stabbed, although there are a few unanswered questions. In the first place his sword had not been drawn. He made no attempt to defend himself— unusual for a character such as Sir Anthony. Secondly, why did he return to the house in secret? Normally he would have ridden up the main drive alerting his servants to be at the front porch to relieve him of his horse, and to welcome him home. Thirdly, why did he enter the house through the library door, which must have already been open, or was opened for him from within? It cannot be opened from the outside. If it was opened who opened it? Although it doesn't answer all the questions the 'surprised thieves' explanation seems plausible. The thieves had probably opened the library door for a quick escape. And the silent arrival of the squire took them by surprise. He saw the open door as he came home. He immediately investigated and was killed.' Lampard pressed further, 'Your assessment would have been more plausible if these thieves had stolen something. Nothing of value was missing other than so far unidentified papers. And why was the library wrecked?'

Weston replied, 'The interruption led the thieves to panic and they ransacked the library in frustration. If you frustrate the common sort they react with a violent urge to destroy. For them if you cannot take, destroy. If you succeed, destroy, if you fail, destroy.'

'Thank you Walter. Have you any questions of me?'

'Yes, who is the Lord Protector sending?'

'A Colonel Luke Tremayne. He commanded the troop of cavalry that dismissed the Parliament in January. He is a hard man from Ireland, charming but ruthless, who is very close to the Protector.'

Lampard was reasonably well pleased, regretting only the potential friction that the personality and opinions of pastor Gibbs might cause. Luke Tremayne might have doubts similar to his own, but his men had reached plausible conclusions. He felt confident that he could defend their stand, and his position. He was not so confident about his dealings with Rutter, and very recently with a stranger who wore a golden cape. For the moment he would carefully monitor Colonel Tremayne's investigation and act when he thought it necessary.

6

Luke told Will of the gooseturd's end and the innkeeper arranged for the victim's discreet burial. The next day Luke settled his newly arrived men, cornet Roger Pennock and sergeant Andrew Ford at the Three Keys. Later they met with Will at the Black Swan to plan a course of action.

Luke was a soldier. He would not move from one position until the present one was secure, or conversely, completely untenable. He would work outwards from the most plausible explanation. The evidence accumulated by the authorities pointed to the work of a gang of cutthroats and his recent interview with Jake's murderer did nothing to change his opinion.

'Andrew, with Will's assistance find out all you can about the bands of knaves that operate in this area. See if you can confirm what old Jake's killer told me. I will talk to the local military commander to put him in the picture and seek his assistance. Roger, I want you to interview the local civil authorities. We cannot ignore the rumours that this was a political assassination. I will also visit the Hall and see what the family and household can add to the picture.'

Luke was about to leave the Black Swan when Eleanor Pyke the landlord's wife approached him. 'Thank you sir for saving us. The women in the group that you helped feel we should repay your kindness. The younger ones may do this in their own way but I can help you solve squire's murder.'

'That is very kind of you Goodwife Pyke but I am sure your husband has given me all the information that I need.'

'Rubbish. Will knows nothing. He tells you all he thinks you need to know without betraying the King's cause and there are aspects of village life—women's business—of which he is totally ignorant. A village woman inspired by a religious fanatic murdered squire. I told your Colonel Baxter. Talk to him.'

'Enough woman,' Will interjected, 'The wives and wenches of this village are divided over the preaching of Amos Hogg. Some are completely obsessed by this tickle-brained cur to the detriment of many a local household; and others like my Nell think he is the Devil himself.'

Luke sent a trooper to Noakes Hall to announce that if it were convenient he would attend the family at three the following afternoon. His man returned to indicate that Sir Robert was absent and that Lady Elizabeth could not receive him until a week hence. Luke had noticed that the investigating officers had not interviewed the family at all. He did not know whether this was in respect of the delicate situation, or a realization that they would receive little co-operation from such devoted Royalists. Luke was prepared for the same lack of cooperation, which seemed already evident in their failure to meet him immediately.

Luke visited Thomas Baxter at his headquarters in Taunton that afternoon. Luke explained his mission to the local commander, presented his letter of authority and asked for Baxter's assistance. Baxter then, at Luke's request, outlined the activities of three groups that threatened civil order—the gooseturds, the blue-coated Royalist militia, and the Children of the New Dawn. Luke was most interested in the religious sect.

'Tom, the landlady of the Black Swan told you that a village woman who had become a member of this group murdered the squire.'

'She did, and I agree with her. I was about to take action when I received notification that you had been appointed to pursue this matter.'

'Is there any evidence to support Goodwife Pyke's claim?'

'I was appointed to assist the civil authorities in the Taunton area to contain civil unrest. In the short time I have been here religious fanatics have caused most trouble. The Protector's policy of toleration is a disaster. You must agree with me Luke. You served until recently in Ireland where the military command had to cashier hundreds of troops infected by this religious poison.'

'There is a major difference between soldiers who must conform to military discipline which often conflicts with their conscience, and civilians exercising the freedom that the Lord Protector has guaranteed.'

'Amos Hogg is using that freedom to destroy law and order, and the security of the state. He believes he is John the Baptist preparing the way for Christ's immediate return. His Children of the New Dawn are disruptive. They refuse to doff their hats to superiors, take oaths, or pay their taxes. They break up football matches, alehouses and church services. According to Goodwife Pyke their activities had already divided Charlton Noakes. At the Easter Day football match between the Hall and the Village three persons wearing the yellow and orange colours of the sect ran off with the ball. Teams and spectators joined in the chase that ended in the violent beating, near unto death, of the ball snatchers. If they had been outsiders and not locals they would have been killed, and I am not sure that they would have survived if one of my patrols had not happened on the scene.'

'Are these fanatics concentrated more around Charlton Noakes than in other villages?'

'Yes, Hogg has considerable support in a large town like Taunton but Charlton Noakes is the one small village where his group is very active and successful. Talk to the minister. The Sunday before you arrived they brought the church service to a premature end –admittedly for that hotbed of Royalist Anglicans a popular outcome. Three enthusiasts entered the church, refused to remove their hats and accused Parson Gibbs of deluding souls. The intruders claimed that they were God's messengers who had come to eject the devil's priest. They dragged Gibbs out of the pulpit and when officers of the church came to his aid a scuffle broke out. The minister had no option but to dismiss the congregation only a few minutes into his hour-long sermon.'

'Come on Tom there is many a sermon we ended. In the early days of the war both of us removed papist leaning clergy from the pulpit. Such activities are relatively harmless.'

'Luke, you do not appreciate the real danger of this sect. The Children of the New Dawn are prepared to assume earthly power in anticipation of their returning Lord by the selective killing of the current establishment.

To kill the local squire fits this pattern of selective assassination, and given Amos Hogg's personal history it is a likely explanation for the squire's death.'

'Hogg was a local lad who became somewhat demented?'

'Yes, and there are several direct links with the squire. Hogg, according to village gossip was an illegitimate son of Sir Anthony whom a well-paid midwife had failed to strangle at birth. Her botched attempt resulted in a deformed body and mind. As a child Hogg had dreams and delusions, often predicting calamities. His ravings were largely excused as the babble of a moonling until they became directed against Noakes. Sir Anthony had Hogg constantly in the pillory or publicly whipped behind a cart driven around the village. Most villagers thought that Sir Anthony was cruel towards the young want-wit but they gradually tired of his constant rant of doom and gloom. Hogg's earlier activities created mild disorder but after terms in the House of Correction where he was badly treated he became even more distracted. He began to depict the county's then senior magistrate as Satan himself.'

'Ten years ago your explanation of Noakes's death would have made sense but Noakes has been a nobody for a decade or more.'

'You are thinking as a sane man, but to Hogg the man who had tormented him in his youth, remained the eternal incarnation of evil. He recently preached that when Christ returned the first local casualty would be Sir Anthony. Slowly the idea of anticipating Christ's actions became central to Hogg's philosophy. He did not need to wait.'

'How does Goodwife Pyke relate all this to a village woman?'

'Hogg preaches regularly in the woods adjacent to Noakes Hall and he has made many female converts. Despite his unimposing appearance he exercises a charismatic power over his followers, especially the older women. They would do his bidding.'

'A most unlikely ladies man?'

'Yes, years of abuse and imprisonment left him hunched and crippled. He walks with a pronounced limp. He hides this unimpressive body with the vivid colours of his apparel—the brightest yellow jerkin over the most vivid orange shirt and breeches with matching yellow stockings. The colours represent the new dawn and the glorious and golden age into which he will lead God's people. His followers testify to their commitment by wearing as much yellow and orange as they can.'

'Did Goodwife Pyke name her suspect?'

'No, I only had a brief chat with her.'

Luke thanked Tom Baxter for his assistance and rode back to Charlton Noakes with three troopers that Baxter had seconded to Luke's investigation. He dropped into the Black Swan and sought out Eleanor Pyke.

'Thank you Nell for what you said earlier. You convinced Colonel Baxter that the followers of Amos Hogg are the major suspects in the squire's murder. Why do you think a village woman is involved?'

'A number of the womenfolk of this village including many of my friends, and several of the girls who work here, have foolishly fallen under Hogg's influence. His advocacy of free love and belief that women must be the equal, if not the dominant partner in a relationship is very appealing. When Will told me what you discovered from the gooseturd concerning Tom Hasting's hatred of the squire it all made sense.'

'How do you link Tom Hastings with an Amos Hogg convert in the murder of the squire?'

'Mary Miller. She's devoted to Hogg. As a teenager two decades ago she had been a younger friend to Tom Hastings and Agnes Napp. She was in love with Tom but he was besotted with Agnes. Mary never forgave Sir Anthony both for his treatment of Agnes, and for his hounding of Tom into a life of crime. The squire ruined any chance she had of replacing Agnes in Tom's affections. She started her working life as a servant at the Black Swan and has stayed here providing sexual favours to this day. She didn't marry. She hoped that Tom Hastings might return to normal society and she would be his wife. Mary saw her sexual activities as a necessary and not unpleasant supplement to her income. She has known her customers for years and helped both fathers and sons overcome their sexual problems. Despite her advancing years she remains popular, not only with her men but also with their wives and daughters. She makes anyone in her company feel important and wanted. Her religious conversion has only highlighted her generous characteristics, except with regard to Sir Anthony.'

'Has Mary said or done anything that might suggest she is the murderer?'

'She told Susannah Thorne one of the other girls that work out of the Black Swan that Satan's officers, the established gentry of England would soon be eliminated and that the death of Sir Anthony was divinely ordained. She was convinced that his assassination would simultaneously atone for her sins, avenge her friends, eliminate evil, and hasten the actual coming of the Lord.'

'Why did Susannah Thorne repeat this conversation as I gather the Hogg supporters in this village do not see you as a friend?'

'Susannah has been taken to a few of Hogg's meetings but is in no way a convert. She was a special favourite of the late squire and visited him once a month originally up at the Hall but latterly in Taunton. My husband had orders from the squire to protect young Susannah. But there is more, Colonel. Apparently Mary approached Susannah to suggest that if she were unable to fulfil her regular liaison with the squire then she, Mary, would be happy to take her place. On the top of the earlier conversation on the need to eliminate the squire Susannah thought she should tell me.'

'Thanks Nell, I will talk to Mary Miller immediately.'

7

LUKE VISITED MARY MILLER that evening, and combined business with pleasure. It had been weeks since Luke had left behind his London diversions—the youngish women at the Black Dolphin and the buxom wench at the Golden Acorn. Mary was different. She was his age—twice that of his London acquaintances. And she was no fool. She immediately challenged Luke as to his motives.

'Why does a fine upstanding man, and I can see that for myself, want to bed a mellow woman when there are the likes of Susannah Thorne available.'

'Two reasons, the males of this village tell me you are the most satisfying wench, and secondly I want to know about the village and squire's murder.'

Mary's hands were already caressing his erect member and he had begun suckling her hardening nipples. Mary surprised Luke with her sensitivity, sensuality and ability to make him feel even more lustful, and eventually, very satisfied. She was a very willing partner and clearly enjoyed the encounter unlike some of those London wantons who lay back immobile. She had the knack of being able to extend Luke's ability to perform well beyond his usual limits. This would certainly not be their last encounter. After their vigorous activity had subsided Mary held him gently by the testicles and fondled the now soft and flaccid penis.

'Mary, in your work you learn many secrets. Can you help me?'

'Why would I help you? I hated the squire. He got what he deserved. I am a friend of Tom Hastings, and I am a Child of the New Dawn.'

'Which makes you, Mary, doubly suspect. The village blames Tom Hastings for the murder; and the army command thinks it's Amos Hogg.'

'Colonel Baxter is a fool. He does not understand Amos— and that is why I will help you. Amos teaches that God's children must prepare the way for the coming of the Lord by establishing the rule of the Saints on earth through the extermination of traditional authority. He believes the Lord Protector, who grants him freedom to preach, is establishing the rule of the Saints and that the army is his weapon. If you uncover the squire's murderer you might destroy those in the establishment who if they did not commit the murder at least have condoned and concealed it. Tom and Amos would not have hesitated to kill the squire for their own good reasons but they didn't. I hate them being unjustly accused. I'll help you, so that I can help Tom and Amos, not for any sympathy with the squire.'

'You hated the squire. Was it only because of his treatment of your friend Agnes, and the exile of Tom from the village?'

'No, there was more. In his younger days the squire was calculating and ruthless in the pursuit of women. He cuckolded half the married men in the village and no young girl was safe. Agnes was one of dozens to suffer such a fate although in later life the squire made sure that the girls did not produce children-once or twice with fatal consequences.'

'The squire was a womaniser?'

'Perhaps worse. For over a decade young girls, several a year, have just disappeared from the village. Giles Yalden is very concerned about it because he thinks it might be related to the rape and murder of his sister. He has publicly raised the issue with the Constable—a man he would never talk to in normal circumstances.'

'Are you suggesting that the squire was a killer who disposed of these girls after he had abused and degraded them?'

'I don't know but the relatives of these girls tell a similar story. A wealthy gentleman promised the girls a new life. How many wealthy gentlemen would the girls of this village come across? And in several instances they were to meet their new benefactor up at the Hall.'

'This mystery man could have been any of the many visitors to the Hall over the years and not in any way related to the squire.'

Luke moved the conversation back to the murder. 'Mary, who do you think killed the squire?'

'I am reluctant to name her as she is a friend—but if it helps free Tom and Amos from suspicion then I must. You might also see my accusation as stemming from professional jealousy as Susannah is the most popular wench at the Black Swan and has powerful clients.'

'Susannah Thorne—and powerful clients?'

'Susannah visited the squire each month for the last five years. The night the squire was murdered she told me she had a very important customer late that evening.'

'We know that the squire was on the road most of that night. Your suspicions could only be proved correct if she was waiting for him at the Hall and murdered him immediately on his arrival. Why would she kill the squire?'

'Squire had strange habits. Maybe he wanted her to do things that the Lord forbids.'

Luke and Mary had struck such a rapport that Mary's gentle caressing had recreated Luke's lust and the means of satisfying it. He followed her guidance and with tongue and fingers stimulated her to the point that her violent convulsions and unrestrained screams of delight transported him to a new level of enjoyment and fulfilment.

Much later they went down stairs and enjoyed a flagon of Will's special beer. Just as Luke was leaving Mary whispered to him, 'Come back tomorrow morning. I will take you to meet with Mother Sparrow. She is the local cunning woman whom the parson is trying to discredit as a witch. She will help you.'

'Why would a local witch help a Cromwellian officer?'

'Old Jake was her husband.'

Next morning Mary led Luke past the Church and along the road that ran through Winslade Wood. At its far end was a small thatched cottage. There had clearly been a small settlement of some four or five other houses in the area but these had been levelled several years earlier.

Mary noticed Luke's interest, 'The squire demolished the settlement as it encroached on his woods but he was unwilling to alienate Mother Sparrow.'

The old woman was waiting at her door and welcomed her visitors. 'You need the old arts to find squire's killer?'

'Not your arts, old woman, but your knowledge of the village,' replied Luke.

'A Cornish lad like yourself cannot be a non-believer and from what Mary tells me you may be loyal servant of old Noll Cromwell but you are no Puritan. What do you wish to know?'

'Has anybody visited you in recent months for help to destroy the squire?'

'Colonel, that won't help you. For forty years the men of the village have visited me for spells and potions that might prevent the squire molesting their womenfolk. In fact in recent years this has declined and there have been none in the last few months. Nor have any women approached me to abort the squire's illegitimate child. This murder, despite what Mary thinks has nothing to do with squire's sexual activities.'

'Well where do you think I should be looking?'

'You should seek an answer in the two extremes—his political friends and his political enemies.'

'His enemies I can understand but why his friends?'

'This is a deeply Royalist village. Most of the menfolk belong to a secret militia led by Giles Yalden, which does the bidding of the Sealed Knot. But there has been much discontent with squire over the last six months. He stopped the locals joining Penruddock's uprising and he has spurned several leading Royalists and excluded them from whatever he and his friend Lord Lidford have been planning. Giles Yalden has been quite distressed by what he suspects as betrayal of the King's cause. As Cromwell's man this should delight you, but I imagine the Parliament and the army are also divided in these troubled times. However a day or two before the squire was murdered Giles sought my help for an old war wound. He seemed agitated and yet confident. All he said was that his suspicions regarding those up at the Hall had been proven correct and action was being taken.'

'Thank you Mother Sparrow and I am sorry that I did not arrive in time to save your husband.'

'Your swift revenge against his killer is why I will help you which despite your scepticism I will do through the traditional arts. I will place a hair or fingernail of your suspects inside a clay ball and bake them. The one that cracks open first is your killer.'

'How am I to get the hair or a fingernail of all the possible suspects?'

'You don't have to worry. Over the decades I have built up a large supply of these necessary items. Come back later this evening and I will name the murderer.'

Later that evening Luke set out on foot from the Three Keys for the old woman's cottage. As he reached the section of the road that was surrounded on both sides by Winslade Woods his years of experience alerted him. At least two men were following him from the shelter of the woods. He felt comforted that he wore his heavy cavalry sword and his ever-ready dagger and that he had taken precautions. Luke was a man of immense height and strength and the sabre wielded with ferocity was a deadly weapon. He pretended he had heard nothing and while increasing his pace he remained alert. Suddenly two men emerged from behind him wielding their cudgels. They underestimated Luke's strength as his first blow cut one cudgel in half and his second opened up a wound across the chest of the other attacker. Luke was in control when a horseman galloped up the road from the direction of the village. The assailants fled, and Luke turned to welcome his sergeant, Andrew Ford.

'Thanks Andrew, but I certainly don't think this was an attempt to kill me. Maybe it was an attempt to delay me. Ride to the cunning woman's cottage. We may be too late.'

Andrew rode towards the cottage and Luke ran as fast as he could. Luke could see the flames darting through the thatch. By the time he reached the house he saw Andrew emerged through the falling timbers dragging an unconscious women.

'Are we too late? Is she dead?'

'No sir, she has a nasty blow to the back of the head. She was knocked out, the door locked and the house set on fire. In ten minutes she would have been burnt alive. There is no sign of her coming to at this stage. What's that in her left hand?'

Luke carefully opened her clasped hand and found there some crumbled clay. In the light of the burning cottage he discerned amidst the clay a nondescript brownish hair. He turned half jokingly to Andrew. 'Well, sergeant this may be the hair of Sir Anthony's murderer. Pity it is not bright red, or silver or jet black.'

'You believe such rubbish?'

'Not in itself but it may give us some vital clues but we will have to wait until Mother Sparrow wakes up.'

Several days elapsed and although the old woman emerged from her coma she had no memory of the events surrounding the attack and the firing of her house. Luke fearful of her safety had her placed at the Black Swan where Nell Pyke and Mary Miller looked after her, while one of Luke's troopers mounted guard at her door. Luke and Will met in the latter's parlour to consider the most recent developments. Someone was fearful of what Mother Sparrow might tell Luke but was it related to squire's murder?'

8

To soften the stark reality of his military rank and status for this sensitive Royalist household Luke dressed for his formal visit to the Hall as a civilian. He wore a dark blue long sleeved slashed doublet and dark blue trunk hose that was fastened at the knee with pale blue ribbons. The padded sleeves had pale blue circlets at regular intervals. A large white lace collar covered his chest and similar lace was rolled back over the end of his sleeves. His dark blue stockings ended in shoes that were beribboned in light blue. He wore a sash of pale blue and his black felt hat was banded with light and dark blue silk all of which highlighted his deep blue eyes.

He cantered up the High Street and turned towards Noakes Hall. He saw to his left the villagers working away in the common fields. It was surprising that a wealthy village on the edge of Taunton Vale, one of the most enclosed agricultural regions of the country, still maintained this open field system where an individual's land was scattered in a number of small strips over two or three fields. He noticed as he approached the manor that its western boundary adjacent to the common fields was clearly delineated with a deep ditch and a thick hawthorn hedge along the man made ridge.

A mounted man met Luke at the gatehouse of the Hall. He introduced himself as James Clark, steward of the estate. Luke followed him along the curving driveway towards the manor house. The steward's appearance, given Luke's pedantic obsession with appropriate dress, intrigued him. Clark wore his snow-white hair long in the cavalier fashion but it was topped by a small brimmed, high crowned black hat. Clark wore a grey doublet with brownish grey breeches and black stockings held up with black ribbon. This sombre vision was alleviated by a small white lace collar whose drawstrings hung down over his chest, the hint of lace cuffs at the end of his sleeves, and a large silver buckle in the centre of his hatband.

Will had told him that James Clark succeeded his father as steward and ran the Somerset estates, and the Noakes Hall household for Sir Anthony but was a very unhappy man. Sir Anthony ignored all the advice to consolidate and save and was always quarrelling with his son Robert. The steward was caught in the middle and usually received a tongue lashing from the son after each incident. He was already seeking other employment, as he would not work for Robert whom he despised and distrusted.

Luke noted the heavy cover of trees that surrounded the northern and eastern edges of the home park, and the large kitchen and herb gardens at the side and back of the house as the road curved past these and brought him to the front of Noakes Hall. He only had a moment to glimpse the large formal gardens that stretched away from the front of the house before he dismounted, and had his horse led away by an obliging servant.

Clark took Luke into the Great Hall, an immense room with a gigantic fireplace and an equally impressive staircase. Before he had time to admire the exquisite panelled walls and intricate parquetry flooring he was ushered into a small parlour. From here he could see the detail of the formal garden with its rectangular ponds and beyond them, down a gentle slope, the many hedged fields—some grazing sheep, others with crops of young wheat or barley, and a few still fallow. In the distance he saw Charlton Mere glistening in the afternoon sun and beyond it Winslade Wood. His mind reverted to the house itself. He pondered on the opulence represented in the building and recalled its past.

Sir Anthony's great grandfather a lawyer in the reign of Henry VIII was rewarded for his services with large estates of recently confiscated church lands. Sir Anthony's grandfather and father expanded these estates, and extensive land ownership was quickly reflected in magisterial and political power. His grandfather, the formidable Sir Jasper, demolished the original abbey buildings and spent a decade in supervising the building of Noakes Hall. It was a magnificent manor house built in the late Elizabethan style, which concentrated on a long rectangle design. Sir Jasper imported honey coloured limestone from the south of the county and slate for the roof from the north. He was obsessed with light, and every room had large glassed windows.

Luke's reverie ended sharply as Clark suddenly emerged from a concealed door at the opposite end of the parlour and invited the Colonel into the inner room from which he had come. 'My Lady, will see you now.'

Luke could not believe his eyes. ''Pon my troth, Elizabeth Hanes, you look the same as you did twenty years ago. I did not imagine that you were the Lady Elizabeth of Noakes Hall.'

'Likewise Luke, you have so many relatives of the same name I only vaguely considered that you would be the monster's special envoy.'

Luke ignored the reference to his leader. He was in the presence of the girl he had lusted after as a boy. He regained his composure and offered the widowed gentlewoman his condolences. Her mourning clothes enhanced Elizabeth's appearance reflecting her beauty, wealth and dignity. On her head she wore a tight fitting black coif embroidered with the thinnest of silver thread and edged in the same manner, which accentuated the roundness of her face. She wore a black bodice embroidered in black silk and silver thread, with both her underdress and overdress of the same rich black silk and fine lines of silver, differing only in the patterns of the embroidery. A collar of black lace fell from her neck. Luke saw glimpses of her golden blonde hair protruding from under the coif. Most outstanding were her deep green eyes which were very close together, a situation that led to much teasing when she was a girl. Luke remembered the many fights he had defending Elizabeth from these taunts. She was also extremely tall for a woman—only an inch shorter than the towering Luke.

Elizabeth Hanes was the daughter of Lord Hanes, one of Cornwall's largest landowners whose home estate lay adjacent to that of the Tremayne's. As children Luke and Elizabeth had spent a lot of time together. Luke went to school on the Hanes estate and was taught with Elizabeth and others by her family's schoolmaster and chaplain. Just after he left for the Netherlands his father had written to him with the dreadful news that Lord and Lady Hanes and their three sons had all died in a dreadful fire that had consumed Hanes Manor. The only survivor was Elizabeth who had been staying with an aunt. Elizabeth Hanes as the sole heir of her father's vast estates was at that time the richest woman in England.

Elizabeth was surprised to find herself quietly excited by the handsome visitor. Although nearly twenty years had elapsed she felt a glimmer of those feelings that had led her to cry herself to sleep, night after night, when her girlhood hero, Luke Tremayne, left for the Dutch wars.

She eagerly asked, 'Where have you been all this time? The last I heard was the shocking news that when you returned from Holland you joined the Parliamentary rebels. It was a great blow to your father.'

'I am surprised Elizabeth that, given what your chaplain taught us as children that the Church of Rome was our great enemy, you did not foresee that I had no choice. I saw the atrocities that Spanish Catholics committed against our Dutch allies and then to discover that my own King was negotiating with Irish barbarians to bring a Catholic army into England was too much. I fought in the civil wars up and down England and then spent over five years in Ireland until I was summoned to protect Oliver Cromwell about six months ago. My term as garrison commander had just finished when I was ordered here.'

Distracted by Elizabeth's outstanding appearance he uttered softly and with immediate embarrassment, 'Beauty is so eloquent.'

'Luke, you surely don't still collect proverbs as we were encouraged to do as children?'

'Time passes away but sayings remain. Now, what have you done since we last met?'

'After the family died my guardians, given the great wealth I inherited, were determined to marry me off as soon as possible. There was some danger that I might become a ward of the King and find myself betrothed to some foppish courtier whom His Majesty could not afford to support. My guardians quickly arranged my marriage to Anthony, a man who had just lost his wife and who was the most powerful figure in Somerset. His power and my wealth were seen as strengthening a legitimate family dynasty. Prudently my father left very precise instructions and my marriage agreement reserved for me considerable rights, which I fear will affect the immediate future, if they have not already done so.'

This last comment led Luke to focus on his mission.

'Elizabeth did anything happen on the last day of your husband's life that might be relevant?'

'The only event of that day was the arrival of a courier from Lord Lidford after which Anthony told me he would return home immediately and not wait until the next morning.'

'Was this behaviour unusual?'

'No, the West Country Royalists have been a little more active in recent times including Anthony. They refused, however, to join that silly uprising of Penruddock, which has brought the army down upon us. In the last four months Anthony saw more of his friends and acquaintances than for the previous five years. Never a day passed without a visitor, or Anthony visiting friends or going to distant Fairs. It was not unusual lately for him to suddenly ride off in the middle of the night, or to receive visitors after dark in the library, alone and in secret. Sometimes he told me who they were, other times he did not. Consequently his last sudden return home and the finding of his body in the library conform to this pattern.'

Luke was well aware that the government was concerned by the reports of greater activity among the Royalist gentry of the Western counties. This was why Cromwell appointed his most senior officer as Major General for the whole region and why he, in turn, had sent Baxter, an expert at maintaining internal order through a blend of charm and coercion to the area around Taunton. Sir Anthony was believed to be the focus or even the instigator of much of that activity.

Luke wanted to press Elizabeth further regarding Anthony's activities and the names of his nocturnal visitors. However he sensed her loyalty to her husband, and her acceptance of his to Cromwell, would silence her on vital points. So he changed his approach.

9

'Elizabeth, my information at the moment points the finger at brigands or religious extremists. Would you agree?'

'No, Anthony was murdered on orders of the Protector, or at least people close to him and I suspect that your mission, whether you know it or not, is to cover up that truth. Cromwell overreacted to Penruddock's rising. A minor riot easily suppressed by local gentry, most of whom were Royalists, led him to impose military government on us, which I now hear is to be extended across the country. Recent activity by Anthony and friends probably panicked the Government. Their agents have infiltrated our circles and no one knows what lies they feed to your leader.'

Luke winced, but Elizabeth continued. 'If Cromwell did not order my husband's death that viperous upstart Lampard may have acted on his own. Lampard feared that when the tide turned Anthony would have him executed. Maybe Lampard mentioned his fears to his lackeys—lackeys who would kill in order to ingratiate themselves with their master. How can you serve such people Luke?'

Luke did not answer, but the question was rhetorical. Elizabeth was enjoying the situation but she suddenly changed direction. 'If Anthony was not killed by his political enemies then you may need to look to this household.'

Luke was taken aback by this change of direction and immediately feared he was being led by the nose but he played along. 'Who do you suspect?'

'My stepson Robert. In recent years he and his father were estranged. Robert had an eye to his inheritance and totally disapproved of his father going increasingly into debt. I discovered from my maid Tamsin Pyke that it was common gossip in her father's inn that Robert had done a deal with that crook back cur Rutter to sell him much of this estate, and threaten the very existence of the village. Given Rutter's record the tenants would lose their land. Robert would move to Devon or Cornwall. He was becoming increasingly desperate because Anthony continued to mortgage more of the property. Rutter would have to pay off the creditors and then find the sale price. Either Rutter had to find more, or Robert would receive a lot less. Both had motives to remove Anthony.'

'Enough to murder one's own father?'

'Who knows, but it gets worse for Robert. My marriage settlement gave Anthony the use of the Hanes estates while he and I remained husband and wife. On his death these do not devolve to his heir but revert to me, and if I should predecease him to our daughter Lydia, not to his sons. To my knowledge Robert did not know of this arrangement. Robert is left with some of the original Noakes land—one third remains with me as Anthony's widow. Robert's residual inheritance is heavily mortgaged and much of it already promised to Rutter. Actually Robert will have access to a tenth of the land that was available to Anthony. Maybe Robert discovered this and was so furious with his father that he struck him in a fit of rage. Or his friend Rutter may have been driven to get his hands on the lands promised him before Anthony increased their level of indebtedness. I hope Robert is innocent, but you must get to the bottom of his dealings with Rutter.'

'So, you revert to being one of the richest women in England; and Sir Robert is reduced to a debt ridden almost landless gentleman. But is Robert even the rightful heir. What about Nicholas?'

'I never met him. He went to Spain a decade before I married Anthony. He wrote regularly to his father but after our marriage any communication Anthony may have had he kept to himself. Something went amiss five or six years ago. He would not tell me what happened but by the way Robert behaved from that time on he clearly saw himself as the heir. At the time I spoke to Dr Basset believing that Nicholas had been killed, and that maybe this was too difficult for my husband to acknowledge. Stephen Basset raised the possibility that Nicholas had become a Catholic, even a priest. There was no way a Spanish educated Catholic priest would inherit the estates of Sir Anthony Noakes whose grandfather had been such a hero against the Spanish Armada. When I put this to Anthony he did not answer.'

Luke thought it prudent to cease the interrogation and ended proceedings with a rather lame and hollow protestation to Elizabeth that he would find her husband's murderer. As Luke left the Hall Elizabeth felt she had treated him a little unkindly by her constant denigration of Oliver Cromwell. Perhaps she had overplayed her hand both in the attacks on his leader and in trying to cast suspicion on Robert. Next time she would be more diplomatic but it had been very easy to fall back into the habit of her teens and tease that strong and handsome Luke Tremayne. Would she revert to other attitudes of that period? She was decidedly restless.

Luke on his departure was in a very good mood. To rediscover his schoolboy sweetheart created a warm and sensual feeling. He was stirred.

Sadly the mood did not last. On reflection it was replaced by the unpalatable fear that Elizabeth was lying. Fair without, false within. She certainly had not told him all she knew. She might be a major player, if not in the murder at least in what increasingly appeared to be a Royalist conspiracy. She was also too keen to cast suspicion on her stepson. Luke knew nothing of the mature Elizabeth or how the loss of her family may have affected her personality. He must not allow the past, and the ease with which it had just flooded the present, to cloud his judgment.

Elizabeth had given him no useful information. He already knew that the West Country Royalists were unusually active but his superiors did not expect a Royalist uprising. Almost to a man the Royalists had refused to rise a few weeks earlier when the opportunities and chances of success were so much better than the present. Something else was afoot. To discover what Sir Anthony had been up to in the months before his death would complete a major part of the puzzle. His recent activity might provide a clue to his murder.

The secret rendezvous after dark in his library was a habit, which was known to many. This knowledge may have been used to attract, and then murder the squire. Perhaps he was the victim of Royalist infighting. His suspected role in keeping the local gentry out of Penruddock's rising may have provoked some extremist to assassinate him. This may explain why

Elizabeth tried to direct attention away from her Royalist friends toward Parliamentary supporters like Lampard and neutrals such as Robert.

Nevertheless there could be a grain of truth in Elizabeth's suspicion that the assassination was the work of government agents. Cromwell's decision to send him on this mission had disconcerted him from the start. Was he a scapegoat sent to cover up government involvement in the murder? No, he trusted the General. However government agencies were more than tainted with corruption. He wondered how Cornet Pennock's enquiries in that area were progressing.

10

Roger was ordered to probe the activities and interests of Lampard, Rutter, Weston and the other Parliamentarians who governed the county. He tried to put himself into their situation. One of them may have been forced to take direct action after years of hatred and conflict with a defeated enemy who would not lie down, yet at the same time did not commit any acts of sedition that would have enabled his legal removal. Sir Anthony who had been squire for forty years was one of the privileged Royalist leaders who surrendered in battle and his capitulation articles preserved all his rights, provided he did not again bear arms against the victors. He had scrupulously adhered to these conditions, a reason many advanced for his refusal to join Penruddock's rising.

Roger was a Cornishman of slight build with a sun burnt olive complexion and dark brown fiery eyes. In civilian apparel he wore the black and dark grey colours expected of the son of a reforming parson and his hair was cropped. The only concession to not being his father was the bright red band around a high brow, small brim dark grey hat. He looked fifteen rather than twenty-five. He was naïve and inexperienced. His mannerisms were decidedly feminine—the source of many a bawdy jibe from his fellow soldiers. He was a boy amongst men and completely unsuited to the military environment. He lacked confidence and immediately convinced himself that he lacked the status to interview most of the county leadership.

But he would visit the local minister, Henry Gibbs, a conservative reforming cleric who wanted to impose a Presbyterian system on the English church. There would be no toleration, and the church would be run by a combination of lay elders and the clergy. Gibbs resented the Episcopal structure of the English Church and rejoiced in the removal of the Bishops. He despaired of the church under the Protectorate. It embodied the three great evils of the time. The local gentry rather than the clergy determined appointments and took much of the tithe. The state tolerated divergent views when there was clearly only one truth. And the community had little time for God's ways. Gibbs's life was shaped in opposition to the great forces of the day, the landowning gentry, the great majority of Christians who did not conform to his limited view of the truth, and the bulk of the population who were more concerned with surviving this life than preparing for the next.

Roger's father held similar views to Gibbs. They were acquainted in their mutual advocacy of the Presbyterian cause. Roger therefore introduced himself quite deliberately as the son of the Reverend Theophilus Pennock. This pedantic salutation stopped Gibbs. He was about to pre-empt Roger's inquiries by denouncing the sins of the world and of the current regime to its military representative. Yet here was a soldier who might have views similar to his own. He allowed his visitor to make the running.

'Sir, you have a reputation for telling the truth despite its consequences. Two decades ago you were imprisoned under Archbishop Laud, and now the new military command is unhappy with your views. But I am not here to judge but to ask you a simple question. Why was Sir Anthony murdered?'

'Cornet, this village sees me as part of the Government but I stopped endorsing any government following the King's execution. I despised Charles but monarchy is ordained by God and cannot be removed by man. All the experiments since have been a disaster but I remain in this position because I am doing God's work, and the return of the Royalists would bring back the Bishops—an even greater evil. By default I support the current local leadership who are genuine supporters of the Parliament, although they only pay lip service to the Protector. He needs them unless he increases the army presence in the county. This he may be doing, to the great alarm of Lampard and his friends but I agree with them that Parliament must control the army and not the reverse.

Forgive this longwinded response to your question but I do not wish to be seen as betraying my colleagues and becoming an informant to my enemies. But the Government's representatives in this county apart from the

Westons do not reflect God's ways. I work with them, but I despise them. They have risen to the top because most of the gentry of this county are Royalists, and as such are debarred from office. We have ungodly villains in positions of power.'

Roger found comfort in the honesty of the man that sat opposite him and was now relaxed enough to notice the minister's appearance. Gibbs was of medium build and very thin— both in general physique and facial structure. He wore a long black coat that distinguished clergymen of his ilk, and a close fitting black cap. A small white lace collar and miniscule cuffs were the only adornments visible. Henry Gibbs looked every part the theologian and scholar. He had little understanding of the pastoral role and no time for sinners. He would never have understood one of Luke's maxims that a house-going parson makes a church-going people. His ideal task was to assist saints such as Walter Weston come closer to God. He had no rapport with the ordinary villagers of Charlton Noakes.

Gibbs finally addressed the question. 'The murder was political, and Cromwell had the right instinct in sending you down here to unravel the behaviour of his godless supporters. Since parliament was dismissed and the Protector has made it known that he would promulgate a new list of magistrates Sir Edward Lampard has been very tense. He called a meeting a week or so ago to ensure that his men had their story clear regarding this investigation. The local constable, Walter Weston, is an honest godly fellow. I would believe whatever he told you. His son, Hugh who was one of you until about five years ago can also be relied upon. On the other hand Sir Edward Lampard and William Rutter would stop at nothing to maintain influence with the government and protect their positions. They would remove any one who stood in their way.'

'Are you suggesting that Lampard and Rutter know more about the murder than the official statements reveal?'

'With Lampard I have nothing more to go on than his long hatred of Sir Anthony. Since I came to this parish Lampard has taken every opportunity to harass and humiliate Sir Anthony, although in the months before his death this was not as evident. Despite a decade of such treatment Sir Anthony defiantly survived, and in recent times reactivated the local Royalist gentry, a potential threat to Sir Edward's control of the county. I would not be surprised to discover that "Nodding Ned" Lampard wrote to the Protector claiming to have uncovered a Royalist plot led by Sir Anthony, whose subsequent death resulted from one of Lampard's minions.'

'Are there other plausible explanations?'

'There could be a more personal motive behind the murder, which implicates William Rutter and Robert Noakes—a lust for property. The Westons are appalled at the business activities of these two. Also at a recent meeting with Sir Edward, William Rutter did not reveal the total truth. Weston reported accurately on the investigation that he undertook. Rutter failed to mention that on the night of the murder he also visited the murder scene and according to Clark who thought I should know, spent considerable time in rummaging through the papers scattered around the library. When I raised the matter with Rutter he dismissed it as part of his duty as High Constable but that he had not wished to upset Weston's feelings by appearing to check on his activities. He did not think it was relevant to inform Lampard, as his conclusions were the same as Weston's. Whatever arrangements Robert Noakes had with Rutter involved the transfer of land, land that Sir Anthony refused to sell, but which I have heard subsequently was very heavily mortgaged. Yet again these parts are lawless and Sir Anthony may have fallen victim to a gang of cutthroats, but if he was, they were not local. It was well known that Sir Anthony had no valuables at Noakes Hall.'

'Thank you parson, you have been a great help.'

'Young man, what I have told you I know to be true. There are other rumours circulating through the village that if true, which I doubt, might have some bearing on your investigation and may negate some of what I have just said.'

'The noise of the parish sometimes contains much truth as those old ecclesiastical courts often proved.'

'And much falsehood as well,' muttered the former victim of such courts.

Roger cursed himself for being insensitive by referring to an institution that had imprisoned Henry Gibbs for his stand against the Bishops, based on the gossip of his parishioners. He need not have feared that this indiscretion would bring the conversation to a close. Gibbs was anxious to relay the gossip.

'The first rumour concerns the bacon brained Amos Hogg. Sir Anthony mistreated Amos. This persecution created the feeble mind that now so easily spews out blasphemy. His parents, God-fearing people, have harboured resentment against the late squire for decades. Goodman Hogg is a member of that illicit royalist militia that is well represented in this village. He could have used the activities of that organization to cover an act of personal revenge. On the other hand one of Hogg's deluded followers out to destroy established society may have struck the blow.'

Gibbs continued. 'The second rumour concerns a distant cousin of Sir Anthony, Sir Tobias Noakes, who lives on an isolated estate on Exmoor and is widely believed to be a key member of a ring smuggling goods from the Americas, Wales and Ireland. This contraband is unloaded on the isolated beachheads of the Bristol Channel and stored on Tobias's farm, and from there distributed to the more settled areas of the county. The illegal import of Irish cattle was Tobias's specialty. He often visited Sir Anthony, and many Irish cattle have found their way onto local estates. If Sir Anthony was part of this group and fell out with members of the gang, retribution would be swift. Smugglers are an unforgiving group. But there is no evidence that Anthony was part of such a gang. However when Sir Anthony was the dominant magistrate no prosecutions were ever launched against Toby. Wilder stories see Noakes Hall as a network of secret rooms and tunnels stuffed full of contraband. This, if believed, might have attracted cutthroats and brigands.'

'Are you suggesting that the official explanation of the murder may be valid?'

'Yes, if a gang of knaves believed these rumours they may have invaded the Hall in the absence of the squire to search for secret tunnels and their hidden treasure, and on being disturbed, killed the squire.'

Roger was pleasantly surprised at the information the preacher had given him. The land deals of Noakes and Rutter and the high politics of Lampard demanded immediate investigation. The other stories might only be malicious gossip but they could give credence to aspects of the official verdict—brigands looking for hidden treasure. If Colonel Tremayne were here he would probably see an explanation of these rumours in the axiom that much power makes many enemies and then immediately counter it with the view that when out of office, out of danger. The latter had not proved true for Sir Anthony.

11

NEXT MORNING THE SOLDIERS were at the Three Keys in the upper room that had become their headquarters. The church bells had just stopped summoning the workers from the fields for a Puritan version of prayers for a successful harvest. Roger winced as he anticipated Gibbs's tirade against sin and imagined the congregation preferring the traditional homilies on the fruitfulness of God and His bountiful rewards.

With the bells silenced Luke and Roger pooled their information. They were almost immediately interrupted by the sound of a galloping horse. Luke looked out of the window. The horseman stopped outside the inn and asked the whereabouts of the Colonel who was investigating the squire's murder.

Luke went down the stairs to meet him.

'Colonel, I have come from the Hall. Lady Elizabeth has been shot.'

Luke felt sick. 'Is she badly hurt?'

'I do not know but she was well enough to send me here, and ask for your urgent attendance on her.'

Luke raised his whole unit and ordered them fully armed. He had no idea where the would-be murderers were. They might try again—at any time.

The soldiers quickly donned their mustard coloured leather coats and pulled on long cavalry boots. Over the coats they affixed black metal breast and back plates. They checked their baldrics to ensure that sword, containers of powder, and snap sack were firmly attached and slung carbines across their saddle. Over close fitting knitted Monmouth caps they finally adjusted their pot helmets with their protective brims at the front and tails at the back.

They wore brightly coloured sashes around their waists in the distinguishing colours of their regiment—red for Luke's officers and dark green for the troopers seconded from Baxter. The colonel was dressed like his men except for a soft black felt hat displaying the bright red hatband of the regiment into which a swirl of red and white feathers had been inserted and instead of a trooper's carbine Luke carried a pistol. Lady Elizabeth's courier rode on to inform the civil authorities. The soldiers galloped to the Hall.

Two hours earlier Lady Elizabeth began the early morning ride that took her around the perimeter of the estate, and through the considerable stretch of Winslade Wood that fell within the manor. For years she had taken the same route. From the edge of the forest she used the track that eventually would lead to the Devon Road. She turned left at the manorial boundary and progressed north alongside the ditch that marked this border until she came to the shores of Charlton Mere. She followed its southern edge until she reached the Manor stream and then cantered along its bank back to the Hall. Every villager knew Lady Elizabeth's routine. They also knew that this strong-minded woman always rode alone. It was her period of solitude before she joined the noisy and busy world of family, household and the wider world.

This time of solitude helped her cope with her problems, some of which had been intensely personal. Anthony had gone through years of depression. He drank too heavily and his personality lost its generosity. Given his condition Elizabeth had taken over much of the politicking although to the outside world she ensured that Anthony appeared the active agent. In reality he had regained some of his old political energy and even acumen in the last few months in support of a project she had sponsored, a project that brought her closer to her cousins—powerful figures both in England and abroad at the King's court.

The spark had long gone out of their marriage although Anthony continued to treat her appropriately. Her decision to cease conjugal relations with him five years earlier had not helped. Despite their differences in age their marriage for the first ten years had been very satisfying, both emotionally and sexually.

Anthony had a string of sexual liaisons with women of the village but this was almost a requirement of men of his status. His serious involvement with several gentlewomen was less acceptable. He was an adulterer and a womaniser. It did not affect their relationship until his constant womanising infected him with the pox. From that time on there had been no sex between them. Anthony firmly held to the traditional view that men could not transmit venereal disease. Women were the creators and transmitters of the pox, and men the innocent victims. Elizabeth insisted on a common sense approach advocated by a few foreign experts that men did transmit such diseases. Anthony eventually accepted his wife's view and the decline in his sexual dalliances might have been due to this as much as to his advancing years. Nevertheless Sir Anthony continued a regular dalliance with his favourite, Susannah Thorne, until a week or so before his death.

Elizabeth's long abstinence might explain her surprisingly carnal feelings towards Luke. Despite occasional flirtations, the deeper private longings due to the cessation of sexual activity went unfulfilled. A married woman of her class could find no socially acceptable release. She mused on the pleasurable possibilities of her new position as a widow but realized her exalted position would deny her the freedoms enjoyed by those of lesser status. Completely lost in a sensual reverie she did not hear the shot but she felt a hot searing pain as something cut across her forehead. Blood gushed down her face. She slumped against her horse, which galloped off uncontrolled through the forest. When she came to she was on the forest floor. Her head ached and when she tried to stand up she felt faint. Fortunately she failed to rise. She suddenly became aware of the sound of many feet not far away. Not quite realizing what happened to her, and initially thinking that a stray bullet from some poachers had accidentally hit her she was about to shout out to her potential rescuers. Then she heard the chilling comment. 'Are you sure you got her?'

'Yes, right between the eyes', another more distant voice answered.

Elizabeth felt even worse. Someone had tried to kill her. She passed out again.

An hour later she regained consciousness and dragged herself slowly and with great trepidation to the edge of the forest. Fortunately she was seen by one of her tenants who was repairing a hedge and the alarm was raised. Taken back to the Hall she told Clark untruthfully, that she had been accidentally shot by unknown hunters, and subsequently thrown from her horse. He immediately sent to Taunton for the doctor and summoned Nell Pyke, the innkeeper's wife who dabbled in the healing arts to come to the Manor and to bring Mother Sparrow with her. Clark took steps to inform the authorities and organized a search for the delinquents. Elizabeth insisted that Luke should be the first to be advised and requested he attend her immediately.

Luke was admitted to the great hall and followed a servant up the large impressive staircase. He was met by Tamsin Pyke, Elizabeth's personal maid, and ushered into the bedroom. Elizabeth ordered the four or five servants that were fussing about her to the far end of her rather large bedchamber although Nell Pyke and Mother Sparrow ignored her and continued throughout her conversation with Luke to administer their herbal ointments.

She could not hold back her emotions as befitted a woman of her status and amidst a flood of tears and violent shaking she hysterically screamed, 'They tried to kill me, Luke. They tried to kill me.'

After she regained her composure she recounted her story during which time Luke gently held her hand. He was pleasantly surprised at the intensity with which she squeezed his in response. She dozed in and out of consciousness, and then slept for several hours. All the servants except Tamsin withdrew but Luke did not leave Elizabeth's side. As she awoke she gave Luke a big smile and once again took his hand. She then began to tell him some of the intimate secrets of her more recent life; as if she was still in the fantasy world she had drifted into just before she was shot. She sat up in bed and drew Luke to her and kissed him gently on the lips. Momentarily the warmth of the emotion overcame Luke but he realistically put her increasing sensuality down to the cocktail of medication given to her by the doctor and the women. As was her place Tamsin kept her head bowed throughout but quietly smiled to herself in witnessing a side of her mistress she had never seen.

They were jolted back into the real world by the sound of a heavy coach and countless horsemen galloping up the drive. Luke looked alarmed. Was this another attack on Elizabeth? She had risen slightly in her bed and could see the drive from her window and visibly relaxed. 'It is a friend, Luke. The coach belongs to Richard, Lord Lidford; but why has he brought so many retainers, and why has he come here at all?'

Elizabeth stopped herself. Richard, Anthony and she had been in constant contact and met regularly, but they did it through discreet channels, never with an ostentatious display of status or power. Something was seriously amiss.

12

Luke bounded down the stairs and raced across the great hall to the front porch where his men were assembled. Lord Lidford alighted from the coach and made to enter the Hall. Luke blocked his path. Lidford exploded.

'Stand aside, I am Richard Pelway, Lord Lidford, and I must see Lady Elizabeth immediately. Is the Hall under military occupation?'

Lord Lidford was the youngest son of a Duke. His eldest brother inherited his father's title and all the lands that went with it. The young Pelway however made a fortune in London property and was titled in his own right by Charles I for his generosity in giving land to the Crown. During the War he raised and financed his own regiment of horse that remained undefeated until it confronted Cromwell's own cavalry. Lord Lidford surrendered on the battlefield and received very generous terms in his articles of capitulation from Cromwell, who had considerable admiration for this fellow cavalry commander.

Lidford was a powerful figure. By birth he was connected with the high aristocracy, both those that remained in England and those that had fled abroad. He retained his mercantile interests and connections in London, both of which continued to prosper. He was a man with an immense network and considerable wealth. He was now well into his fifties and had been a widower for almost twenty years. He was of slight build and with an olive skin that he inherited from his Spanish born mother.

He was the very picture of aristocratic opulence and elegance. He wore a heavily padded brocade doublet in dark green with the slashes worked in gold and revealing an apricot lining. His cuffs were of the most intricately worked white lace. His Venetian breeches were of the same matching green. He wore a dark green three quarter cape that just revealed a large white lace collar that covered most of his chest. His wide brimmed, moderately crowned soft black felt hat was almost hidden by the mass of dark green feathers. When Lidford gave a command people reacted. Even Luke found himself quickly responding to the aristocrat's question.

'No, my lord. We are not occupying the Hall. We are here to protect Lady Elizabeth. There was an attempt on her life this morning.'

'Jesu, is she badly hurt? I knew it. We are all in great danger.'

Luke introduced himself as he escorted Lord Lidford to see Elizabeth. The peer clearly knew all about the colonel's activities. At the door of the bedroom Lidford asked Luke if he could have a few minutes alone with Elizabeth. He explained that if Elizabeth agreed to his suggestions they could shed light on aspects of his investigation. Tamsin admitted Lidford to the bedchamber. Luke stationed a trooper outside the door and returned down the stairs through the great hall and into the small chamber where he had waited for Elizabeth only the day before.

After some time Tamsin told him that Lord Lidford and Lady Elizabeth were ready to receive him. When Luke entered the room Lidford spoke.

'Colonel, I will not reveal the secrets of my friends but I can inform you of some activities with which the Protector would be pleased. Elizabeth tells me that you are aware, although you could never prove it, that Anthony and I co-ordinated the activities of the Sealed Knot in Somerset and Dorset respectively. I came here today heavily armed and in haste to warn Elizabeth that there is a plot to wipe out the leadership of the Sealed Knot. Anthony was the first victim, then a week or so ago my coach was ambushed and all those on board killed by sustained musket fire. Unexpectedly I was not aboard and my nephew, who had taken my place, was murdered along with the servants. Hence my large escort today. I did not relate it to the Knot or to Sir Anthony's death until this morning when I heard that Sir Thomas Odam, our leader in Devon was shot dead while hunting. At the very time Odam was killed his manor house was ransacked. Two nights ago my servants disturbed several persons attempting to break into my study.'

'My lord, this is very alarming news but why should the Lord General be pleased to hear it? I am sure he is not behind such a campaign of political assassination.'

'I do not know who is behind it but I know why and this would explain the Protector's interest in Sir Anthony's death, and the ransacking of three houses.'

Elizabeth confessed, 'Anthony, Richard and Sir Thomas Odam have spent the last three months developing an united front among the royalists of the Western counties to deal with the government of the Protector. He has the armed power to implement his will and attacks on his Government simply bring even greater hardships upon us. The Protector, unlike his Parliamentary predecessors, and some of his current supporters, is meticulous in adhering to the treaties of capitulation and thereby protecting our property and position. The King is in no position to help any one. For the time being we accept the Government of the Protector as the best option available, and will oppose any Royalist attempts to unseat him at this time as counter productive. Anthony informed the Protector that this was the intention of the Sealed Knot. This is probably why his death provoked Cromwell to send you here.'

'All this seems plausible, but what are the murderers still looking for?'

Elizabeth looked intently at Richard who replied, 'The gentry who support this position have made a signed declaration as to their position. These are contained in three county lists. I gave the Dorset list to Anthony some time ago and he received the Devon list from Sir Thomas the day before he died. We assume he had the three lists with him when he left Devon on the day of his death. These lists were to go to the Protector as a sign of good faith. Widespread personal and political mayhem will result if outsiders obtain these lists. We must find them at all costs.'

'Who would gain most from these lists?' asked Luke.

'Almost everybody. The majority of political factions in the nation do not support the Protector. Cromwell's parliamentary and army enemies would use the lists as proof that he was negotiating with the Royalists, and many Royalists would see our action as betraying the King. On every side there are groups undermining the fragile stability that Cromwell has brought in order to change the regime to their liking—republicans, parliamentary gentry, renegade elements in the army, and royalist extremists who seem to be getting encouragement from foreign elements at the King's court in Paris.'

'Where do we start looking?'

It was Elizabeth who answered. 'When the library was ransacked on the night of the murder I assumed the killers were searching for the lists. I sent servants to our estate in Tiverton to see if Anthony had hidden them there before he came home. They found nothing. He must have had the lists with him the day he was killed. He could have hidden them anywhere between Tiverton and Charlton Noakes.'

13

Lord Lidford and his large entourage departed and Luke, having persuaded Baxter to provide protection at the Hall for Elizabeth from early that evening, eventually returned with his men to the village. He was uneasy with what he had just been told. It explained the Protector's interest in Sir Anthony yet he was no nearer finding the squire's murderer. He still could not rule out the local suspects who for personal reasons may still have killed Sir Anthony before the political assassins found their target.

Luke considered his priorities. Should he concentrate on the murder or the lists? He was deeply troubled. Who could he trust? Were Lidford and Elizabeth telling him the truth? Was he being misled by his emotions—feelings for his boyhood sweetheart, and respect for one of the King's most capable cavalry commanders?

His instincts told him that Will Pyke was one man he could trust. As he ambled towards the Black Swan to bring Will up to date he reflected on his unlikely friend and ally and consciously reassessed his friend. Will was a very small man with a slight limp. Grey haired and clean-shaven he had a large face with a double chin and sported rather large ears that often protruded from his range of different coloured Monmouth caps that his wife Nell knitted for him. Although the colour of the cap changed daily the rest of his apparel did not vary. Over a greyish shirt he wore a brown coloured jerkin—a hue that his wife called puke. His breeches were a dull grey, Rats colour, obscured by an even darker grey apron.

Will was outgoing and gregarious, a man of unlimited energy, with a great sense of humour, a disgraceful tongue and a very optimistic outlook. He enjoyed the life of an innkeeper and was a great advertisement for his establishment. He drank heavily and believed that life was to be enjoyed. His ability to sift the tittle-tattle of his customers and the underlying causes of the brabbles and arguments that often climaxed in his inn made him a reservoir of community knowledge. This information provided him with the facts to exercise power and leadership—a role he exercised within his basic political and personal opposition to the current government and his loyalty to the late squire, and to the King.

It was in respect to this that Luke decided not to tell Will the nature of the missing documents. 'The squire lost some valuable papers between Tiverton and the village on the day he died and Lady Elizabeth has asked me to help find them.'

'Cuds-me, pity that prating gooseturd churl is dead. That pestilent knave followed him the whole way. By heavens that scurvy villain would have known where squire stopped.'

'We still have Tom Hastings,' Luke lamely replied.

Roger also had his problems, and took the opportunity of the leisurely amble back to the village to ponder his situation. A younger son of an impoverished cleric had limited opportunities for suitable employment. The army had provided an unexpected career and unlike the men who trotted slowly beside him he had never seen, let alone taken part, in armed conflict. Garrison duty in London was relaxed, and his secondment on this mission surprised and worried him. His only link with Luke was that they were both Cornishmen. But what if Luke had more serious motives and intended to make a proper officer of him? Was the Colonel out to test his loyalty to the Protector? This did worry him. He was neither an experienced officer nor a devotee of the Protector. If times changed, and he was still unfortunately in the army he would have no difficulty in changing sides. What he had seen locally of the Government supporters did not encourage his loyalty.

It had been a hard day for Roger. He was not used to standing guard and patrolling the grounds of a large estate. Luke had insisted that his entire unit, officers included, should guard Lady Elizabeth until Baxter could send his militia. This had taken up the whole day. Roger was tired, and did not intend to discuss work with his colleagues over dinner. He would excuse himself and slip away to the Black Swan where the ale was better and, according to his troopers, the women generous. He also missed the London establishments that relieved the boredom of army life.

Roger sensed hostility as he entered the Black Swan but most people were too busy or too drunk, or both, to notice the callow youth who looked even younger than he was. The Black Swan was a large inn with an immense entrance hall in which drinks were dispensed. The inn was the social centre of the village. The hall was furnished with several tables and benches and with adequate space for dancing. A number of small drinking chambers led off from the hall, which catered for particular groups or special occasions. At the back of the hall were the kitchen and a few service rooms. Up the stairs that led out of the hall were the bedchambers of the household, visitors and servants.

Roger was amazed at the range and quality of the drink. It included the strongest beer, a range of herb-flavoured ales and the local specialty a homemade cider that had absorbed a considerable amount of livestock. Rumour had it that the body of a missing local had been disposed of in the very cider being sold that evening. It had the consistency of a thick soup.

Will, as the landlord, immediately saw in the boyish faced Roger the opportunity to make money. Will hoped his friend Luke who had just left would not come looking for the lad before the girls had extracted as much money as they could. Will had great respect for Luke but every group had a misfit. Will saw that Roger was a soldier only in name, and sensed that his experience was limited. If he had known that he was dealing with the sheltered son of a Puritan cleric his assumptions and prejudices would have been confirmed.

After many drinks, and mutual groping with several of the girls it was physiologically evident that he was ready. The more popular girls were already engaged so it was the youngest and least experienced wenches that cavorted with this drunk, and slightly belligerent young man. In his drunken haze Roger remembered what he had heard about the girls at this inn and if a woman was good enough for Sir Anthony Noakes and Sir Edward Lampard she was good enough for Roger. He demanded Susannah Thorne.

THE SPANISH RELATION

Susannah was not there and before Roger caused any further trouble in selecting an object of his lust, he passed out. He passed in and out of consciousness for much of the night. He vaguely remembered being in a small chamber with at least three women lustily singing the bawdy song of the young smith and the damsel that let him use her forge.

Roger was later to hear to his great embarrassment that he had attempted to provide actions that corresponded to the words. When he awoke late next morning he was in nothing more than his shirt and someone had evidently helped him release those weeks of sexual tension. He felt overcome with embarrassment and was not sure how he would recover his clothes and pay what he owed for whatever had gone on during the night. Before these problems overwhelmed him the door burst open to reveal Sergeant Ford with his clothes.

'The Colonel is waiting, sir.'

The Cornet dressed, and on confronting the landlord was told that his bill had been paid. When he left the Black Swan he realised that it was later in the morning than he thought and that the Sergeant's visit was not an early morning reminder but the result of an irritated Colonel trying to find a missing deputy. Luke had been warned when he selected Roger that the young man lacked experience and discipline. Luke had no problems with his deputy frequenting the Black Swan and its wenches. After all he had set the example. What annoyed him was that it was two hours after the time scheduled for a meeting. You can have as many women as you like but do not let it interfere with your job. Secondly, given the events of the previous day the thought that Roger had been killed or kidnapped had passed through his mind.

Roger suddenly realized he was in trouble. Luke did not mince words.

'I selected you for this mission to try and give you some experience. From today you are on reduced pay and if there are any other breaches of discipline I will reduce you to the ranks. Our lives are under threat all the time. To wander off alone especially into what is a seething den of Royalists and criminals was indiscreet if not foolish. It is fortunate that the landlord is a friend, and told us you were there. Having emptied your purse he ensured that no harm came to you. Government soldiers are hated in these Royalist villages. If you must drink alone go into Taunton where the Protector's men are objects of admiration.'

'Sir, I protest. Surely a visit to the women at the Black Swan does not warrant a reduction in pay and the threat of loss of rank.'

'Roger, are you stupid, or still drunk? You are not being disciplined because of your sexual adventures. You are being disciplined because you reported for duty two hours late, and in a state that is not acceptable. You are in no condition to interview respectable citizens in the name of the Protector. I am standing you down for the day from this inquiry and you can report to the officer in charge at the Hall and take your turn as you did yesterday in patrolling the grounds and protecting the household. Report back here at the proper time tomorrow morning. Dismissed.'

14

After dealing with Roger, Luke visited Walter Weston for news of the Constable's investigation of the attack on Elizabeth. Walter was the exception in the discordant gossip that plagued Charlton Noakes. Most had a good word for him. Will admitted that the Constable was an honest man, despite the company he kept. This general approbation was surprising as Walter was a Puritan, supported parliament, represented the law, and was very wealthy. He owned more land in the parish than the squire. Weston Farm, comprising the southern third of the parish, consisted of a dozen large enclosed fields, the portion of Winslade Wood to the east of the Devon Road (which provided the farm's western boundary), and a third of Charlton Mere.

The Westons lived in a large farmhouse in Church Street, a continuation of the High Street. The house was a Somerset longhouse, a rectangular structure three times as long as it was wide. It was of whitewashed cob with a slate roof. It was opposite the rectory which facilitated a close friendship between Walter and the parson Henry Gibbs. Without Walter's support the progress of religious reform in Charlton Noakes would have been even more pitiful than it was.

Luke knew that despite their political, religious and class differences Walter and Sir Anthony Noakes had never publicly criticised each other. This needed probing. If there was a special relationship it may have coloured the Constable's report, or it might conceivably have had something to do with the murder.

When Luke arrived at the farm Walter was in the orchard. He wore a dull brown doublet and matching breeches with black stockings. There were no slashes, no visible buttons, no edgings of gold or silver or for that matter any other colour. As he got closer Luke noted the one concession to fashion was a large lace collar and turned back lace cuffs on his sleeves. He was bareheaded and his grey hair was cropped.

Walter received him with genuine pleasure and they gravitated to a low stonewall that surrounded the rows of pear and apple trees. Walter had developed his cider and perry making into a successful commercial enterprise that serviced many of the alehouses and taverns of Taunton. 'Colonel, I was expecting you following your deputy's visit to Hal Gibbs. You have read my report?'

'Constable, before I ask you about Sir Anthony what is the latest regarding the attempted murder of his wife?'

'It was well planned and carried out with military precision. Old Dick Smith, the head gamekeeper up at the Hall, helped me. He knows Winslade Wood like the back of his hand. As a youth he was the most successful poacher in the parish and rather than punish him Anthony's father, Sir William, made him a gamekeeper. Dick believes that there were six to eight men in the woods that morning spread out along the route that Lady Elizabeth took. There were another three or four men posted as lookouts between the first group and the road. After the shooting these men methodically criss-crossed the woods looking for the corpse. They failed to find Lady Elizabeth's unconscious body because by sheer chance, one of Baxter's patrols entered Winslade Wood at the critical time. Alerted by their lookouts they dispersed without the troopers being aware of their existence. This was no gooseturd frenzy, it was a military operation.'

'The army?'

'No, not at all. It was probably the work of the part-time Royalist militia that acts for the Sealed Knot. What is confusing is that Sir Anthony and Lady Noakes were the public face of the Sealed Knot. Why would her own men turn on Lady Elizabeth? If they are responsible perhaps they also killed Sir Anthony. This attempt on Lady Elizabeth would appear political, and carried out by a well disciplined unit.'

'Mother Sparrow hinted that the local Royalists are divided and that Giles Yalden was very unhappy with those up at the Hall. Maybe he had orders to remove both husband and wife. The murder of the husband and then the attempt on the wife could hardly be a co-incidence. Perhaps the attempt on Lady Elizabeth is our best clue as to who murdered her husband?'

'I know this village. Despite all his weaknesses and the political and religious passion that has been engendered in recent years I cannot see any local murdering the squire –not in the way it occurred. As a soldier you must have seen horrible disfigurements but I have never seen such a brutal bashing. Anthony's head was reduced to pulp.'

'Apart from Will Pyke you are the first person I have spoken to who seems to sincerely regret the death of the squire, and I have learned that despite your political differences you and he were never enemies.'

'The Noakes and the Westons have lived in this village for a century and a quarter. The Noakes as squires, and the Westons, originally as blacksmiths. My father obtained a bit of land and he, and then I increased our holdings. When I was a boy there was less of a barrier between village and Hall. Young Anthony joined us village lads in the usual juvenile pranks. As we got older, lads in the group incited each other to do more and more outrageous things. On one occasion, as a result of a dare Anthony and I chased deer in Selwyn Forest. The gamekeepers caught us and accused us of hunting the King's deer. I distracted them and Anthony escaped. I was severely beaten to make me divulge the name of my runaway accomplice. I said nothing. When I was brought before the magistrates Sir William Noakes, Anthony's father, persuaded his fellows on the bench that there was no evidence that I was hunting and that my trespass was accidental, as the forest boundaries were not marked. I was given a bond for good behaviour which I later discovered was guaranteed by Sir William. Anthony and I rarely spoke after that. Our friendship was somehow suspended rather than destroyed or developed.'

'I have read your report. Do you still think a gang of cutthroats murdered Sir Anthony?'

'I am not sure. The shattering of his skull by some heavy instrument suggests a spur of the moment, irrational killing but the subsequent attack on Lady Elizabeth raises doubts. Colonel, I must confess. I have prayed daily since it happened seeking the Lord's forgiveness for my dereliction of duty. When I arrived at the Hall James Clark told me he had cleaned up the murder scene. He had found Anthony's sword broken in two and carefully placed on the desk in front of him. Clark saw this as a symbol of dishonour or treachery and he would not allow his master's death to be cloaked in such innuendos. I acquiesced in removing the broken sword and placing another in Anthony's scabbard. I later realised that the failure of the squire to draw his sword might raise questions. Lampard picked it up immediately and I had to emphasize in my report that it did raise a question. The broken sword and the attempt on Lady Elizabeth suggest a political execution, yet the callous, head splintering assault does not fit that picture.'

'If political, why?'

'Colonel, you are aware of unusual activity amongst the Royalists. You may not be aware of similar behaviour by the parliamentary gentry. Something big is being organized. I am excluded from these activities. My religious views are such that I would be forced to reveal any activity that I thought was against God's will, or that undermined a government that I believe is divinely sanctioned. Secondly, although I am called Mr Weston I am simply a successful yeoman. Goodman Weston is my real status. Given the ways of the world my son is genuinely accepted as a gentleman, I am not.

My guess is that the gentry of the West Country are uniting in some major enterprise. I can see only one target of such an enterprise—our Lord Protector and his army. The King failed to understand, the Republic failed to understand and now the Protector is committing the same mistake. The gentry rule the western counties. They are the magistrates and the members of parliament. Until the wars they also controlled the armed forces of the county. They resent and will destroy any outside force that attempts to coerce them in the name of outside, albeit higher interests. Lampard believes the Protector sent you to investigate what was going on in the county and the role he, Lampard, is playing.'

'Do you have any specific evidence to support your view of the situation?'

'Royalists and Parliamentarians are meeting together. In the last three months I have heard nearly all my Parliamentary colleagues say nice things about Sir Anthony Noakes. His name has cropped up in most discussions in a favourable light when until recently he was despised. I also know from a comment that Lampard dropped recently that he has been in personal communication with Sir Anthony. If you can find out what they have been up to, you might have an answer to why Anthony was murdered.'

'Is there anything else you can tell me?'

'Luke, what I have said suggests a political explanation but there is another possibility. When I said my acquaintances on the Parliamentary side have suddenly been saying nice things about Anthony, there is one exception—the High Constable. He has publicly threatened the Noakes family.'

'Everywhere I go I hear complaints about the High Constable. Is anyone that bad?'

'Rutter is evil. If Hal Gibbs needs an example for his sermons of a life that leads to damnation William Rutter is the perfect model. He has no morals, he has a vicious personality and he will use any means to gain his ends. During the war he was a contractor to both sides at the same time. He raised provisions from the parishes, on the security of I O U's, which were redeemable from the headquarters of the occupying army, headquarters that seemed to move further and further away from the provisioning villages. He took goods without receipts, and terrified farmers into compliance. He seized goods and property, claiming untruthfully that the parishioners were in debt to him, and ruthlessly used bailiffs illegally to enforce his seizures. He raised far more than the troops needed which he then sold on the market at exorbitant prices. I could go on. Rutter is capable of committing every crime in the book. You must investigate him. My son can help you with the details.'

'As someone born and bred in the village and a school friend and lifetime neighbour of Sir Anthony are there aspects of his past that could have led to his murder? Are there deep family secrets?'

'No, apart from the consequences of his overindulged sexual appetite and the truth about Nicholas, Sir Anthony's life, the good and the bad, is an open and reasonably respectable book. The one area of mystery is the Exmoor connection.'

'Tell me more.'

'A nephew of Sir Jasper, Marcus Noakes, was knighted by King James for reasons that were never clear. Sir Marcus lived a lonely and isolated life on Exmoor on a sprawling but poor estate, Black Top Manor. Yet he and his son, Toby, the current squire were never short of money. I heard Anthony once say that although the King might make a knight, he could not create a gentleman. For decades Marcus and Toby embarrassed Sir Anthony. Yet in the last five years the cousins have come together. Sir Toby now visits Noakes Hall several times a year.'

'Are these Exmoor Noakes smugglers?'

'I don't think so. It has long been the noise of the county that smugglers and pirates land their contraband on the northern coasts of Devon and Somerset and use middlemen to move goods through Exmoor into the towns. Maybe the Exmoor Noakes turn a blind eye to such activity. Sir Marcus and subsequently Sir Toby were never investigated which led some to suspect that Anthony was using his legal and political position to protect them. His enemies claimed he was protecting his own involvement. However in the ten years since Anthony lost power his successor Sir Edward Lampard has not questioned Toby either.'

'But if it were true and Sir Anthony was involved, a breakdown in the smuggling partnership could have provoked the killing.'

'Maybe, but there is no evidence, even if the Exmoor family assisted smugglers, that Sir Anthony had any part in it. It was not in the nature of the man. There is more in the other rumour associated with Sir Toby.'

'Which is?'

'Ten years ago when you were besieging Bristol the Royalists who had flocked to the city with their moveable wealth, feared that it would be looted by the soldiers of the Parliament. They decided to move it for safekeeping. One night a small group of horsemen escorted through the Parliamentary lines two wagons laden with the jewellery and plate of the Royalist families of the West Country, and the silver and golden vessels of wealthy churches of the city. The officer in charge of this unit was a Captain Tobias Noakes.'

'Surely if Noakes absconded with the treasure it would be easy to prove and justice rendered accordingly.'

'Not so simple. Another Royalist troop of horse which came out of the city to disrupt Parliamentary lines found one wagon empty, young Toby semi-conscious under it, and rest of the group dead. Toby claimed that they were ambushed by Parliamentary cavalry, his men killed and the treasure stolen. At the time the loss was accepted as one of the misfortunes of war. After the war when the gentry on both sides came to discuss the incident the Parliamentarians denied any knowledge of the episode. The Parliamentary Colonel in charge of the area where the ambush was supposed to have happened was one of our God fearing, bible spouting Ironsides whose discipline over his men and his knowledge of their movements was above the ordinary. He claimed that none of the besieging troops left their positions that night. Whatever the truth there has been a persistent rumour that somehow Toby purloined the treasure and it remains hidden for safety in the secret chambers of Noakes Hall.'

As they chatted Luke noticed a horseman turn off the road and make his way to the house.

'It is Hugh. Please join us for dinner.'

15

Walter escorted his guest into a long thin hall with a large fireplace and beside it the narrow stairs that led up to the sleeping chambers. Luke was reminded of his childhood home. On the ground level all rooms were long and thin consisting of adjacent parlours that led off the hall at the front half of the house. The rear half of the house consisted of the kitchen and other service areas.

They dined in the hall in front of a fire that seemed unnecessary on such a warm day. After the meal Luke and Hugh moved to the parlour. Their common experience in the New Model and their admiration for the Protector created an immediate rapport.

'Why did you resign from the army?' Luke asked.

'I was at Naseby, saw service in Scotland and Ireland and then at Worcester—one might say all the major battles of the New Model. After Worcester I thought our opponents would accept the inevitable, and our Parliamentary leaders would create a better nation. I wanted to be part of that rebuilding at the county level and help my fellow soldiers readjust to a golden age. I was mistaken.'

Hugh seemed lost in painful memories and after a long silence asked, 'You remain loyal to the General?'

'To the general, yes, but to the governments that the army has helped install, no. We fought to protect the Protestant church and the rights and privileges of the gentlemen of England to be represented in Parliament and not be subjected to arbitrary taxes. We beat the King countless times but he refused to budge. His execution was essential to break the deadlock. But the Republic was worse. The corruption was unbelievable. Those politicians used their new power for personal gain and dishonoured all the army agreements regarding the treatment of soldiers—Royalists and our own. The Nominated Chamber of the Godly, which followed the 1653 dismissal of the Rump, was another tragic experiment. Saints could no more agree to put the national above personal interests than the sinners.

Our only hope for stability still rests with the army led by the Lord Protector but it is currently being undermined by the influx of civilians into the administration, especially those with Royalist connections. The proposed extension of military rule across the nation on the model we have here may yet save us. However my experience over the last few weeks has raised further misgivings. Your father suggests that something is going on among the county elite, irrespective of their stand during the Wars, and that the Protector and the army may be their target.'

'I agree. As a lawyer to gentry from both sides I have sensed a rapprochement over the last few months. My own situation proves the point. Some months ago the ultra-Royalist leaders Sir Anthony and Lady Elizabeth Noakes, made me, a former officer of the New Model, their lawyer.'

'Can I ask you something very personal but I do have a reason, and it vitally affects the course of my investigation.'

Hugh flinched with nervous anticipation.

'I gather from my various informants that you are the fantasy of many local women. Lady Lydia is besotted with you and my deputy repeats with obvious envy that the voluptuous Susannah Thorne regards you as her most satisfying partner. You have been a regular of hers over the last year or two?'

'Yes, probably twice a month.'

'Do either of you have the pox?'

Hugh reacted with a hint of anger and embarrassment. Luke knew that Hugh was not happy and immediately explained the reason for his indelicate question.

'If Thorne is clean, and an elderly gentleman who visits her monthly for the last five years has the pox why did he not infect the wench?'

'Come on Luke, although as a soldier you and I know differently the learned medical profession does not believe that males can transmit such diseases. I imagine that the infected male continued to have his way with the girl. She must have taken precautions. Failing that you have two other choices. Either he had aberrant tastes, which were satisfied without sexual intercourse, or he did not visit her for sex. You refer to Sir Anthony Noakes or Sir Edward Lampard. And I can add a further touch of mystery. Over the last few months neither gentleman has been available for business meetings on the evening of the last Wednesday of each month. They both claimed a prior commitment in Taunton and Susannah Thorne is missing from the Black Swan on those very same Wednesdays.'

'Are you suggesting that these leading gentlemen engaged in some animalistic threesome?'

'Not at all. It's political not sexual. Meeting Susannah at least in recent months was a cover to enable the leaders of the rival factions to meet in secret.'

'Do you know where they met?'

'No.'

Luke felt that while he could eventually force a confession out of Susannah Thorne, loyalty to her former squire might make it a prolonged and difficult task. The last Wednesday of the month was a week away. He would follow Sir Edward. It was reasonable to assume that Sir Anthony would have been replaced. It would be a coup to catch Lampard and the Noakes replacement together. It would give him some leverage in dealing with the county's most prominent politician. The more he thought about it, the more he began to believe in a gigantic plot brewing against the Protector. He could trust no one except Will, a royalist; and the man across the table. He decided to act.

Hugh Weston was dressed totally in black but allowed himself the ostentation of a slashed doublet edged in silver thread, slashes which revealed a red silk lining. The end of his breeches just below the knees and the top of his stockings were held in place by equally bright red ribbons while he sported a large collar and large cuffs of the finest Honiton lace. Unlike his father he wore his dark brown hair reasonably long to the point that it covered some of his collar. On his entry to the house he discarded his long black cape with its matching bright red lining. His large hazel eyes were piercing and sparkling. He had a generous and lively personality that belied both his profession and ancestry. Yet it was his loyalty and vision that appealed to Luke.

'Hugh, the Protector's cause may be under serious threat. I would like you to help me if the situation worsens. I will use my authority under the Protector to recommission you, as Captain Weston. I will send the relevant papers to Whitehall immediately and inform the Protector personally of what I have done. For the moment keep it to yourself. I will not call upon you unless it is absolutely necessary. Do you accept?'

'Yes, I left the army because I thought I could do more good here. Now it looks as if the army once more must save England and the Protector.'

'Thank you. On the more specific issue of my investigation, who murdered Sir Anthony?'

'Initially I believed it was Rutter or one of his henchmen because of his shady dealings. But since father confessed about the broken sword, the attempt on Lady Elizabeth's life and the intense politicking amongst the gentry of all persuasions I incline to a political explanation. This leaves us with a very broad field. Maybe there were Royalists who opposed what was going on, or even Lampard may have seen the writing on the wall and considered that if the gentry families were re-united Sir Anthony rather than he would be their natural leader. If Sir Anthony were out of the way Lampard would then be the obvious choice. If it is a plot against the army maybe some of our comrades uncovered it and immediately struck against its potential leader.'

The discussion with Hugh had lifted Luke's spirits. There were two immediate tasks—to follow Lampard and hopefully catch him in such a situation that he would be forthcoming with information, and secondly to probe into Rutter's past. As he left the farmhouse in the late afternoon, he felt as if he had been hit from behind with a heavy instrument. It took him several seconds to realize that it was only an effect of an afternoon of cider drinking. He was not an experienced cider drinker and decided that in the future he would to stick to ale.

A Week Later

Luke was not going to miss the opportunity. On the Wednesday afternoon he sent Andrew in light disguise to locate and then follow Sir Edward

Lampard. He would shadow Susannah Thorne. His conviction that he was on the right track was strengthened when Roger who had become Susannah's lover announced that he would eat with his fellow soldiers that evening, as Susannah had to go to Taunton and would not be back until late. Roger was surprised that none of his comrades were eating at the Three Keys.

Roger would have been further alarmed if he had known that Luke was intending to follow the tantalising Susannah to Taunton. Luke quickly realized that it would be more useful to provide her with an escort. He caught up with her cantering towards the town and offered to ride with her. His offer was readily accepted. Susannah thought Luke, given his deputy's interest in her, was taking advantage of this co-incidental meeting to probe the relationship. Both avoided the subject but Luke took the opportunity to question her concerning Sir Anthony. Susannah, for her part was determined, to reveal nothing until the beginning of St Swithen's Week and appeared a little muddled as she sorted out what she could or could not tell him. Her enterprise that very evening would widen his horizons immensely but she would remain loyal to the late squire, whatever the cost, and tell Luke nothing that he did not already know.

'Thieves caught in the act butchered Sir Anthony.'

Luke could see tears trickling down her cheeks, but he persisted. 'The weakness in that account is that everyone knew that there were no valuables in the Hall.' Luke hoped he might provoke a response regarding hidden treasure but it did not come.

'Maybe squire was bringing something with him that night.'

Luke reacted inwardly. Did Susannah know more than she was revealing? By the end of the evening he would have an answer. When they entered Taunton and progressed along West Street heading for the centre of the town Luke pretended he had reached his destination and tethered his horse at the first inn he encountered. He dismounted and followed Susannah on foot.

She turned down a side street, tethered her horse and entered the Four Bears, one of the more salubrious taverns of the town. Luke walked casually down the other side of the street and nearly fell over Andrew who was half hidden in a recessed doorway. Andrew indicated that Lampard was already inside. The two soldiers followed, bought their pints and studied the layout of the inn. There was no time for any elaborate plan. They were no sooner seated at a bench than Susannah left an up stairs room at the top of the stairs and joined other women in an adjoining chamber. She would not be present at any political discussion.

A direct approach was called for. The soldiers rose from their bench, drinks in hand, and nonchalantly climbed the stairs and stationed themselves outside the room that Susannah had just left. They would enter the room and uncover two overt political enemies in a covert alliance. Luke was elated, and then he froze. There was a pistol pushed against his ear. Four or five armed men had appeared from nowhere. Andrew and Luke were hustled down the back stairs to a cellar where they were pushed down a ladder and locked in. No words were spoken.

'I'm a fool, Andrew. I should have realized that if this design is as important as the Westons think the parties involved would protect the secrecy of the meeting. Who replaced Sir Anthony? I would be content if it were Lidford or Elizabeth. If it is anyone else the plot becomes complex, although it might help our murder enquiry. Perhaps Sir Anthony was murdered because others were not happy with his performance at these meetings and wanted him replaced, or maybe the very fact of these meetings led to his death. They would certainly have alienated some on both the Royalist and the Parliamentarian side. On the other hand I would imagine that Lidford or Elizabeth would continue Anthony's approach. Damn, damn, damn.'

'Relax Colonel. In following Lampard earlier I passed dozens of drinking places. Just around the corner there are a large number of men in the livery of Lord Lidford. Some of them I recognised from the other day. It seems a bit of a co-incidence that there is a meeting here and Lidford's men are close by. Lidford is the Royalist up stairs.'

Andrew's views made Luke feel better. The Sealed Knot still controlled the local Royalists or at least continued to speak for them. But it did not help his murder enquiry. The soldiers settled down to await developments. Some hours later the bolt on the door was released. They waited a few minutes and felt their way in the dark up the ladder. When they opened the cellar door they saw that it was opposite an external exit through which they quickly departed. They recovered their horses and somewhat crestfallen rode quietly back to Charlton Noakes.

16

Roger did not know that his visit to the Black Swan coincided with Will's discovery of a vital piece of information. This clue came Will's way, accidentally, a minute or two before Roger arrived. The women who worked from the Black Swan were arguing about their relative sexual appeal. Mary Miller upbraided the newest recruit, young Martha Rodd, about displaying herself in the village street for all to see, and allowing men to have their way with her up against a neighbour's door.

'In almost twenty years I have never swived for all to see,' Mary gloated.

'Liar,' the young girl replied.

'I saw you in Goodman Napp's doorway the night the old squire rode through village.'

Will pricked up his ears. It confirmed what the murdering gooseturd had told Luke. Before Mary could reply Will summoned Martha into the front parlour. 'When exactly did you see squire ride through town?'

'Five or six weeks ago. It was a Thursday. Willie Calf, a servant at the Hall is my only regular and Mr Clark only frees him from his duties on Thursday evenings.'

'What did you see?'

'Squire galloped past but I heard him suddenly stop just after he passed us but Willie had my attention.'

Will was excited.

'He stopped?'

'Yes.'

'Where, for how long?'

Will could have shaken Martha. She had no idea of the significance of what she said. After all she was a beef-witted drumble who filled in her days tending the community's geese on the village green. Several of her older sisters had disappeared, according to village gossip, to the bawdy houses of London. The family had a reputation for being lewd and loose although one sister Annie had risen out of the mire and was a personal maid up at the Hall.

Recently Will gave Martha an evening job as a scullery maid. She was short and plump and her immediate appeal to men lay in her more than ample breasts that were scarcely concealed under her light green woollen bodice, and her thick inviting thighs. She wore no petticoats. Her big but listless brown eyes, and a trusting and innocent personality reflected a somewhat naïve generosity. Her long strawberry blond hair was never effectively contained under her tight fitting white linen cap. She always looked untidy. Will did not notice her dirty brown skirt and rather grubby tawny apron.

Will repeated his question, 'Where did squire stop?'

'I was well into the porch and could not see but by the sound it was several houses down the High St and as there were several horsemen in the street I didn't hear him start up again. Mary might know more. She was further down the street.'

Will waited until Mary had finished with her current visitor and quickly entered the small parlour from which a man had just emerged. 'What landlord, you want to be naught with me? You'll have to pay like the others.'

'Enough, all I want is the truth. When you were on the street as Martha claimed did you see the squire?'

'No, I had my back to the street.'

'Do you think your partner saw anything?'

'No, old George is nearly blind, and he always shuts his eyes when he is swiving.'

'Did you hear anything?'

'Several horsemen galloped past while I was with George.'

'Did they stop?'

'The first man did. I heard him dismount two or three doors further down the street.'

Will was cross. Had Luke yet questioned any of the villagers? The Thursday of the murder was a pleasant evening. Others may have seen the horsemen. Someone may have seen squire dismount. He had stopped at one of perhaps four of the smaller houses lower down the High Street. Their doors were not far apart. If he could pinpoint the house the missing lists may be found. He would take matters into his own hands.

Roger's arrival deflected Will from his investigation. With the aid of the women he might make a large profit from the naïve cornet. At the same time he would let his friend Luke know of Roger's whereabouts and potential predicament should his other clients manifest their anti-army feelings.

Next morning Andrew arrived to collect Roger. Will asked him whether Luke had questioned the servants up at the Hall and the customers of the Black Swan and the Three Keys. Andrew confessed that this had not been done but with the landlord's help he would start. Will volunteered to make some discreet enquiries of the villagers as to their activities the night the squire was murdered and meet with Andrew later that day.

Will was troubled. Who should he trust with the details of the squire's stop over? Could he trust Lady Elizabeth? He sent a message to Lord Lidford.

When Lidford received the news from Will he was both elated and alarmed. The gooseturds who followed Anthony from Tiverton to Charlton Noakes would know where he stopped. Yet how could Lidford get the information he wanted? If the gooseturds were told about the lists they would be in a position to coerce or blackmail him, or worse still to obtain the list themselves, and sell it to the highest bidder. This might explain why Anthony rode through the village when he was in a hurry to get home. His diversion was to give the lists to someone he trusted.

Several days elapsed in which Lidford consulted with Lady Elizabeth. Will was surprised to receive an invitation to the Hall to meet Lord Lidford and Lady Elizabeth and even more surprised when he was ushered into a parlour off the great hall and not received at the back door by one of Mr Clark's lackeys. He still had serious misgivings about talking to Lady Elizabeth but plainly Lidford had initiated the move. For the moment he would hold his tongue. Lady Elizabeth entered the chamber resplendent in her mourning apparel accompanied by his daughter, her personal maid. Father and daughter smiled at each other but the deferential couple did not speak. Lidford arrived a few minutes later and nodded to Lady Elizabeth who spoke.

'Will, thank you for your loyalty to my husband. We need your help again. Anthony left Devon with an important list of names, which should it get into the wrong hands could destroy the King's cause. We need to retrace his steps and hopefully recover the lists. Tom Hastings knows where he went. Can we get these details without putting ourselves at the mercy of this knave, who for all we know murdered Anthony?'

Will hesitated.

'My Lady, for that pestilent dissembling villain money is his only language. Suggest that squire had on his possession, a family heirloom, a gold ring encrusted with precious stones worth hundreds of pounds. You are desperate to recover it for personal reasons, and given your new found wealth, of which all the region would by now be aware, you are willing to pay double its value to the person who brings it to you. And for any other possession of Sir Anthony that they may come across in recovering the ring you will pay an appropriate bonus.'

Lord Lidford protested, 'It's too dangerous. Tremayne should be consulted before we go further. We may need his help. Wait until you have questioned those villagers who were in the High Street that night. They may be able to pin point the exact house at which Sir Anthony stopped. And you will not need Hastings.'

'I'll wait, and then get Mary Miller to arrange a meeting for me with Tom as soon as possible.'

Will had every intention to consult Luke and question any villagers who were in the street on the fatal evening. However on his way back from the Hall he met Mary coming up the High Street. He mentioned that he wanted to see Tom and she confessed that she was then on her way to meet him. Later that afternoon before Will's customers descended on the Black Swan Mary suddenly appeared in Will's parlour declaring that Tom was in the back chamber.

Will, forced to put Lord Lidford's reservations to the back of his mind went straight to the point. 'Jehu, Tom, help us to help your brazen faced self to a fortune. Squire had with him the night he was killed a precious heirloom, a jewel encrusted triple gold ring that has not been found. I, and others know that you and your scurvy knaves followed him that night. You may even have killed him. That is not my concern. Lady Elizabeth wants the ring back and will pay double its value. You are the only one who knows the route the squire took from Tiverton to Noakes Hall. Sir Anthony and you were seen by several villagers riding down the High Street not long before he was killed.'

Hastings could hardly believe his good fortune. He now understood the message taken from Lidford's courier. Sir Anthony probably had a meeting with an unknown person to sell them this particular heirloom. Although it might be established that he and his men followed Noakes from Tiverton and through the village they could only be guessing about what happened next. He would be in no hurry to reveal details, especially the brief stop the squire made in the village. It was so quick that only something small like a ring could have been exchanged. His mind was already racing. He could hardly contain his gold lust. 'I find the ring and I get double its value. What's the catch? There is a price on my head and I could be arrested as soon as I deliver the goods. It would be better for me to find the ring and fence it through my normal channels. What tricks are you up to Will?'

'God's blood Tom, no tricks. Lady Elizabeth wants the ring. You know where squire went. She will pay better than any of your fences. If you find anything else belonging to Sir Anthony when you find the ring she will pay even more.'

'Why should I help the Noakes household after what that toad Anthony did to me?'

'Money, Tom. If you recover this ring it will be worth more than six months of your petty robberies.'

'I'll think about it,' mumbled Hastings as he hurried away already committed to ransacking two or three houses at the end of the High Street.

Will immediately realised he had allowed things to get out of control. He had acted too quickly. Hastings would need to be shadowed and the activities of his men continually monitored. Will had no time to seek the approval of his superiors. Would he call on Giles Yalden or his new friend Luke? After all Lady Elizabeth wanted the Protector's men informed and time was of the essence. He sent to the Three Keys and asked Luke to come to the Black Swan immediately. He checked that Hastings had departed. He had, and the speed of the exit worried him.

Half an hour later Luke and Andrew arrived. They were greeted with catcalls and bawdy comments suggesting that they were out to rival their colleague's performance earlier the previous week. The landlord took them into a private room and sought their assistance. After hearing the details of the plan Luke was furious.

'I cannot believe that Lord Lidford approved this harebrained scheme. I can see why you are a landlord Will, and I am the soldier. God! you have given the initiative to Tom Hastings without having in place the men to follow his every move and prevent him causing more havoc. It was so unnecessary. Your girls had located the squire's visit to one of three or four houses. We could have searched these houses and may have found the lists without involving Hastings.'

17

Between Roger's first visit to the Black Swan, and Will inviting Luke to meet him as a matter of urgency Roger Pennock had lost all interest in the investigation. He and Susannah Thorne were obsessed with each other.

Susannah had seen Roger from afar and was anxious to meet him. He was a comely lad unlike most of the locals. He was half the age of the other gentlemen she satisfied. Her parents were away for several days at the funeral of a kinsman so she invited Roger to visit her on the following Monday. Given the rollicking he got at the Black Swan and the bawling out from his colonel, Roger could not conceal his lustful anticipation of this clandestine meeting. She became the focus of his continual self-abuse, as the Reverend Gibbs would have described it.

The meeting with Susannah did not terminate after the usual short-term release of built up lust. Susannah slowly rebuilt his desire. She used her hands, lips and tongue to reawaken every manly fibre in his body and succumbed again and again to the thrusting of her creation. She was not in love with this attractive and responsive soldier but their relationship was mutually satisfying, and he would be her passport to a better life. They spent the night together. Next day they met twice and enjoyed bursts of uninhibited lust, but on the following night Roger would have to wait until near midnight as Susannah had to be in Taunton in the early evening.

Roger was in a dilemma. He was besotted with Susannah. He had never met a woman like her. It was not only her sexual prowess. She was kind, considerate and loving. He was surprised at her awareness of events, both local and national. But she had slept with many men in the parish and certainly had a long-term relationship with two of the notable gentry of the county. For the moment he killed off these negative thoughts and enjoyed her company. After all if Sir Anthony and Sir Edward did not feel tainted by their acquaintance with her, why should he?

Susannah dreamed above her station. She had saved much of her earnings, and her gentlemen patrons had been very generous. She realised that a single woman could not safely leave money in a box hidden somewhere in her parents' house or at the inn. She had asked Hugh Weston to look after her money. The popular lawyer regularly gave her a receipt for the money she deposited with him. She did not realise that she was worth a lot more than Roger. She would run away with him to London. It was time for her to settle down, marry and have children. She was not going to spend all her life as a harlot. It was more lucrative than simple service but she was not going to finish up like Mary Miller. After all there was only room for one Mary Miller in the village. Susannah had neither Mary's generosity nor tolerance. Susannah's provocative appeal to males and a somewhat arrogant attitude to other females made her unpopular with the village women.

Susannah had an immediate problem which Roger could solve. On her return from Taunton they made love again and again, and then she quietly cuddled him in her arms.

'Roger, I need your help.'

'To do what?'

'Some weeks ago, when I was at the Black Swan, a horseman knocked on our door here. Father answered and a sealed letter was thrust into his hands with a request to give its to Lady Elizabeth in St Swithen's Week. The fairs and markets associated with St Swithen's begin their monthly cycle through the neighbouring parishes the day after next. Would you take the letter to the Hall for me?'

'Of course. When did this happen? Who was the horseman?'

'It was squire on the night he was murdered.'

Roger was surprised but it never entered his head to immediately inform the Colonel. There were more important things to do as he clambered on top of Susannah, and her caressing hands led him home.

After Luke's outburst the three men sat momentarily in silence. There was a realization that Will had blundered and the landlord confessed that Lidford had only approved the enterprise subject to Luke's agreement. Hastings should have been followed at all times. He was a loose cannon. Before they began to redress their mistake they were interrupted. Roger and Susannah burst through the door. Their appearance appalled the trio. The couple were as white as a sheet and both were visibly trembling. Clearly they had been through a shocking experience. Will was quickly pouring strong spirits down their throats.

'My God, it's horrible. We are lucky to be alive,' exclaimed Roger just before he fainted.

Susannah had stopped trembling and calmly she told her story. 'An hour ago Roger and I went into Winslade Wood. While we were there Roger suddenly put his hand over my mouth. I'm a noisy lover. Horsemen led by Tom Hastings passed within a few yards of us heading for the village.'

'Heaven forgive me,' uttered Will.

'We headed for home but saw one of Tom's men stationed on the far side of the way where he could see who came up and down the road. When he looked up the road we threw ourselves behind an adjoining wall and wriggled to the back of the house. It was being demolished. A man called out, "It's not here .The slut must have it. Your squire gave the ring to his harlot." Tom replied, " Let's find her and cut it from her finger." They mounted their horses and were about to leave when Rover the neighbour's dog came bounding home from his nightly wanderings and picked up my scent. He sniffed his way through the bushes and when he found me he started to bark with tail wagging and demanding a game. Tom heard the commotion. "What have we got here my hearties?" Just as he moved towards me a ginger cat appeared from nowhere and Rover went after it. Tom turned to his men and told them to go find the whore.'

During Susannah's calm description of events Roger who had recovered with liberal gulps of Will's special West Indian rum was anxious to continue the tale.

'We went around to the front of Susannah's home and found the door hacked in, and drawers and cupboards emptied all over the floor. Wall hangings were slashed, crockery shattered. The floor slates had been prised up and great holes smashed in the walls. We immediately headed this way

THE SPANISH RELATION

for help but on passing the neighbour's house we heard groaning. Their door had also been smashed and there was a similar scene of destruction. Far worse, there was an old man with his throat cut, blood everywhere, and a younger woman severely cudgelled.'

Will spoke, 'God's Mercy, that will be Christopher Jenkins and his wife. I will send Nell and Mother Sparrow, to see what can be done.' Will, visibly upset, called his wife, and sent one of his servants to inform the constable. Luke asked Andrew to send one of the troopers to Colonel Baxter to inform him that the gooseturds had been active in the village. While Susannah was being consoled by some of the other women Roger joined the men in the parlour.

'God's truth, this bloody business is my craven clapper brained fault,' lamented Will. 'Young Martha heard the squire stop in the village that night. The clay brained churls following him probably saw the diversion but could not be sure exactly where he stopped. Cods-me, Roger it was lucky, that you and Susannah were not at home. Both neighbouring houses, the Thornes and the Jenkins were possible hiding places to Tom Hastings. Goodman Jenkins and his wife had been servants at the Hall before they moved into the village. The squire always found work for Jenkins to supplement his earnings. They were a family that the squire could trust—and the whole village knew that Susannah had a special relationship with Sir Anthony. We know the dissembling toad spotted rogue did not find the non-existent ring but did the venomous varlet find the missing lists?'

'Ask Susannah,' whispered Roger.

Susannah was called back to the room and she recounted her story of the squire's visit. Luke was the first to speak. 'Did Hastings get the letter? Why did you hold on to it for so long when it were clearly intended for Lady Elizabeth?'

'My father was certain that the instructions were to hold it until St Swithen's Week. Roger was to take it to Lady Elizabeth next Sunday.'

Luke fixed a disapproving eye on Roger.

'All right, but do you still have it? Are you sure Hastings missed it.'

'I will get it for you,' replied Susannah as she left the room. After a few minutes she returned and placed a thick sealed letter on the table in front of Luke. 'As soon as my father gave me the letter, and especially when I heard of Anthony's murder I knew that whatever was contained in the letter could be very important. I do not know why he wanted me to wait seven weeks until St Swithin's week, but the least I could do for a man who protected me was to do as he asked.'

Luke cut the seal and satisfied himself that the letter contained the three missing lists. 'Susannah, the recovery of this letter is very important. It is the culmination of Sir Anthony's work over the last few months and affects the security of the state. I will take it to Lady Elizabeth.'

Luke waited for Andrew's return and they headed for the Hall.

18

Will was still worried. The order to execute Lady Elizabeth haunted him. He had loyally served the Sealed Knot which was led in Somerset by squire and Lady Elizabeth and in neighbouring counties by Lidford and Odam. So, who ordered the killings? Lidford and her ladyship clearly continued to act for the Sealed Knot, and Sir Anthony and Sir Thomas Odam were dead. Had there been a split in the leadership of the Knot? Had her ladyship, before her execution was effected, managed to wipe out her rivals? Did she and Lidford murder squire and Odams?

Will could not accept this. He had known Sir Anthony all of his life and Lady Elizabeth for nearly twenty years. He never once doubted their loyalty to the King. Will's daughter, Tamsin, worshipped her mistress but in recent months had alluded to some tension between husband and wife, especially after visits by Sir Toby Noakes. But hardly at an intensity as to provoke murder. It was all too much for the usually buoyant and optimist innkeeper.

Then it hit him. The Royalist network had been infiltrated. The order he had passed on to Giles Yalden had come from the enemies, and not the leadership, of the Sealed Knot. He had been a beef witted fool. He must warn everybody involved and stop the lists being given to Lady Elizabeth until the situation was clarified. He sent his son Daniel to ask Lord Lidford to be at Noakes Hall as early in the morning as he could as the future of the Sealed Knot was in great danger. Will galloped after the soldiers whom he overtook at the gates of the Hall. He was in two minds as to how much he should reveal to these men whom except for the investigation of his beloved squire's murder were sworn enemies to all he stood for. Then he remembered Tamsin's gossip of that morning. He would leave out the politics and concentrate on the personal. 'Luke, I know who tried to murder Lady Elizabeth. I can say no more until I talk to Lord Lidford in the morning. Don't deliver the letter until Lord Lidford clears up a few loose ends.'

Luke for a moment wondered if this was a ploy to provide an opportunity for the letters to be stolen but he trusted Will. Andrew offered to ride on to the Hall and leave a message for Lady Elizabeth to expect them and Lord Lidford in the morning. 'No, Andrew, you and I should not be split up. Will ride on to the Hall and leave a message with your daughter to inform Lady Elizabeth of what is planned. It will look less suspicious in case we are being watched. Let's get back to the Three Keys and have my troopers guard this document. We will meet at the Hall in the morning.'

Luke stationed his men around the manor. Will and he were ushered into the parlour off the great hall with which Luke had become very familiar. The innkeeper was ill at ease and remained standing unable to bring himself to sit in the presence of his superiors, even if it was a Cromwellian colonel. Lidford eventually arrived with the rumble of his coach, and the raucous shouting of his entourage. He displayed a slight degree of irritation as he entered the parlour.

'What is the meaning of this, sirrah? A peer of the realm summoned to a meeting by an alehouse keeper. You had better have an acceptable explanation for this outrage, or my men may be forced to teach you a lesson about keeping your place.'

Will blanched, but replied quickly, 'My lord, forgive my churlish behaviour but when you hear my story you will understand. May I have words with you alone and then, with your approval, I will tell everyone what I know.'

Lidford and Will went back into the great hall but did not shut the intervening door. Even from that distance Luke could tell that the peer was visibly shocked. They returned to the parlour just as Lady Elizabeth, with Dr Basset, entered from the opposite door.

'Good morning gentlemen, I understand that the lists have been recovered. Excellent news. But why is Pyke here? And why my lord have you come all this way?'

Lidford replied, 'Elizabeth, please listen to Pyke, he has an alarming tale to tell.'

'My lady, forgive me. I don't know who ordered the attempt on your life but I played a part in it.'

'By my troth, Will, why?'

'Two days before your husband died the Sealed Knot told me that a traitor had been discovered amongst its leadership. The guilty person had been sentenced to death by the King and I was to have our men carry out the sentence. You, my lady, were the traitor.'

'But Will you know that Anthony and I led the Sealed Knot in Somerset as does Lord Lidford in Dorset.'

'My lady, I am as his Lordship suggests an ignorant alehouse keeper. I do not know what goes on in great houses. I obey orders. I was shocked to read your name but assumed that squire was taking his orders from the King. Then when squire was killed I wondered whether the Knot had ordered a different agent to deal with him as another traitor, or that perhaps you had had squire killed before his men could get you. I was confused as to Lord Lidford's role but in the end he was the only person I could turn to.'

Elizabeth attempted to speak but the detail of Will's account and her continued weakness from the attempt on her life proved over whelming. She fainted, and gracefully slid to the floor. Her servants were summoned and Tamsin helped half carry her to her bedroom, giving her father a most frightful glare as she went by. Luke was first to break the silence.

'Did you not think to question the order?'

'Colonel, you should be the last man to ask such a question. If you received a direct order from the Protector to act against your family I am sure you would obey. Obedience to lawful authority is all we have left in these troubled times.'

Luke persisted, 'So what created doubts?'

'Zounds, nothing's been making sense. I could not trust Lady Elizabeth so I sent news of the squire's stopover in the village to Lord Lidford yet he consulted my lady who then sought my help. Your role added to the confusion. Fore God, why did the leaders of the Sealed Knot trust the

Protector's envoy? Why did squire's murder in this violent age interest the Protector in the first place? It all pointed to some Royalist arrangement with the Government which Giles Yalden has long suspected. Then it hit me the orders had not come from the Sealed Knot but from its enemies within the Royalist ranks.'

'They certainly did not come from the Sealed Knot,' affirmed Lord Lidford who turned to Luke, 'Can you get the lists to Whitehall? I must immediately inform everyone of the breach in our security and try to rebuild our network.' Luke could not help conceal a smile. To have the enemy so disconcerted and clearly in disarray could only help the Protector.

Lidford turned to Will. 'Take no orders except those that come through your daughter, and immediately contact our men in the field and rescind that regarding Lady Elizabeth.' He then turned to the room in general, 'Give my apologies to Lady Elizabeth. I must leave now in order to repair the damage. Good day to you all'. As Lidford passed Luke his face lit up as he whispered, 'I hope you and your man were not seriously inconvenienced at the Four Bears?'

Luke also was about to leave and accompany Will back to the village when Tamsin came running after him. 'Colonel, my lady would like to see you before you leave.' She whispered to her father, 'Don't wait, he will be here all day.'

Tamsin caught up with Luke and escorted him back through the house to Lady Elizabeth's bedroom. Elizabeth had already been disrobed by her coterie of servants and assisted into bed. She signalled Tamsin to leave and then arose, clad only in a long, almost transparent chemise with an exceedingly low cut neckline, and placed the bolt across the door herself. Before Luke could compose himself Elizabeth entwined herself around him and began kissing him ferociously and thrust her tongue deeply down his throat. Luke was not slow to be aroused and was visibly moved by this passionate display. They cavorted together on a large rug in front of the fire that was roaring away on this colder than usual morning. Their hands and lips explored each other's body. She dragged him on top of her and for the first time in five years she felt the thrusting of a loveable man. They exploded together. It seemed hours later when after much cuddling and caressing Elizabeth spoke.

'There are things I must tell you.'

'And I have questions for you.'

'You start.'

'Some days ago you told me intimate things about Anthony which suggest his visits to Susannah Thorne were a cover. I proved this the other night when we followed Susannah and Sir Edward Lampard to a meeting at the Four Bears. Lord Lidford just confessed to have been there in place of Anthony. What is going on Elizabeth?'

'In the last few months the Sealed Knot considered it prudent to inform its enemies of a temporary rapprochement with the current government. This rapprochement would backfire if the old rivalries were rekindled in the struggle for power under the new dispensation. Anthony and Nodding Ned Lampard were simply keeping each other informed. Until our lists were with the Protector, and he had responded, it was unwise to go public regarding meetings with long term enemies.'

This only covers the last few months of Sir Anthony's association with Susannah. What about the previous four and a quarter years?'

'What I intended to tell you explains it. It is not news to me but it will soon become public and will affect one of your officers, and this entire household. Hugh Weston will read Anthony's will next week, using a copy, which he made and had Anthony sign as soon as he took over our affairs. I have sent a message to London where Sir Robert has been hiding since his father's funeral to return for the reading.

'How does the will explain Anthony and Susannah?'

'Susannah is Anthony's daughter by Agnes Napp. Agnes died in childbirth and Anthony had the baby seized and after an appropriate lapse of time had it fostered out to another village couple, the Thornes.'

'Does Susannah know?'

'No, not even the Thornes know. They assumed Anthony was placing an illegitimate child of one of his servants.'

'So, Sir Anthony to avoid suspicion saw his daughter on a regular basis under the cover of a sexual liaison.'

'Yes.'

'It still doesn't make sense. How do you visit a whore monthly for five years and not have sex, and retain any credibility with the girl? She must have thought he was strange.'

'I never asked.'

There was a long pause with neither party wishing to comment. Elizabeth broke the embarrassing silence. 'The Thornes and Cornet Pennock should come to the Hall where you and I will break the news to them. It might be less suspicious if you escorted them here the day after tomorrow.'

Talking was exhausting and they fell back into each other's arms. Luke experienced the truth of the adage that where love is greatest words are fewest. When he finally left her bedroom he felt both privileged and slightly disconcerted. He realized that he was besotted with Elizabeth but knew he had to be careful not taint the honour of the woman he loved. Regular and open visits to Mary would keep the gossips on the wrong track. To be honest he wanted both relationships. Mary had awakened aspects of his sexuality that he did not know existed and the exercise of his new confidence and knowledge impressed and satisfied Elizabeth.

19

SUNDAY AFTERNOON WAS A good time to talk to the servants at the Hall. For a few hours most were released from their daily routine. Luke wandered around the Hall chatting with groups of servants deciding that Willie Calf and Annie Rodd, both of whom were resident on the night of the murder, deserved further attention.

Willie Calf was an indoor servant who wanted to be a stable hand. He loved horses and since the arrival of Luke's troop in the village dreamed of joining the cavalry. Luke took advantage of Willie's dream. He took Willie to his tethered horse and lifted the youth into the military saddle and led him around the stable courtyard. Luke recounted some of his own adventures and in the process questioned the highly elated and talkative lad.

'Willie, tell me about the night your master died.'

'Twuz Thursday night. Tiz my time off. I was at the Black Swan most of the night. When I got back to the Hall the Constable was already here and squire long dead.'

'What did the servants think happened?'

'We were more betwaddled by the loss of two of us at the same time.'

'What do you mean?'

'Mr Robert's personal groom and Mr Clark's deputy have not been seen since that night. The lads think they saw too much and were killed. Mr Clark says he dismissed them for thieving. Mr Robert was in a real blather when he heard and it caused yet another argument with Mr Clark.'

'Mr. Clark and Mr. Robert argued a lot?'

'All the time. They all did. Lady Elizabeth and squire were the worst.'

Luke reached a tethering post and helped the boy dismount.

'Willie, show me the stables and Sir Anthony's fine horses. I need to talk with the stable boys.' A group of grooms were sitting on bales of straw and showed interest in Luke's very large cavalry horse. 'Lads, I have been asking Willie about your squire's murder. He tells me the household was not a happy place in the months before the killing.'

One of the boys responded.'Zackly, Lady Elizabeth was tetchy and squire a pisspot, a real slack abed. Her Ladyship took charge and had us up at all hours of the night to get her horse ready or to attend that of a late night caller.'

'Where did she go?'

'Into the wastelands.'

'Did you know any of her late night visitors?'

'Most were local squires and a regular was Lord Lidford.'

'They be lovers,' a sniggering boy interjected.

'Were there any other events around the murder, or in the months before that appeared strange?'

The sniggerer continued.

'Anyroad on the night of the murder there were a lot more horses coming and going than Mr Clark lets beknown.'

The first groom interjected.

'Mr Clark had his own visitors at night and kept them secret from the family.'

'Who visited Mr Clark?'

'His brother-in-law Giles Yalden, in recent weeks a stranger who I've seen at the Black Swan with Danny Pyke, and backalong I got a glimpse of a gent with a golden cape.'

'I see one of you walking a fine Friesian horse. I had one in the Low Countries but they are rare in England.'

'That's Black Meg, Lady Elizabeth's favourite.'

Luke was momentarily speechless. He felt an empty feeling at the bottom of his stomach. Lady Elizabeth was the mystery horseman who met the Whitehall messenger and disappeared in the coppice? He reverted quickly to his line of questioning.

'Your masters all have a theory about the squire's death, what do you lads think?'

The sniggerer spoke,'Tiz family. Lady Elizabeth ordered it, or Mr Robert lost his temper yet again and went too far.'

'Thanks lads, look after my horse while I go up to the Hall and talk to some of the wenches.'

Annie Rodd according to other servants was a long tongued babbling gossip. She was also aggrieved. She had been one of Lydia's maids and when Lady Elizabeth's maid left to marry Annie expected to take her place. Tamsin Pyke who had little experience was appointed instead. Annie blamed her fate on the unpopularity of her loose living family. Luke was old enough to be Annie's father but he still made a big impression on the young maid who enjoyed being selected by this handsome and charismatic soldier as his special informant. Annie let go a torrent of gossip that in essentials agreed with Willie Calf and the stable hands.

'Annie, was there anything else about the night of the murder that may help me?'

'Hereaway there was a lot of coming and going late that night. I heard horsemen come up the main drive and from along the manor stream and I saw one disappear into the wastelands. Mr Clark says only squire and his murderers came that night. He lies.'

'Who murdered the squire Annie?'

'Twer Lady Elizabeth.'

'Come, that's just gossip. Why would you think such a thing?'

'Lady Elizabeth was very cruel to squire. He was sick and sad, and often distracted with drink. She bullied him and would not let him leave his chamber unless she, Dr Bassett or Mr Clark were with him. Lady Elizabeth was squire. She spoke to important visitors in the library well into the night. She also saw a lot of Lord Lidford. They were lovers. Squire was a cuckold.'

Luke was again disconcerted. The gossip regarding Elizabeth and Lord Lidford was so common that perhaps it was true. Maybe he should enjoy her body but not to get himself too involved. It was a soldier's privilege to love and leave.

'Were there other visitors?'

'In the last half year Sir Toby came about once a month and spent the time drinking with Sir Anthony. After he left Lady Elizabeth and squire argued. After this last visit, just before they went to Tiverton, Lady Elizabeth was furious.'

'Was this because Sir Toby was encouraging the squire to drink too much?'

'In that last shouting match between squire and her ladyship Mistress Lydia's name was often mentioned.'

Luke sensed that Annie had given him some promising leads. He continued probing. 'Annie, what's the gossip regarding Sir Robert?'

'When I first came here both Lady Elizabeth and Mr Clark told me never to be in a room alone with Mr Robert and if he touched me or made lewd comments I was to report it immediately. Tiz'nt fair. Init. They all hate Mr Robert. One of my sisters thinks he's lovely. He took her to London. He is very kind to all the girls and never did me any harm.'

'When you came here you were not warned about any of the other men, Sir Anthony or Mr Clark?'

'No, only Mr Robert'.

Luke arrived back at the Three Keys late in the afternoon and had just finished briefing Andrew on what he had gleaned when they heard the sound of many horses arrive at the inn.

Colonel Baxter knocked on the door. Luke responded, 'Come in Colonel, this is a surprise.'

'More so than you think, Luke. It's not a social visit.'

'Serious?'

'Yes, did you send a messenger to my headquarters two days ago with an urgent letter for the army post to Whitehall?'

'No, I always bring the letters personally to your headquarters or send one of the troopers you seconded to me whom you would recognise.'

'I thought so. Two days ago an unknown messenger delivered a letter at my headquarters asking that it be sent post haste on your behalf to Sir John Marks, the Protector's secretary at Whitehall. I remembered when you briefed me on your mission that you emphasized that nothing was to go to Whitehall unless it was addressed to the Protector personally. In addition you also made several disparaging remarks about Marks and the evil influence civilians were having on the administration. Both the manner of the delivery and the address made me suspicious. I took the liberty of breaking the seal and reading the contents. Here is a copy.'

Baxter gave Luke a sheet of paper. For the benefit of Andrew, Luke read its contents aloud.

'27

Situation in hand, Tremayne competent but contained, greater danger from within, France the problem.

23'

Luke turned to Baxter, 'What do you make of it Thomas?'

'It could be Royalist, parliamentarian or Army. Sir John Marks is the middleman who will distribute it to 27. Who is 23?'

'Are they friend or foe?' added Luke.

Andrew interrupted, 'It's Royalist. Lampard could use the government post and send it direct to Whitehall. There would be no need for secrecy. An army source would legitimately and openly use the system. A Royalist agent used our system to get a message urgently to someone on the Council of State. If they relied on a traveller heading to London it would take four days. Our express post along the Bristol Road can get a letter from here into the Protector's hand in 26 hours. And it is probably someone who knows your manner of working. After what you heard this afternoon Noakes Hall is the source. Maybe Clark or Basset but I think Lady Elizabeth Noakes is 23.'

Luke brought Tom Baxter up to date with the information he received from Willie Calf and Annie Rodd. Baxter uttered aloud what the others were thinking. 'If the tall horseman who met the London messenger and then disappeared into the coppice just outside the parish was Lady Elizabeth then a person who receives communications from Whitehall may also be the person who sends communications to Whitehall. I agree with Andrew. She wrote the letter I intercepted.'

Luke was flushed with excitement and apprehension. 'The letter makes sense. Whatever the secret Royalists on the Council of State are planning this letter is suggesting that they hold fire. The situation in Somerset is contained. Even though I am seen as competent in what I am doing it is not central at the moment to their plans. They don't see me as the enemy. Other royalists are stirring the pot. The reference to France may be to the King's court. In essence whatever the Royalists are up to in London and here they are facing problems from other Royalists presumably in touch with the King. Lady Elizabeth is bringing their man in Whitehall up to date.'

Luke was happy to have the letter interpreted but inwardly he was numbed by the major role Elizabeth appeared to be playing. Was she using her sexuality to derail his investigation? Tom Baxter was certainly not happy.

'Given my responsibility for security it is worrying that the Royalists in this county have direct access to someone on the Protector's Council of State. As regards your investigation it complicates any political motivation.'

Luke trusted Baxter and gave him a full account of recent developments regarding the Royalist dealings with the Protector and the existence of potentially incriminating lists.

Baxter offered some advice.

'Send the lists to the Protector by normal army post. It would be there in just over a day. A troop of horse will take four. That's plenty of opportunity for it to be stolen. As we have couriers leaving around the clock it would be difficult for any outsider to know with which courier they were dispatched.'

20

The Thornes were alarmed to find a troop of horse at their door but Susannah relaxed when she saw Roger. Luke explained that they were affected by Sir Anthony's will, and Lady Elizabeth wished to let them know the details before it became common gossip. While they waited for the women to ready themselves Goodman Thorne chatted with Andrew.

The group were shown into the reception parlour where Lady Elizabeth and Hugh Weston were waiting to receive them. Elizabeth was resplendent in her heavily embroidered mourning clothes while Hugh wore the black highly laced apparel of a lawyer and his usual red trimmings. Elizabeth signalled to Goodwife Thorne and her adopted daughter to be seated while the men remained standing. Elizabeth did not waste words. 'My husband's will contains material that might shock and disturb you, but which in the end will be of benefit to you all. There is a reasonable gift to you Goodman Thorne and your wife for looking after Susannah. Susannah you have an annuity of a hundred pounds.'

Roger thought lasciviously to himself that Sir Anthony plainly appreciated Susannah's talents, of which he now had become the besotted beneficiary. Elizabeth placed her hand on Susannah's shoulder. 'My dear, Sir Anthony has been generous beyond all bounds because you are his daughter.'

Roger went green and vomited spontaneously overcome with disgust and revulsion at the thought of Susannah sleeping with her father. Before his angst completely debilitated him Luke brought him into line. 'Cornet, control yourself. Sir Anthony and Susannah never slept together. Is that not the case girl?'

Susannah was in a state of shock. She gave a meaningless nod to Luke. She now knew why a man who was attracted to her and visited her constantly never had sex with her. He paid her four times the usual rate for a cuddly conversation. However in respect for her newly discovered father she would say nothing.

While Lady Elizabeth continued explaining the details of the will Andrew quietly attracted Luke's attention. 'We have all wondered why Sir Anthony did not want the letters delivered until St Swithen's Week. I talked with Goodman Thorne earlier. He is profoundly deaf. I think he misheard the squire's instruction. I think Sir Anthony actually asked that the letter be delivered "within the week" rather than "St Swithin's Week". It makes sense. There was no point in delivering it immediately in case those anxious to obtain it were still around. "Within the week" was probably an optimum time in the squire's mind.'

Susannah and Roger decided to marry as soon as possible. They would ask Dr Basset to marry them according to the traditional rights of the Anglican Church and illegalities in this could be rectified later before any magistrate. Susannah could not stay in the village. Her past, in terms of her activities and her parentage would make life too difficult. Once Tom Hastings knew of the situation there is no knowing what he might do, as she was the daughter of his beloved Agnes. Agnes' parents, the Napps, would find it difficult to cope with the knowledge that for twenty years their lost granddaughter lived only a house or two away. The new squire, Sir Robert, would find it intolerable to live with a half sister who was, in the eyes of the respectable element within the village a common whore and who in the popular mind now added incest to her abominations. With the income assured by Sir Anthony and her own not unsubstantial savings Roger and she could live comfortably well away from Somerset.

Susannah left Charlton Noakes next morning with Dr Basset and his daughter who were going to visit relatives in London. She would stay with them until Roger could join her and then they would marry. Dr Basset who had long known of her parentage undertook this last mission for his departed friend and patron. It removed Susannah from the village before her friends and enemies became aware of the situation. Roger was peevishly unhappy in the temporary loss of his sexual partner but would have been much happier had he known that within a few days he, too, would be headed for London.

Will felt reassured, and at the same time somewhat guilty that he had not queried the order requiring the execution of Lady Elizabeth. Lord Lidford was devising a completely new system so the failure of the old was now water under the bridge. But was it? If Will could trace the movements of the last courier he might be able to isolate locations where the system had been compromised. This could lead him to the infiltrators and possibly the murderers of Sir Anthony.

As the old system was no longer operational he would seek Luke's help. Will had discovered from Lidford that the courier who brought him the message involving Lady Elizabeth was a wagon driver who delivered sacks of barley to numerous alehouses and inns. His load also included ten or so smaller sacks, which were unloaded at designated places. These smaller containers concealed a leather bag in which the instructions were held. The courier who was changed for every journey would only know that he delivered a small container at ten or more alehouses with the special compliments of Lord Lidford.

Luke and Will made their way to Lower Chase one of the villages near Lidford House, in the centre of a barley growing and distribution area. They quickly discovered the waggoner who had delivered the barley on that fateful day. He had taken three days to move from Lower Chase in Dorset, through Somerset to a village in Devon near the home of Sir Thomas Odam. The timing fitted perfectly the murders of Noakes and Odam and the attempts on Lady Elizabeth and Lord Lidford. The waggoner was vague until he recognised Will as the host of the Black Swan.

'I tellee anigh Charlton Noakes your lad Daniel and a stranger hitched a ride on the wagon. Avore ee unloaded your small container they disappeared into the inn.'

Will was breathing heavily. 'Friend, did my son refer to the other man by name?'

'Aah, twuz the same as my granfers, Cuthbert.'

Will was excited and alarmed. Cuthbert Mowle had been staying at the Black Swan since the murder. The opportunity to replace the original instructions with another was patently there as they bumped along the way leading into the village, but what role did Daniel play in this deception? The men found the nearest alehouse and Will drowned his concern for his son in far too much drink re-iterating time and again that Daniel Pyke and Cuthbert Mowle had to be questioned immediately.

21

Before he left with Will Luke organized the delivery of the lists to Whitehall. His own men would deliver the letter to the Protector. Baxter still advised the use of army couriers but nevertheless freed up one of his regular patrols to accompany Luke's men to the edge of his military district. Luke used his special authority for patrols in the adjacent districts to take over the role, while a unit from his own regiment would meet them on the outskirts of London and accompany them to Whitehall. It would take four days.

On his return Luke informed Roger that he would carry the letter to London. Andrew and the three troopers would accompany him from the unit. Luke would remain in Charlton Noakes with an additional secondment of men from Baxter, and the mobilisation of Hugh Weston if it became necessary. Roger was delighted with the news. He would be in London with Susannah within the week.

Roger thought of the last night they spent together in the village. The effect of their new found wealth and prospects of a very comfortable future only enhanced their mutual sexual appetite and performance. Half way through the evening Susannah decided to visit the Black Swan for the last time and farewell her friends. She told them that she was off to London to marry Roger. The young officer could not refuse the offer of free pints to celebrate his coming marriage. He became more and more intoxicated and more talkative. When ale sinks words swim. Before Roger left the

Black Swan well wishers and enemies knew he was leading an important expedition to London to deliver something to the Protector.

Tom Hastings, Giles Yalden, Cuthbert Mowle and Daniel Pyke were very interested auditors. Tom wanted revenge. He had been tricked, and made to look a fool. He now knew there had been no ring, and that the gentry had been looking for a missing letter. The letter must have been recovered and was now about to be sent to London. What else would account for such heavy security? His experience of the army was that it lacked initiative. The soldiers would ride to London along the obvious, direct route. The only variable would be whether they chose to join the Bristol Road to the north or the Exeter road to the south. He could cover both possibilities. There were many places where they could be ambushed between Charlton Noakes and well into Wiltshire, beyond which he had little knowledge. Tom would wipe out the entire unit and put the letter to the highest bidder.

Giles Yalden was also a very busy man. He was in conversation with Will for about ten minutes and later as he was about to mount his horse to depart Daniel Pyke and Cuthbert Mowle detained him. At the end of this conversation Yalden and Mowle departed in opposite directions.

Susannah half carried and half dragged Roger to her house and the drunken snoring of her lover obliterated her last night in Charlton Noakes. Susannah and her adopted parents said their fond farewells and Goodman Thorne escorted her to the Hall to join the Bassets long before Roger awoke.

Roger would leave at twelve noon three days after Susannah's departure to fit into Baxter's schedule. The important letter was put in a leather container and placed in Roger's snap sack. At the last moment Luke called Andrew aside and handed him an object, which the Sergeant placed inside his coat. The large gathering of troops on the green was a big event for the village although it brought back bad memories of wartime occupation. Roger led off with Andrew slightly behind him with the troopers following in a row. Some distance to the rear came a troop of Baxter's men. Roger at least looked the part. His mustard cavalry coat was criss-crossed with various baldrics holding in place his sword, his powder and his snap sack. Around his waist he wore the bright red sash of the regiment and his hatband displayed the same identifying colour. His men including Andrew wore their breast and back plates and their pot helmets. They unsheathed their swords and held them high as they trotted out of the village. Baxter's militia were essentially dragoons without armour. They carried a carbine strung across their saddle and held a shortened pike in addition to their sword and daggers. A green sash that was a multi-purpose baldric and their unit's colours lifted their dull buff coats.

Beyond the village Roger's troopers were redeployed, one out in front of Roger and one each on either side, Andrew fell in behind the cornet. Some of Baxter's men formed a rear guard to Andrew while others galloped ahead or into the adjacent fields providing reconnaissance for the main party. The Somerset part of the journey provided no problems and young Roger basked in the unexpected status of leading armed men through many villages in which the inhabitants, at least the children, lined the side of the road. Late in the afternoon the officer commanding Baxter's men informed Roger that his troop would end the escort at the river that now appeared before them, and that their replacements would pick them up across the bridge. The Somerset escort turned back along the road it had come. Roger rested his men and watered the horses. An hour later he resumed his journey. The new escort were not visible on the other side of the river but Roger expected to find them around the sharp bend the road took after it crossed the bridge.

Roger rounded the bend and was deafened by several volleys of musket fire that killed two of the troopers immediately and badly injured the rest of his group. The three badly wounded soldiers staggered to their feet with swords drawn and confronted their assailants but they could not hold out for long against overwhelming numbers. Just when all appeared lost another group of horsemen emerged who with military precision butchered the men who had attacked Roger. Their operation impressed Andrew. These were experienced soldiers. In fact they appeared to the sergeant, whose loss of blood was now becoming serious, to be uniformed troops whose blue coats and hatbands were clearly evident. Andrew vaguely recognised their leader, a tall man with red hair, who checked that their opponents were dead and then turned towards Roger. The wounded young officer was about to thank him profusely when the red haired one shot him between the eyes at point blank range. Andrew simultaneously felt a searing pain all over his body and realised that several pistols had been aimed at him. He fell to the ground and lay motionless. The battle experienced veteran lay as still as possible, faking death, while struggling to maintain consciousness. He heard the leader shout the orders.

'Round up the officer's horse, bring me the snap sack, check the Sergeant's clothing and above all make sure no one is left alive.'

Andrew sensed a figure about to search and kill him and just before he lapsed into unconsciousness he thought he heard more galloping horses. It was Baxter's patrol that having heard distant gunfire returned on their tracks. They were appalled at the massacre that confronted them. All of Luke's men appeared dead, as were a dozen or so of the assailants. The patrol immediately assumed that Luke's men had put up a heroic fight and that the surviving assailants had fled on hearing them approach. Roger's snap sack was missing and there were no documents on the Sergeant. In verifying the latter it was realised that he was not dead. As one trooper rode off to commandeer a wagon on which to load the bodies the relief patrol finally arrived. They had received false orders from a buck toothed horseman altering the location of the changeover. They were alerted to a problem by the same volley of gunfire that alarmed Baxter's troop.

Two days later Luke was sitting in the front chamber of the Three Keys with Hugh Weston when Baxter appeared and was immediately directed to the other two New Model veterans. He quietly informed them of what had happened. All of Luke's special unit were dead except Andrew who was severely injured and being cared for by military surgeons at the army headquarters in Winchester. Luke was visibly moved, and openly blamed himself for the death of his men. He should have gone himself and not left such a major exercise in the hands of an inexperienced and unreliable officer. Baxter put his mind at rest.

'Your men were outnumbered. They killed twice as many of the enemy before they died—well that is what my cornet initially reported. Just before I came here I received a further report from Winchester. Your Sergeant has regained consciousness and has told a worrying story. The unit was attacked twice, the first time by the gooseturds. Just as they had given up hope a larger band of horsemen arrived, killed all of the assailants, and then shot your badly wounded men. Andrew recognized the leader of the second group as a regular at the Black Swan—a tall man with red hair and a military bearing.'

Hugh spoke, 'This is serious. Two groups determined to get the lists and two carefully prepared ambushes. Why did both groups want to eliminate any evidence of their activity? My God, you don't think it was a rogue element within the army?'

'It can't be ruled out,' replied Baxter. 'Many of our fellow officers do not like the growing power of the civilians and any rapprochement between our former Royalist enemies and our corrupt and ambitious Parliamentary masters is not in the army's interests. How secure was this operation, Luke?'

'Unfortunately not very. It involved Royalists whose whole network has been compromised, and young Roger who becomes indiscreet after a few drinks. Half the Black Swan knew the generalities of the operation—that an important object was being escorted to London.'

'As this enterprise involved the Royalists you should let them know immediately. The loss of the lists could create great instability in the region,' said Hugh.

While they spoke another soldier galloped up to the inn, and sought out Colonel Tremayne. 'Sir, this letter has just come by military post from Whitehall itself and had to be delivered to you personally.' Luke took the letter and broke the seal, which all the soldiers recognized as that of the Lord Protector of the Commonwealth of England and quietly announced, 'General Cromwell received the lists early yesterday.'

'So you took my advice after all and used the army post', smiled Baxter.

'No, but Roger and Andrew were decoys. They carried blank papers. I used the method that Sir Anthony had used in the first place to inform the Protector of what was going on. My courier was a harmless old minister travelling to London with two young women. Dr Basset carried the genuine lists.'

Baxter left. Luke and Hugh made their way to the Black Swan and told Will the whole story. Will was very upset to hear that Andrew had been badly wounded and was distraught to hear of a tall red headed man. He became a little unsteady on his feet and let out a cry of anguish and disbelief.

'By St George, I am at a loss. The man described by Andrew is my friend, Giles Yalden, the leader of a Royalist unit that carries out the orders of the Sealed Knot. They made the attempt on the life of Lady Elizabeth when I passed on those false instructions. A few days ago I received orders from Lord Lidford to activate Yalden's unit to follow your men and come to their assistance if necessary. Good heavens, either they have become a rogue outfit doing their own thing or they are taking orders from another source. I personally gave Yalden his instructions the night before your men left Charlton Noakes. I must let Lady Elizabeth and Lord Lidford know what has happened.'

'No,' replied Luke, 'I will let them know officially. It appears that your unit has been turned. Do you have any idea who might be behind it?'

'No, but it seems obvious that the milk livered miscreants who compromised the network in the first place, and murdered the squire and Odams are behind it. We decided that Daniel and Cuthbert Mowle needed investigation. You must not waste any time. With Andrew wounded and your men dead are you getting replacements?'

'Not in the short turn. I need men who already know the situation. Will, I have a proposition for you. I am about to activate Hugh into the role of Captain Weston, and my new deputy. Would you replace Andrew as the third member of the team with the rank of Sergeant?'

'Zooks, I would die rather than be part of the Protector's army but I feel responsible for the attack on Lady Elizabeth and now for the massacre of your men. Until we uncover the venomous varlets who are undermining our Royalist cause, and who murdered Sir Anthony, God forgive me, I will join you.'

Hugh commented, 'Our first priority should be to find out what the gentry of this county are up to, and whether it is a threat to the Lord Protector? While Will follows up the problems within the Royalist ranks namely Yalden, Mowle and his own son we should examine Lampard and Rutter as a matter of urgency.'

Will, Hugh and Luke finished their pints in absolute silence. All three pondered the implications of their new partnership. Hugh and Luke left, but Will drank well into the night trying to drown his concern for his son and his friend Giles.

22

LUKE REPLACED HIS MILITARY and gentry apparel with clothes provided by Will—olive green jerkin, dark brown breeches with matching stockings, and a tight fitting dull brown woollen cap. This would not fool the inhabitants of Charlton Noakes but would help Luke melt into the crowd when he followed the major suspects. He also moved to the Black Swan. The Three Keys where he had lodged with his old unit no longer held any appeal. The Black Swan had more to offer. He was closer to Will, he could keep an eye on the customers and enjoy the wider range of food and beers not available at the Three Keys.

Mowle and Daniel regularly drank together for about half and hour each evening and then disappeared. They returned an hour or two later and resumed their drinking. Will was anxious that Daniel's role should be clarified. On the night after he moved to the Black Swan Luke followed the two friends. On leaving the inn they walked down the middle of the High Street towards the church and when they came to a fork in the road they separated. Luke did not see where Daniel went and was forced, despite Will's anxiety, to follow Mowle who continued past the church and headed for Winslade Wood.

Just after Mowle entered the woods Luke heard the sound of a barn owl which was immediately responded to by another. The second caller was not as adept at mimicking the bird as the first. The wood was clearly occupied, and sentries were warning their group of Mowle's arrival. Luke froze. He stopped tracking Mowle and retraced his steps back to Charlton Mere followed its southern shoreline until he reached the manorial boundary ditch and traced this back into the woods. Luke crawled slowly and concentrated on listening for movement. He edged his way into the middle of the woods and eventually saw the flickering of lanterns and the muffled sound of voices. He moved closer but a stifled cough within yards of his position indicated that he had nearly run into one of the lookouts. Assuming that these sentries were spaced some distance apart Luke crawled as close as he could to the cougher. He continued on until he reached the edge of a small clearing. There was Giles Yalden addressing some twenty men. Mowle then stepped forward and thanked the men, praising them for their efforts. Luke boiled within. These men massacred his comrades, seriously wounded his friend Andrew, and tried to assassinate Elizabeth. Those he could distinguish in the flickering light were villagers of Charlton Noakes with whom he had drunk on many occasions.

Suddenly the forest came alive with frenzied hooting. The gathering disappeared in a flash and even Luke's attuned ears did not hear Yalden's men depart. The cause of concern became obvious. Men, boys and dogs from the wasteland hovels emerged in search of rabbits and the odd pig that the village swineherd may have failed to contain for the night. Luke retreated to the boundary ditch and followed it back to the southern edge of the lake from where he headed west until he found the road. As he reached the causeway where the road dissected the lake he was forced to halt. Just in front of him Mowle emerged through the church gate. He must have escaped into the manorial lands, circled round the lake and followed its northern shore through the glebe until he met the road. Luke was amazed. Mowle had travelled twice the distance and continued to outpace him as they both headed for the Black Swan. This was a very fit man. Within the hour several of the villagers he had seen in the woods joined those already drinking in the landlord's parlour.

The next night Luke again followed Mowle, as Daniel, much to his father's chagrin, remained at the inn. Luke thought he was in for a repeat of the previous evening as Mowle again headed for the Wood but there were no owl calls. Luke risked detection by running some distance so that he could keep his quarry in sight. Mowle crossed the wood, entered the manorial grounds and took the major path leading to the house itself. Although Luke did not know it, Mowle followed the path that Sir Anthony took on the night of his murder particularly in leaving it at the orchard. Mowle hidden from the house by this move also disappeared from Luke's sight. Minutes later he reappeared crawling through a hole in the hedge and sprinting quietly towards the house where for the second time in recent months the library door was open.

Luke was torn between continuing to watch or to confront Cuthbert Mowle. His military intuition was to march across the garden and arrest the intruder. Mowle could be a threat to Elizabeth. Love, combined with his sense of military duty made the decision easy. He drew his dagger, the only weapon that went with his disguise, and was about to run briskly across the garden to the door when Mowle re emerged. Mowle skirted quickly around the formal gardens in the front of the Hall and disappeared into the trees of the park.

Luke was pleased with his two nights of surveillance. Mowle was not only connected with Giles Yalden and his Royalist militia but also clearly had contacts within Noakes Hall. The household had not told him all. The murderer may be a member of the household and ready to strike again. Luke fluctuated between anxiety over Elizabeth's safety and angst concerning her possible complicity.

Next day Luke followed Mowle to his employment. Will told him that Mowle usually ate a large breakfast and left the inn about a half hour after day break and headed toward Taunton. Luke left the Swan just before sunrise and waited in the roadside coppice just beyond the Gap. After an hour hidden among the trees Luke saw Mowle ride through the Gap. Not far behind him came a group of villagers. Luke joined them so that his pursuit of Mowle was not obvious. Luke was suddenly alerted when on reaching Taunton, Mowle went straight to the Four Bears. Luke hoped this experience at that inn would not be as disastrous as his earlier visit. Mowle tethered his horse outside the Four Bears indicating a short stay.

A man emerged and mounted Mowle's horse. For a moment Luke did not recognize him but noting the rider's mannerisms and body language Luke became convinced that it was Mowle. The man who went into the Four Bears was a labourer in a grey jerkin and blue green breeches and a burgundy Monmouth cap. The man who emerged was a gentleman of the highest quality. His black doublet slashed, back and front, the slashings edged in gold to reveal a bright white lining. His black trunk hose and black stockings were both tied with bright white ribbons, which also bedecked his shoes. The lace around his collar and sleeves was excessive. He wore a large brimmed, low crowned black felt hat with a matching white hatband, which was enhanced by a mass of white feathers. The labouring Mowle had hidden his hair under his close fitting cap, in his gentry guise he revealed masses of long black hair worn provocatively in the Cavalier style. And what stopped Luke in his tracks was that he wore a short golden cape.

Luke was confused. The wench at the Wiltshire inn told him a stranger in a golden cape had saved him from certain death. Why did Mowle save his life, follow him to Charlton Noakes and then murder his men? There were many golden capes in England. Was this the same man?

Luke followed Mowle along a busy road crowded with people going to or coming from Taunton. After an hour Mowle left the road through the impressive gates of a place, which Luke ascertained from a fellow traveller, was Eglin Place, the residence of Lord Eglin. Mowle spent the rest of the day visiting the homes of another three peers and four gentry. He stayed at each for less than a quarter hour. When Mowle turned back towards Taunton, Luke with eight names in his head, returned post haste to Charlton Noakes. He sought Elizabeth's advice on the information he had uncovered.

After some delay, because the gatekeeper did not recognize the labourer as Colonel Tremayne, Luke was admitted to the familiar chamber off the great hall. Elizabeth swept down the stairs and came across the great hall looking every inch a noblewoman of striking beauty and bearing. Luke could hardly contain his feelings as she entered the parlour, her face wrinkled by an inquisitive smirk. She was about to tease him regarding his appearance when she quickly gauged that he was in a serious mood.

'What's so urgent Luke that you visit me in such disgusting apparel?'

Luke told her of his adventures on the first night out and of his travels of that day. It was prudent for the moment not to reveal the discovery of the second night—that Mowle had visited Noakes Hall.

'Elizabeth, is there any connection between these names?' Luke handed Elizabeth the list he had compiled during the day. She read the names and commented, 'I'm not certain about two of the gentry but the four peers and the other two gentry are Papists. Lord Eglin is the senior Catholic aristocrat in Somerset. Perhaps your friend Mowle is a Catholic priest bringing the mass to these isolated believers.'

Given his obsession Luke did not need much to convince him that Elizabeth was right. Priests were very adept in donning disguises of all types to keep ahead of the persecuting Protestant magistrates. He took his leave of Elizabeth and trotted home to the Black Swan where he informed Will of the day's discoveries.

Will sipped his beer slowly and eventually spoke, 'Pittikins, this dissembling and dangerous traitor is not a priest. There are many Catholics scattered around Somerset especially in the area you visited today. Despite the efforts of the authorities they have been continuously serviced by several priests, which the Papist peers have been able to protect and conceal for decades. If he is a priest then the provision of the mass is not the reason for his visit. Obviously he had no time today to provide such a service. There is something else going on and I do not like it. First the Royalist gentry come together, then the supporters of Parliament and now the Papists. It looks as if somebody is rallying all sections of the Somerset gentry and aristocracy to some end. If I were the Lord Protector I would be very worried.'

23

Luke was worried. The plotting gentry demanded his attention as much as the murder investigation. Discover Mowle's true identity and he might clarify both situations. Luke decided to return to Eglin Place and talk to the locals. He approached the gatehouse asked the servant who barred his way if there was any day work available. The servant appeared friendly and was happy to relieve his boredom by talking to a stranger.

'His Lordship hires labourers once a year at the Fair and baint need others.'

Luke asked him about his work which the gatekeeper's assistant was willing to whinge about at length. Luke tried an indirect question. 'Lord Eglin gets important visitors. Yesterday I saw a high and mighty gentlemen go through these gates?'

'The Spanish gentleman. Never understood his name but twuz told that if a man wearing a short golden cape approached the gate I was to take him to his lordship.'

'Spanish, was he?'

'Init strange. When goldie cape met my lord he talked in the ways of this county, not like you. And not like a Spaniard.'

'Has he been here before?'

'Too many questions, nosebag. My mother scollared me never to ask what boils in another's pot.'

'Curiosity killed the cat, but I was surprised to see a man of such quality riding alone, and if he is Spanish you are in trouble. If war with Spain comes Eglin Place could be seen as a nest of traitors.'

Luke knew immediately he had blundered.

'Stranger, go before I set his Lordship's dogs after you. Lord Eglin may be Papist but he only inherited the title because his gramfer's two older brothers died fighting the Spaniards at the time of the Armada, and his own brother was killed by the Spaniards in the Netherlands a few years backalong.'

Luke beat a hasty retreat. As he did so he saw just ahead of him a female servant who had just left Eglin Place armed with two empty baskets. Walking briskly he drew level with her. She wore the apparel of in-servants of the aristocracy—a tight fitting white coif, long sleeved black bodice and an underdress of the same colour. Her overdress that was open at the front was grey which would have revealed the black underdress if it had not been hidden by a long greyish brown apron. She had traces of white lace at her collar and sleeves. Luke recognised her as a senior servant. He was right.

Her initial reaction to Luke was fear. 'Varlet, I have nothing for you to steal, and doan-ee touch me or I'll scream and my Lord's servants working behind these hedges will help me.'

'Forsooth good woman I mean you no harm. I need advice. Your lord's reeve offered me labour, but I've heard that this is not a good place to work?'

'Stupid question, fellow. I have no idea how outservants are treated. I work for the house steward and prepare meals for the household.'

'And for the important visitors as well.'

Luke observed that this woman warmed to her sense of importance and that flattery might be rewarding.

'Yesterday when I was talking at the gate a man with a golden cape went through just before noon. You prepared his meal?'

'I prepare the meal not serve it but I heard that visitor was in a hurry and had a little wine and left.'

'Who was he?'

'The Count of Varga y Verganza.'

'A Spaniard in Somerset with war looming?'

'Can't say. He has a Spanish name but he talks like me. I would have thought him a wealthy local. Good day to you sir, I shop hereabouts.'

Luke had not noticed that they had reached the village. He was immediately impressed with the large number of alehouses which would be frequented at the end of the day by Eglin's day labourers and outservants.

He would return in the evening and extract as much information from the drunken rabble as he could.

Then it hit him. A man with a Spanish title who spoke English like a local and a man who had visited Noakes Hall in a clandestine manner. Cuthbert Mowle alias the Count of Varga y Verganza must be Nicholas Noakes. No, there were too many loose ends. Why did he not make himself known and claim his inheritance? What part if any did he play in his father's murder and his brother's constant disappearances? Why was he visiting the Catholic households of the area? Luke returned to Taunton, put Baxter in the picture and sent an urgent report to the Protector.

The sun was almost down when he returned to the village. The first alehouse he came across was tiny, and made the Black Swan look respectable, even puritanical. To enter Luke had to step over a man befuddled in drink who lay in a puddle just outside the door. Luke was about to enter but was pushed aside by a group of drinkers who emerged from the alehouse and pissed on the recumbent drunk. This explained the puddle in an environment in which it had not rained for days.

There was one big room in the centre of the alehouse with a large fireplace. The beer was served in one corner and apart from one table the only furniture were benches placed around the walls. There were two tiny rooms, hardly bigger than cupboards at each end of the entrance hall. All of the customers gathered in the larger room.

The noise and the stench almost overcame him as he encountered a plethora of sexual encounters, drunkenness and violence. In one corner a woman was strung up by her heels and attached by a rope to a beam. Her dresses had fallen over her head and as the mixed group around her swung her from one end to the other they poured beer into her private parts. From what Luke could pick up over the general uproar she was too hot for her husband and had to be cooled down before enjoying other company. At the other end of the chamber there was mass singing about the euphemisms for the male and female genitalia—the cuckoo's nest and the cucumber. The Cuckoo's Nest was a popular song in this situation as it encouraged mass participation and the acting out of the words was a prelude to sexual activity. This incitement to fornication was reaching a climax when one of women singers espied the handsome stranger.

THE SPANISH RELATION

The gathered throng completed the chorus and the woman approached Luke and whispered seductively in his ear the next verse which ended, 'So gently lift your hand into me cuckoo's nest.' At which she took Luke's hand and placed it up her skirt as the group once more bellowed out the chorus. Luke was thinking, somewhat slowly how to extricate himself from the situation when a man appeared from behind him and struck his hand away from the woman's body and was about to put the other around his neck. The assistant gatekeeper of earlier that day intervened.

'Stop it Jimmie, twuz Meg's doing, but stranger you might save yourself from further trouble by shouting us drinks.'

Luke readily provided the drinks but unfortunately his wellendowed purse interested the spectators and their further demand that he drink a health with them made him anxious. Would he go for safety or principle? Jimmie did not give him much time to reflect. 'Do-ee drink, damnation to Baptists, Quakers and tub thumping Independents?'

Luke could drink to this without much dent to his principles. He had always thought the Protector had been too tolerant and these groups especially the Quakers had been a threat to army discipline in Ireland.

'Come on stranger, refill our pots so that we can drink more healths.' Luke complied, and when the assembled group was ready Jimmie took centre stage again. 'To His Majesty King Charles.'

Not only did Luke fail to raise his pot he poured his beer on the ground. All eyes turned to Jimmie. 'Dang I. You be a scurvy Parliament boy. Taunton turd. Come on ole muckers let ee be taught a lesson.' At this point Luke had his dagger in one hand and luckily had picked up a thick staff that had been left against the wall, in the other. While the group hesitated as to who would make the first assault the gatekeeper intervened.

'Stop it Jimmie the constable and the watch are just outside dragging stinking old Jacob out of his puddle. They be in here in a moment and I don't want to join old Jacob—even if you do. This stranger has a fat purse. Let's punish it and not him.' Jimmie responded in a mildly threatening tone, 'The night is young. He will keep, but in the meantime let him lose his money through his own incompetence. Let him play sixpence in the pot.'

Luke had seen variants of the game. A beer pot was placed some distance from the end of the table. Luke was to place one hand under the table with a coin in its palm. By hitting this hand from below with his other hand

- 119 -

he was to propel the coin into the pot. At a closer distance it was relatively easy. Where Jimmie had placed the pot made it difficult. Every coin Luke flicked into the pot he kept until he had to hazard it again, everyone that missed went to Jimmie and his friends. As the drink began to have its effect Luke thought about escape. He noticed that several of the candles had been extinguished in order to give some privacy to the acts of frenzied fornication that seemed to be occurring all over the room. As he attempted to propel yet another coin into the pot, Meg, the woman who had approached him earlier during the rendition of the Cuckoos Nest whispered in his ear.

'Sweetie, there be but two candles still alight. Anywhen I put out the one at the other end of room you snuff this one and escape. If you need to hide, go past four doors on this side of the street and push open the fifth. Wait for me there.'

All went according to plan. Luke escaped during the confusion, as most were too drunk to follow him. He was not surprised to find his horse gone. He clearly needed a bed for the night and as a gentleman he should reward the girl who had aided his escape. As they noisily and aggressively enjoyed each other's bodies they could still hear the bawdy rendition of the Cucumber from inside the alehouse which proclaimed universal female satisfaction with any man 'who knows the uses of his cucumber.'

24

While Luke was following Mowle, Hugh prepared to question William Rutter, the man he believed was the murderer. Hugh hated this malicious and ill disposed rogue who through sinister means and unlawful practices had accumulated immense wealth. Over five years Hugh had represented dozens of people against Rutter but failed to bring him to justice or gain compensation for his clients. Rutter covered his back, and guilt could legally be proved only against one of his dim-witted minions. He kept well ahead of the law. For a layman, Rutter possessed an extensive knowledge of legal practice and of every loophole that existed. Hugh had to be content with adding to an extensive dossier on the criminal activities of this errant rascal.

Rutter was a Londoner. He was an orphan, brutalised as a child and saved from utter degradation by a new master who treated him like a son. This relationship lasted little more than a year and the master died leaving the boy a sizeable amount of money. Hugh unreasonably believed Rutter murdered the master and forged the will.

In the early years of the war Rutter moved west. As a bailiff he began a reign of terror falsely seizing goods, and returning them at a price. Victims paid up to recover the goods rather than launch an expensive legal suit. Illegal seizure and the inability of victims to finance legal proceedings was a weakness in legal practice that Rutter exploited to the full. Embezzlement, forgery, refusal to pay debts, undervaluation of property when buying and over valuation when selling, and extensive sheep and cattle rustling gradually added to his estate. Rutter utilised slander, blackmail and physical force. He acted illegally, and dared the victim to take him to court.

Hugh was convinced that some magistrates, or at least those in the local area turned a blind eye to Rutter's activities. He knew that Rutter had a very close relationship with Sir Edward Lampard, the county's power broker. How else could you explain Rutter's appointment as High Constable? It was common to appoint a poacher as gamekeeper, but a criminal as a law enforcement officer was unusual.

Despite his prejudices Hugh had no evidence against Rutter in regard to Sir Anthony's murder. Rutter had hoped to increase his holdings in Charlton Noakes by buying the freehold fields in the valley. The village believed that Robert Noakes also promised to sell Rutter significant amounts of manorial land, the very land that Sir Anthony had heavily burdened with debt. Hugh reflected on Luke's view that the need to obtain the land before the debts accumulated further could have given William Rutter a motive for murder.

Was it significant that on the night of the murder the documents relating to land transfers and tenancy agreements as well as the will were stolen? The murderer may have believed that these documents would incriminate him. Hugh who had made copies of all these documents knew that there was nothing in any of them to help identify the murderer or his motives. Lady Elizabeth's marriage settlement and Anthony's will might surprise some people, but a thief would not know what these contained until he stole them.

Hugh felt depressed about the situation but was suddenly propelled into action. His servant announced that the High Constable, Mr William Rutter was waiting to see him. Hugh winced at both titles, the man was no gentleman and only the distraction of the times allowed him to get away with the claim, and he was High Constable through corruption. Hugh refused to receive Rutter in his study parlour. They met in the entrance hall where Hugh usually spoke to servants.

Rutter's appearance was a contradiction. He was a short man and his slight hump, stooped bearing and a gigantic head created the impression of a large dwarf. His mass of curly brown hair, worn long, hid the loss of his left ear. Village gossip held it was sliced off in a drunken brawl. This was untrue. Rutter never drank to excess. He had taken to heart the proverb that when the ale is in the wit is out. And Rutter lived by his wits.

Rutter took his usurped status as a gentleman seriously and overdressed the part. There was nothing subtle in his apparel. He was dressed from collar to toe in light blue—a light blue, long sleeved doublet, matching breeches and stockings. He had a very large white lace collar and exaggerated lace cuffs. His stockings and breeches were tied with light blue ribbons and his shoes were likewise decorated. He wore a low crowned black felt hat with a light blue hatband. The doublet including the sleeves were padded and heavily slashed to reveal a darker blue lining. Each slash and the edges of the doublet were embroidered with silver thread—a London rogue dressed as a cavalier courtier.

Before Hugh could express the necessary formal welcome Rutter spoke.

'Weston, I'm 'eartily sick of the rumours and lies circulatin' frough the village concernin' my activities and ya're in a position ter put a stop ter them.'

'How can I be of assistance?' Hugh mockingly responded.

'Do they fink I killed Sir Anfony?'

'I can't answer that question. Colonel Tremayne is aware of the gossip that you wished to purchase manorial land and that Sir Anthony stood in your way. In other words you had a motive.'

'Bleedin' gossip. Years ago the purchase of estate land would have been ter my advantage but Sir Anfony so burdened it with debt that it is now not viable. As the Noakes's lawyer ya kna the exact amount of funds I would have to find to buy even a small portion of the estate and free it from debt. Ya despise me Weston but at least ya kna that I aint stupid about money.'

Hugh had to admit that Rutter had a point. Sir Anthony had ruined the estate. 'I will certainly pass that on to the Colonel. How else can I help?'

'I need to see Sir Robert. As the family lawyer tell 'im he must meet wif me before week's end. Or I will inform ya as Tremayne's deputy of certain of Robert's activities that ya would then have ter investigate.'

'You're still the blackmailer, Rutter, despite your fancy clothes.'

'Be that as it may, me last question, can Tremayne over ride decisions of local officials?'

'If what you really want to know is whether Tremayne can legally undo any of your crooked decisions and override your authority the answer, thankfully, is yes. Whether he would use the Protector's authority to stand up against the united opinion of the county magistrates is another issue. If I were you Rutter I would co-operate with the Colonel. You could give him information willingly rather than wait until I discover it and begin criminal and civil proceedings against you. Of course that assumes that the army will not take you under its jurisdiction and have you executed. If lucky they might ship you to the Americas as a servant to some other upstart.'

'Oo is the bleedin' blackmailer na?' retorted Rutter.

Neither man indulged in the civilities normally so important in social intercourse. Little Boy Blue, as Hugh nicknamed his unwelcomed visitor simply turned on his heels and left. Hugh reviewed the discussion. He concluded that Noakes and Rutter had fallen out and maybe Luke who would show less antagonism to Rutter may be able to elicit more on that front. Most urgently Robert Noakes would need to be found and questioned before Rutter located him. The motivation Luke attributed to Rutter for the murder of Sir Anthony would not hold up. Hugh quietly cursed himself. If he had done the figures himself he would have realised that to buy land within the manorial estate in its current state of debt would be financially suicidal. He also sensed that the ever-active criminal mind of Rutter was assessing the power of the new player in local politics and deciding whether he would co-operate with, or attempt to destroy Luke Tremayne.

This was exactly what Rutter was thinking as he rode quietly back to his farm. Could he do a deal with Cromwell's agent? He could offer considerable information about all the suspects in return for a lack of interest in his own activities. He would sacrifice Robert Noakes but Sir Edward Lampard was very dangerous and very powerful. The Colonel would need strong evidence against Lampard before Rutter would join in for the kill. It was unfortunate that Tremayne had enlisted young Weston as his deputy. The do-gooder would influence the Colonel against him. He must see the Colonel immediately to counter the lies.

Hugh was about to leave his study and prepare for dinner when his servant delivered a message from Noakes Hall. He was required to be present at noon the following day for the transfer of a lease to the widow of Christopher Jenkins who was murdered by the gooseturds. In preparation for that meeting Hugh examined his copy of the tenancy papers. He knew as a boy growing up in the village that Sir Jasper had been very generous to the villagers granting them long leases on their houses and the associated gardens and orchards, which brought with it the right to use the common fields of the village for agriculture, and to use the common, the green, part of Winslade Wood, and the wastelands to the north of the village to graze their stock and to gather berries and wood. Almost a century earlier Sir Jasper divided his lands in two. One half was enclosed behind the ditch and hedge and this manorial estate was owned by the lord of the manor and farmed directly by him. The other half he ceded to the villagers and their descendants for ninety nine years with the simple requirement that during that period every new lessee would provide the Lord of the Manor with one black feather. The important aspect of this was not that they received their house rent-free but that such occupancy gave them rights to the common lands on which their income and survival depended.

Hugh read the old parchment and became increasingly agitated. For most of the period ninety-nine years had been a long way off and the villagers gave little thought to what would happen at the end of the period. But Sir Jasper had spelt this out very clearly. After the expiration of ninety nine years, the person currently holding the lease would remain in possession until his or her death at which time the Lord of the Manor would either confirm the lease for another ninety nine years on the same conditions, or terminate the lease and all the rights associated with it. The final clause worried Hugh.

> *'All the above will be rendered void if the village should be destroyed by accident, or by the unanimous decision of the signatories or their descendants. In such a case the Lord of the Manor will rebuild the village in a place that he will determine, and at his cost. He will allocate the rights that are attached to village habitation at his discretion. Whatever is his determination it shall be in place for such time as he shall determine at the beginning of the tenancy.'*

Sir Anthony had made clear that he would renew under existing conditions as he saw the agreement as a formality and treated the inhabitants of the village as freeholders. The agreement would expire on Lammas Day next, ten weeks away. What would Sir Robert do? A frightening scenario suddenly hit Hugh. Rutter had discovered a much better proposition than buying manorial land. He would force the new lord of the manor to transfer all the leases to him giving him the village and its fields. Rutter would control more of the parish than the squire and his father.

Then an even worse scenario dawned on him. If the village were destroyed by accident the scheme could be implemented immediately. Rutter had a motive to remove Sir Anthony before the expiry of the leases. He needed a compliant Lord of Manor should the village accidentally burn. Arson had been a favourite weapon of William Rutter in the past. Had firing young Clark's house been a warning to an individual, or a failed attempt to destroy the whole village?

25

Luke, Hugh, and Will met in the landlord's private parlour the next afternoon. Hugh had spent the late morning at the Hall while Luke slept off his nocturnal adventure. Comparing notes Hugh was not convinced that the Count of Varga y Verganza was Nicholas Noakes. 'Dozens of West Country lads finished up in Spain. Nicholas was so young when he was last in Somerset that it is unlikely that he retained a West Country accent.'

Will disagreed. 'Tiz'nt so. Nicholas served Lord Rimington for over ten years both here, and in Spain. I'm minded as a young man meeting Rimington. When the old scoundrel visited Noakes Hall he came here for some entertainment. Rimington spoke like the lowliest of his servants. By Heaven we had trouble understanding him. In Spain Nicholas would have had a decade or more access to our broad Somerset accent. But I hold with Mr. Weston. There is no proof that Mowle is Nicholas.'

'Rubbish,' interjected Luke, 'this link explains a lot. It suggests why Mowle has friends inside Noakes Hall. It accounts for Robert's disappearance. If he is not the squire what is there left for him? And it puts an entirely different slant on our murder investigation.'

Will interrupted. 'More than you think. D' mind what old Jake's killer told you about the letter Hastings intercepted which he thought concerned the return of an heirloom.

Maybe the message was not about heirlooms but about an heir. An heir, Nicholas, looms. By God, squire rode home to meet Nicholas.'

After a long silence Luke jumped to his feet. 'It's time to act. I will arrest the brothers Noakes.'

'Luke, hold off on Mowle,' cautioned Hugh. 'Keep him under surveillance. Talk to Lord Lidford. We know who subverted the Royalist network but not why. Lidford may know the Count. If Will's interpretation of the letter is correct we need to know who sent it? Did Lidford know its content? Was he party to Nicholas's return? Probe Lidford's role and knowledge on this matter before we act on Mowle. Mowle may be Lidford's agent.'

'Hugh, your lawyer's logic annoys me. Action not words is needed. However you may be right on Mowle but I will take Robert into protective custody immediately, if we can find him. Where is he?'

'London,' advised Hugh, 'Lady Elizabeth just received a letter from Dr. Basset bemoaning Robert pestering his daughter Katherine. Send your men to Basset's lodging and wait for him.'

Sir Robert Noakes was still fuming five days later when he arrived at Noakes Hall escorted by six troopers from Luke's London based regiment. The Colonel was at the Hall to receive them. He seconded the six troopers to his team and stationed them at the Hall. Meanwhile Sir Robert was recovering from his journey and no doubt concocting a series of implausible tales to explain his conduct. He was to receive Luke and Hugh within the hour for what Luke had brusquely described as interrogation.

Robert received them in the inner parlour off the entrance chamber. Luke had only met Robert for a few minutes on his arrival but now had time to study him more closely. Perhaps the slim Mowle may not be his missing brother as there was little physical resemblance. Robert was of moderate height but almost as broad as he was tall—the build of a Welsh labourer. He was very strong in the upper body. His brown face and his enormous calloused hands were those of a working farmer. His moon shaped face, large lips and rather small eyes created a vacant smile. He dressed in the earth colours of his labourers, a rusty brown long sleeved doublet and breeches with black stockings. His apparel was neither slashed nor embroidered. The only concession to his status was a lace collar and claret sash.

'Colonel, I must protest at my kidnapping in London and my current house arrest. By what authority and for what purpose am I here?'

'Sir Robert don't waste my time. You are a suspect in the murder of your father and your arrest is made under the direct authority of the Protector. You ran away because you murdered your father, and you were scared of Rutter.' Luke believed he had also fled from his brother but for the moment he would keep that explanation to himself.

'Colonel, on most accounts you are wrong. What is true regarding my dealings with Rutter is that I will not renew the black feather leases and will replace them with ten-year leases at reasonable rents. It is incredible that in a rich village such as this the Lord of the Manor receives no rents. I will do what nine out of every ten landlords have done. If I receive reasonable rents from the tenants I can remove the debt on the manor lands. Rutter will be able to seek those leases like everybody else. Years ago there was an agreement to sell some of that land to Rutter but as my father increased the debt Rutter lost interest. Yes, I have promised Rutter first offer on any leases that become available, but the offer is to lease, not to buy. This is our sole agreement and it is verbal only. The High Constable wants the option to buy, and for me to put it in writing, and have it notarised.

Yes, I knew about Lady Elizabeth's marriage settlement.

Father told me five years ago when I became heir on my brother's death. I must admit that knowing that my estate would be limited to the debt ridden original Noakes holdings made me angry especially as my father allowed this debt to accumulate further. If this was a motive for murder then I was stupid. I should have killed him five years ago. Financially I would have been much better off. Yes, Rutter also wants me to sell him the rights of the Lord of Manor of Charlton Noakes. I refused because the raising of a substantial income from my tenants in rents and dues is the only means I have of making the estate viable.'

Luke was impressed with Robert's openness and relaxed manner but continued his interrogation. 'Sir Robert, why did you run away?'

'Rutter. He threatened that if I did not offer land for sale and put our agreement in writing I would meet the same fate as my father. At father's funeral two of his henchmen assaulted me and indicated what might follow if I did not comply with Rutter's demands. Time in London would enable me to work out my options, and in my absence I hoped you would arrest Rutter for father's murder.'

'Do you have any evidence that Rutter murdered your father?'

'Only that he threatened to do so on many occasions. He saw himself as the potential owner of Noakes Hall and all its rights, and became increasingly angry at the drain on its assets by my father and his failure to exploit its potential. Rutter considered my father's approach to the estate immoral. Rutter would use any means to achieve his ends but these ends were couched in moral terms. Noakes Hall should go to the diligent Rutter and not stay with the wastrel Noakes.'

'Ambition makes men diligent,' mused Luke, 'but why didn't you complain to the authorities about Rutter?'

'You're joking,—the family's Royalist views would not get me a fair hearing from the Parliamentary gentry who monopolise the local bench especially when Rutter has one or more of them in his pocket.'

Luke decided a white lie might help. 'Sir Robert, Rutter has told us that you were at the Hall on the night of the murder. Why were you there at such a critical time?'

'The man is a liar. I was not there. I timed my return from London to coincide with the arrival of the household in midafternoon of the next day.'

'So where were you the night of your father's murder?'

'I was staying in a tavern in Wells. My companion for the night will be difficult to find. She was a soldier's wife bound for Ireland.'

'I have to admit Sir Robert that before this interview I was convinced of your guilt but perhaps I was mistaken. Nevertheless many in the village and here at the Hall dislike you. Why is Mr Clark so hostile?'

'I blame him for my father's failure in estate management and I have let him know my views. It is the duty of the steward to ensure the smooth running and profitability of an estate. Clark never once stood up to my father's hare brained schemes, never once supported my attempts to rein him in. Yet after every discussion Clark would complain about my father and whinge about how the squire was ruining his reputation as a steward. Clark is a weak man, untrustworthy and duplicitous. He knows my low opinion of him as a person and as a steward. I will be glad to be rid of him.

A more personal situation explains our mutual hostility. He married a much younger woman and about ten years ago she and I began sleeping together. Clark treated her badly. We were lovers for several months. One night she was raped and murdered and her body was dumped in the boundary ditch near our gatehouse. I had been in Taunton that night and Jane had been at the Crown and Sceptre drinking with some of the women of the household. I apparently rode past the body just after she had been murdered by a roving Parliamentary patrol that had penetrated deep into what was then Royalist territory.

Recently Rutter accused me of the deed and claimed he had three witnesses who would swear that they saw me dismount when I came abreast of Jane and then disappear with her into the ditch, where she was found the next morning. Rutter's golden handshake could probably find ten men who would swear to his truth. I had no defence given my Royalist ties and Rutter's influence with the current bench. It was easier to ride with it. My fear was that he would tell Giles Yalden, Jane's brother, who would kill me without worrying about proof.'

Luke was beginning to feel sorry for this unloved victim of vicious blackmail but persisted with his questioning. 'Who murdered your father?'

'While in London I thought about this a lot. At first I believed that one of Rutter's henchmen had done it. They're animals and the shattering of the skull reflected their brutality. Yet this atrocity could have been the manifestation of decades of simmering hatred in someone like Clark. On the other hand the order could have come from stepmother. I gather she has shown an interest in you. You are not the first. Over the years there has been a stream of very close friends who visited when father was away. For the last few years Lord Lidford has been a frequent guest and private companion to the alluring Elizabeth. I should know. My bedchamber is next to hers. She is now free with her beauty and her wealth to have any man in England. Father was getting old and I know that real relations between them stopped four or five years ago.'

'Was that enough for her to risk her position by provoking or even organizing the murder of her husband?'

'It could have been political as well as personal. She bullied my father and treated him as a child. Given his drinking and depression my father was a sick man who contributed nothing. It was Elizabeth who ran the household, and with Lidford, the Sealed Knot. Perhaps father was getting in the way both at home and abroad.'

Luke felt sick in the stomach as he thought about Elizabeth's possible guilt but he was determined not to show his concern at Sir Robert's comments. 'Stepmothers are never popular are they? What about Dr Basset?'

'I do not like Basset. He is a man from the past who believes that prayers and vigils solve all problems. He opposes my courtship of Katherine for no better reason than I am not a devoted Royalist and High Church Anglican. I'll accept Cromwell if he leaves me alone to increase the value of my estates. Basset knew my father's secrets more so than any family member. He might be involved if father was betraying some long cherished principle or alliance. Father's refusal to rise with Penruddock could have upset the old dodderer, but smashing in a skull would not be his style. If father died of poison, then I might suspect the chaplain.'

Luke mused that it would be ironic if Basset had opposed the deal made between the Royalist gentry and the Protector in which he had just played a major role. Luke decided to change the topic. 'What happened to your brother?'

'I have had no contact with my brother since I was seven. Father communicated with him on a regular basis until the death of our mother. After that I was told what father thought I should hear. Five years ago after the arrival of a special courier from Lord Lidford father locked himself in his study overnight and in the morning summoned me to him. With tears in his eyes he told me that Nicholas had renounced his faith, his country and his family. He was now a loyal subject of Philip IV King of Spain who had ennobled him. He had married a Spanish woman and become a Roman Catholic. Nicholas would never return to England and I was to consider myself the heir. To avoid hurt and possible complications we were to inform those who were interested that Nicholas had gone missing on a military expedition and was assumed dead. That his son would fight for Spain against fellow Englishmen was too much for father.'

Hugh who had sat silently throughout the interview intervened. 'Sir Robert, while I am Colonel Tremayne's deputy in this enquiry I am also your family's lawyer so I have refrained from participating. Can you support the claims you make against Rutter, Clark or Lady Elizabeth with more concrete evidence? It would make our task a lot easier.'

'I will let you know if I remember anything of importance. Gentlemen would you like to join me in the other parlour for some wine?'

Luke and Hugh excused themselves and headed, as briskly as was appropriate to the Black Swan.

26

Sir Edward Lampard was anxious. He was certain that Luke's mission was to report to the Protector on his leadership of the county. Why then had the Colonel ignored him? He took the initiative.

Luke was surprised to receive Sir Edward's invitation to dine with him on the following day, and amused that the venue was the Four Bears. He arrived dressed as the Colonel of 7th Cavalry Regiment with his red hatband adorned with a mass of bright red feathers. He was shown immediately into a private chamber, which consisted of one long table groaning with food. Lampard had dispensed with the chairs and had placed a long bench on each side of the table. He was already seated on the far side and rose to greet his guest.

Lampard had a reputation as a conspicuous consumer. His love of food and entertainment helped maintain his network of supporters and informers. His attitude towards the good things of life ran contrary to the austere spirit of the time, a situation that put his political stance at odds with his personal whims. He had been, until the Government abolished it, a great supporter of horse racing. Now he had to lead his gentry friends into the low life of Taunton to bet heavily on cock fighting and boxing.

His appearance reflected his life style. He had a reddish blotched face with excessively thick grey eyebrows and obscenely large lips that gave the impression that he was dribbling. His silver grey hair had not completely obliterated the remnants of his original black locks, which were still obvious around the back of his neck and beside his ears. Hugh had warned Luke not to be taken in by Lampard's relaxed appearance. He invariably closed his eyes both on social and professional occasions, giving the impression of a person dozing after too much drink which accounted for his nickname of Nodding Ned. This demeanour concealed one of the sharpest minds that Hugh had ever encountered. Lampard consumed great amounts of alcohol but like his minion Rutter, was never drunk. He had not risen to the top of the political tree by being a sot although to give the appearance of such often gave him a tactical advantage. Lampard combined a ruthless professionalism with the ability to relax and enjoy life.

'Greetings Colonel. Let us dine.'

He indicated to Luke the spot opposite him at the upper end of the table. Luke who had become accustomed to the simple fare at the Three Keys and Black Swan was amazed at the ability of the Four Bears to provide such a feast. He later learnt that Lampard's own cooks had prepared the meal.

Ned Lampard planned that his guest would be well fed before any serious discussion took place. To whet the appetite there was a choice of fine white bread rolls, or slices of the less refined cheat bread to be used as trenchers to hold the chicken and almond, or goose liver and nutmeg pates. Luke ignored the bread and chose a miniature pastry filled with cod's liver. It was obvious that Lampard intended to slide along the bench and progressively tackle each course that had already been set out sequentially on the table.

Both men moved slightly along the bench to confront the first course brimming over with the choice of large cuts of roasted beef, boiled mutton, fried patties of beans, figs, onions and sage; bream in a cold green sage sauce; eels in thick sweet spices; baked quail; and slices of a pork sausage flavoured with sage, ginger and pepper. Luke hardly noticed the veal tongues, lamb pies and various salads.

Some time later he took the lead from his host and slid further along the bench where he faced hard boiled eggs covered in a mustard sauce; scrambled eggs with fresh herbs, spices and oysters; and bread that had been dipped in yolks and fried. The servants continually refilled Luke's goblet with a nutmeg flavoured amber coloured Malmsey wine although Lampard did not suggest the sweet sherry and sugar enhanced claret so beloved of the English gentry.

Luke began to feel that Lampard's hospitality, as intended, was beginning to undermine his inquisitorial resolution and he noted with alarm that they were not as yet halfway down the table. 'Sir Edward, this is indeed a banquet and it has certainly lived up to your renowned hospitality but before the wine affects my wits I think we should discuss the matters in hand.'

'Certainly, Colonel and please forgive my initiative in inviting you to dine but I believe that a person in my position can help you in your enquiries.'

'Sir Edward, I sense a slight tone of admonishment in your welcome. I avoided you until I knew what to raise with you. The noise of the county is that the murder was political and Sir Anthony's political opponents such as you are prime suspects. I am also aware that many think my mission here is to clear the government, whether it be you, the army or the Protector himself from any complicity in the event.'

'Don't be so sensitive Tremayne. Perhaps the drink has got to you. Yes, I was peeved that you shunned me but I knew it was because of your real mission. You can't fool me. I have run this county for almost a decade and given the distraction of the times, that requires considerable ability and political acumen. Parliament has been dissolved and the Protector is drawing up a new list of magistrates. You are here to assess for your master my efficiency and my loyalty to the Government.'

'Sir Edward, you are mistaken. I am sure others report to the Protector on your activities. Many of my military friends have been destroyed by their involvement in politics. Politics is like a net, the more you stir in it, the more you become entangled. That I do not intend to do. I am here to solve one simple issue—the murder of your long-term rival Sir Anthony Noakes.'

Luke's intense dislike of Lampard got the better of his political acumen. He unnecessarily provoked the magistrate.

'Incidentally I have uncovered information about you that could be interpreted as detrimental to the security of the regime which you have taken an oath to sustain.'

'Information, which you have undoubtedly forwarded to the Protector?' snarled Lampard.

'Yes, and do not think Sir Edward that because you corrupt a young officer in the local military headquarters to prevent my reports going to Whitehall that my second or third copies have suffered the same fate. Hugh

Weston thinks you are the most brilliant man he knows. I am surprised that you did not foresee that a simple army officer would have back up procedures. By now the Lord Protector will know of the issues I alerted him to, and that his senior magistrate in the county attempted to prevent this information reaching him.'

'You would find that difficult to prove. The young officer at Baxter's headquarters clearly misunderstood my request. All matters regarding security, law and order in this county while now the responsibility in part of the army must also have the counter signature of a civilian magistrate. The officer clearly thought that your report fell into that category and put it aside. I simply expressed interest in it, I did not ask for it to be withheld indefinitely.'

'Sir Edward you know that my reports are for the eyes of the Protector only, and are in transit under his specific authority which overrides any other regulation or law. But I suppose it will be your word against that of a junior officer.'

'You don't have any real evidence against me.'

'Sir Edward, if my prime concern was to destroy you politically I would ask why you meet secretly in this very inn with Royalist leaders and why you appointed William Rutter, a known rogue as High Constable of Charlton Hundred? I could make a case that you are both a traitor and corrupt. Need I say more?'

Lampard who had been nibbling delicately on a large pork bone at last opened his half closed eyes and glared intently at the colonel. 'These are serious charges and if there had been any truth in them my countless opponents would have used them against me long ago.'

'Fortunately I am not here to interrogate you on your political views, activity or management. Who do you think killed Sir Anthony Noakes, and why should I remove you as a suspect?'

'If you must continue with this charade I suppose I should play the game if only to free my self of suspicion. I must go back to the issues of high politics that get in the way of your murder investigation. Noakes was seen as my rival and that if the King returned he would replace me in control of the county. Honestly, how likely is the return of that puny minnow, Charles, while Cromwell lives? As you have discovered in recent months Noakes and I were working together—we were allies not rivals. What you threaten to portray as treachery was a brilliant success for Cromwell brought about by my diplomacy. I convinced Noakes and his friends that a declaration, even though for a limited period, of Royalist support for the Protector would be in the interests of the county, the nation and the government. At the same time I have been working on my own Parliamentary colleagues to adopt the same position.'

Luke was annoyed. Lampard could paint himself to the Protector as a Government loyalist who had won over the Royalist opposition. Sir Edward continued. 'The success of Noakes in preventing any real support going to Penruddock convinced me that it was time to heal the wounds of war at the local level and that this would require stability in the centre for three or four years more. The gentry of England must re-establish their dominant role in the political, legal and military system of the nation. Divided, we have allowed the rabble to rise, destroy established religion and advance wild doctrines, and on the other hand we have permitted a centralised state to enforce its will in the country through armed force. I admit that like my new Royalist friends I have no enthusiasm for the government of the Lord Protector but for the moment he provides the stability we need to achieve our ends.'

Luke felt much of his argument undermined and regretted his stupid confrontation. 'Sir Edward, I am well aware of the coming together of the gentry and aristocracy of this county. I am glad that for the time being at least this swell of political activity is in support of General Cromwell, although I am not sure what the Papists such as Lord Eglin are up to. But this does not entirely free you of suspicion regarding the murder of Sir Anthony. If the Lord Protector, as a gesture of his appreciation for Royalist support, readmitted them formally to political life your position would be threatened. Apart from Taunton and few other towns, this county is overwhelmingly Royalist. Noakes and his friends would defeat you and your cronies in any election.'

'These matters were discussed. Sir Anthony and I agreed to share the two seat county constituency if Cromwell restored that traditional method of representation and our friends would divide the borough electorates between them. If the Protector persisted with his new eleven representatives from the county we had a written agreement giving us four each and the other three would depend on the whims of the electorate.'

'You miss the point, Sir Edward. In this scheme you share power with your traditional rival. If Sir Anthony were dead you would be by far the most dominant figure in the county and the Protector would undoubtedly recognize this. What you have presented as a wonderful achievement by yourself on behalf of the Protector could be interpreted by a simple army officer as a brilliant piece of opportunism, which removed the one Royalist threat to your dominance. With Sir Anthony gone there is no senior Royalist left in the county to take his place. Therefore, you had a motive for having Noakes murdered.'

'You are the one who has missed the obvious. Anthony was a has been. He was a sick, ailing drunkard who when he met with me presented papers and parroted a position dictated to him by Lady Elizabeth. She is the Royalist leader in this county but even in these distracted times women cannot stand for public office. No, Colonel I did not need to murder Anthony. Politically he was dead already.'

Luke was not happy to hear of Lady Elizabeth's role. She had concealed Sir Anthony's condition from him. What else was she hiding? His musing was only momentary as Lampard went on the offensive. 'My dear Colonel, I can see why Cromwell entrusts you with missions such as this but be careful. Accusations that you cannot support and speculation that may damage the reputation of important men are dangerous devices that may return to punish you.'

'If that is a threat I can only respond in kind. Important men can be brought down. High places have their precipices. You need to tread carefully. Don't underestimate the resolution of the Protector. If you are guilty I will ignore the corrupt civil administration and subject you to military law. However for the present there is no evidence against you. I have simply raised with you county gossip and elicited your response. Before you put an end to this meal—if you are innocent, then who murdered Sir Anthony?'

'Family. It was either Robert, who has hated his father for years, and was probably deranged by increasing indebtedness and the news of his step mother's property settlement, or the beautiful Lady Elizabeth who had spurned Sir Anthony for some five years, and according to rumour has dallied with Lord Lidford among others. As I see by the expression on your face the beautiful Bess has captivated you. Beware cats that conceal their claws.'

THE SPANISH RELATION

'Why would she have her own husband murdered?'

'Anthony was a total embarrassment. Lady Elizabeth ran the household and the Sealed Knot. Maybe they could no longer trust him. I know his growing friendship with his maverick cousin, Sir Toby Noakes, infuriated her.'

Luke again felt sick at the bottom of his stomach on hearing the allegations against Elizabeth, and he also wondered how Sir Edward knew of her and Anthony's partial estrangement. He was angry and he knew that when a man grows angry his reason rides out. He was no longer in the mood to battle wits with Sir Edward. He thanked his host, drank a health to the Lord Protector, excused himself, and left.

After Luke's departure Lampard closed his eyes and reviewed the discussion. He had been a fool to tamper with official military reports. He could defend himself, as he had not tried to obtain the document. He actually had no idea what it contained. He wanted it delayed until he had a chance to sum up the author. The Colonel annoyed him. Tremayne was a man who would carry out his mission ruthlessly and relentlessly—a man who seemed to have uncovered considerable material in his short time in the county.

Lampard's own research had established that Tremayne had the respect and the ear of the Protector. Any attempt to undermine the soldier's credit would require a major indiscretion or mistake by the Colonel. Sir Edward considered this most unlikely. If he had the time he might be able to build on the Colonel's relationship with Lady Elizabeth. God preserve him from honest men! Walter Weston was enough, and now Luke Tremayne.

Lampard was worried about his relationship with Rutter. Others had tried to establish this connection but he used his legal position to stall any serious enquiry. Tremayne could override any such obstruction. If Tremayne dug deeply with the help of that dangerous whelp Hugh Weston most of Lampard's judicial indiscretions might be uncovered. His protection of the Green Glove in return for their services might be revealed. Lampard was disconcerted by Tremayne's mention of Eglin and the Papists. Sir Edward could not afford any serious investigation in that area or Tremayne would have grounds to accuse him of treason.

If Tremayne could not be discredited he must die, as must Rutter. Lampard dispatched a servant to the Black Swan to locate Tom Hastings. The one positive from the meeting was that Luke had no idea of the real purpose of the Royalist and Parliamentary meetings. Temporary support for his leader seemed to satisfy the otherwise critical and curious mind of the cavalry commander. Lampard smiled, and mused what would the righteous Colonel do if he knew the truth. Perhaps he should be told.

27

Luke went to Baxter's headquarters where he quickly penned an account of his meeting with Lampard and dispatched it to Whitehall. Cromwell would certainly receive stories fabricated by Lampard or his friends so it was wise to get in first. The soldier, despite himself, was becoming the politician.

Luke needed to see Lord Lidford. It was early evening when he arrived at the House still dressed as a colonel of a cavalry regiment. The attire evoked memories for Lord Lidford, of his own successful career in such a role. Lidford welcomed him.

'By your attire I assume this is a formal visit?'

'No, my lord, pardon my impertinence in arriving without an appointment or giving you any indication that I was coming but I think I know who compromised your network but I need to clarify some points before I can be certain.' By now the two men were seated around a small table in an inner parlour and Lidford had dismissed his servants from the room. Luke did not waste time. 'Sir, what can you tell me about the Count of Varga y Verganza?'

Lidford delayed his answer as he considered what he could tell Cromwell's man of secret Royalist activity. His own doubts about the Spaniard convinced him that there was more to gain than lose in a frank answer. 'Some months ago the Count arrived bearing impressive authorization. His papers were signed and sealed by His Majesty Charles II and also by King Philip IV of Spain. He had appropriate letters of introduction and authorization for any action that he undertook. He did not tell me his mission but I suspected he was assessing the political and religious situation in the country should Spain go to war on behalf of Charles II.'

'In what tongue did he speak to you?' Luke asked.

'In rather fractured French. This surprised me as my mother being Spanish I speak his native tongue fluently. Even though I greeted him in Spanish he replied in French. Why do you ask?'

'I will explain later. What was your reaction to his visit?'

'I was troubled that the King should send a Spaniard to Somerset at the very time we were engaged in the delicate negotiations of which you are familiar. And secondly to send a Spaniard here when the Government is attacking Spanish colonies in an undeclared yet popular war would not win many over to the King's cause. I sent a messenger to the King's court to satisfy my concerns. Two factions make up the court in exile—the English and the rest. The Englishmen around the King have no time for a group of foreigners—Scots, Irish, French and Spaniards, who convince Charles that he can be restored to his English Crown at the head of a foreign army. My friends at court believed that Varga was sent here to rally support especially among the Papists for a projected French Spanish invasion to restore the King.'

'I can fill in some of the gaps,' volunteered Luke. He recounted his adventures in following Mowle alias Varga and his visits to papist households, but withheld for the moment, any reference to his suspected English origins.

Lidford was astonished. 'I did not know that Varga had usurped our network, and taken control of Yalden's men nor that he has an ally at Noakes Hall. All I knew for certain was that locals were sounded out regarding their stand should Spain assist a Royalist invasion. People never learn. The Armada and the Civil War proved that when conflict occurs Englishmen, papist or puritan, do not support foreigners, even if they are co-religionists. This probing upset Lord Eglin whose family has a long record in fighting Spain. Eglin informed me of Varga's activities. He also told me that Varga had let slip that he had an agent at the highest level of the county administration. If it is not Lampard it must be someone very close to him.'

It was Luke's turn to be surprised. 'If we could establish links between Varga and Lampard it might throw more light on my murder investigation. Let me revert to that enquiry for a moment. The message that you received a few days before the murder and sent on to Sir Anthony—where did it come from and did you know what it contained?'

'It came as a sealed letter within a covering note by our normal courier from Paris. The covering note simply asked that the sealed letter be sent to Sir Anthony provided it would reach him no later than the following Thursday morning. If this was not possible I was to destroy it. That is why I wasted no time in sending it on.'

'Lord Lidford there is a major twist to the Varga affair. Although Hugh Weston disagrees I believe that the Count of Varga y Verganza is Sir Nicholas Noakes. He may have spoken fractured French to you but in his guise as Cuthbert Mowle and his visits to many of the local gentry he has a very broad local accent, and he visited Noakes Hall late at night and was received briefly by someone in the house—in the very library in which Sir Anthony was killed.'

Lidford placed his head in his hands and for some time stared in front of him. 'These are indeed distracted days. Who do I trust? A decade ago you and I would have met on the battlefield. We knew who was on our side and who was not. I fought to save the King and you fought to defend the Parliament. Where has it got us? I support a Lord Protector against my King. You support a Lord Protector who has dismissed three Parliaments. The rest of the country plots against him. At least I know what I am up against. When it comes to the crunch will Yalden's men support the Sealed Knot or Varga? I suppose that all the Count had to do was to show Yalden and young Daniel Pyke his papers bearing the seal of the King. If he were Sir Nicholas Noakes he would also have family loyalty on his side. Do you think he murdered his father?'

'The broken sword, the murder of Odam and the attacks on you and Lady Elizabeth would suggest a political motive. Nicholas maybe on a mission to eradicate those whom the King has convicted as traitors to his cause. It all makes sense except for the brutality of the murder.'

Lidford reverted to an earlier topic. 'There could be a link between Lampard and Varga. An understanding between the two would fit Lampard's personality and his obsession with power. He is the consummate politician preparing for the day when the Stuarts return. He has already taken steps to protect himself in a Royalist future. Lampard has four daughters and he has married three of them to the younger sons of Royalist peers. His fourth daughter was betrothed to my nephew who was killed in the coach explosion meant for me. Perhaps unlike many of us Royalists Lampard is preparing for an imminent return of Charles II. Somerset's current political leader has no loyalty to your Cromwell.'

Before Luke could respond their discussion was interrupted by the unannounced arrival through a concealed door in the far wall of the parlour of a most beautiful and regal woman attired significantly in crimson and gold, and not wearing her black mourning clothes—Lady Elizabeth. Both Elizabeth and Luke looked astonished and embarrassed. Lidford recognized the awkwardness between his guests and smiled to himself.

'Lady Elizabeth, I have an unexpected visitor. Luke you will stay for supper and for the night?'

After Lidford left the room Luke, overcome with a feeling of betrayal, rejection and foolishness, was lost for words. Elizabeth broke the ice.

'Dear Luke I did not expect you here so soon. Hugh Weston said that the oaf Lampard had summoned you to lunch. You are certainly backing both sides, dinner with Lampard and supper with Lidford.'

'The fortunes of war, no doubt.' Luke lamely replied.

He had wished to add love but jealousy, fuelled by the comments of Lampard and others, reduced his responses to a meaningless babble. His training and status stopped him asking the obvious questions. What was Elizabeth doing at Lidford House? Was she having an affair with Lidford? Were they long-term lovers?

Lidford returned accompanied by two younger women. He introduced the youngest as Lady Mary, his daughter, and her slightly older companion as Grace Rutter. Luke raised his eyebrows at her surname, which was noticed by Elizabeth who gave him a discreet nod. He later ascertained from Elizabeth that when his wife died William Rutter blackmailed a very wealthy yeoman to bring the child up as his own although Grace was always aware of her real father. When Grace became a teenager Rutter persuaded an aging gentlewoman, a distant relative of Lidford to take her in as a servant-companion. On her death bed the gentlewoman recommended Grace as a companion to Lady Mary. Grace was not aware of her father's activities and had come to believe that his inability to have her live with him was due to his highly secret operations on behalf of the government that took him abroad for much of the year.

Luke had not dined at an aristocratic table in the West Country since his youth in Cornwall. It was ironic that the last time he did so Elizabeth was present as the daughter of the house. She was present again today but in what role? Luke's jealousy was further fuelled by the table placements. Lidford sat at the head of the table, and Lady Elizabeth at the opposite end of the table, the place usually reserved for the wife. Lidford must have sensed Luke's distraction.

'Colonel, my wife died in giving birth to Mary. I have never remarried. Not long afterwards my friend Anthony Noakes also lost his wife and although he was much older than I, he took a young wife. The three of us over the years became close personal friends as well as political allies. When I indulged in lavish entertainment, as I am doing over the next four days Elizabeth, with Anthony's approval, became the lady of Lidford House. Elizabeth and I are very close friends—as an older brother and younger sister. So, do not fret young Luke.'

Luke was deeply embarrassed that his demeanour had clearly been so black that Lidford felt forced to make such a statement. All he wanted to do was to crawl under the table— where he would probably be savaged by one of his lordship's mastiffs. He had overeaten at dinner with Lampard and certainly drunk more than was appropriate. He ate little supper, consumed as he was with jealousy and embarrassment. His face was the colour of his sash. As soon as it was politely possible Luke retired for the night. He would have slept more peacefully if he had heard the discussion between Lidford and Elizabeth after he had left the dining hall.

'Elizabeth, Luke's discomfiture in your presence highlights the matter I raised with you before. You must seriously consider your own future and decide whether our brave Colonel has a major role to play in it. He is undoubtedly besotted with you. The look on his face when you came through that door and his immediate assumption that you are my mistress. Devastation was written all over his face.'

'Richard, I am attracted to Luke. It may be his association with the happier times of my childhood, and the exuberance of girlhood love but I do not know the mature Colonel Tremayne. Again my self-imposed abstinence may be another pressure pushing me into his arms. I need time to think. I want to see our cause triumphant, and my daughter married and well maintained before I risk any personal relationship.'

'Lydia is still a child and you should not use her as an excuse. Don't wait too long. I did. Luke would be an ideal companion. Do not let him slip away.'

'You're biased Richard. You see in him the characteristics that made you an excellent cavalry commander. I sense you also see in him the son you never had.'

Elizabeth retired to her chamber. As Tamsin assisted her to remove the magnificent red gown, multiple skirts and bodice, and their masses of silver linings and lace attachments she half thought of seeking out Luke and re assuring him of at least her affection. This was not her house and given her role for the next few days as Richard's surrogate wife it would be inappropriate. Her fantasies that night were decidedly inappropriate. She must either embrace the situation or bring it to an end.

She would bring it to an end.

28

Luke rose late as befitted a guest of the aristocracy. From his bedchamber he could see down the long drive that led up to the large courtyard that provided the entry precinct for Lidford House. Even though it was only Friday, midmorning, weekend guests were already arriving. Luke noted the procession of coaches bearing the arms of the great families and was a little irritated by the noise of brightly liveried footmen assisting households to unpack. His mind went back to his childhood and he mused on the great entertainment that Elizabeth's father had provided. This tradition of conspicuous consumption displayed to a select circle of equals had maintained the unity of the great landowners. Given the restrictions imposed by Cromwell's regime it was one of the few opportunities for the Royalists to meet and plan joint responses to the issues that confronted them. It was also essential for the continuation of their family dynasties as it provided an environment in which eligible young men and women could be paraded before their potential suitors and their respective parents. His reverie was broken by a loud knock on his chamber door and before he could reply Lidford had entered the room.

'Luke, a quick word before more of my guests arrive. Call me Richard, and do not give up on Elizabeth. She was asked to invite you and young Weston for this weekend, in part in order that you might release Robert Noakes from his house arrest. For his father's sake I do not want him to feel snubbed or isolated from his father's circle of friends. Keeping an eye on Robert was only part of my motivation. Weston needs to see more of young

Lydia in the appropriate environment, and you can surely not object to an opportunity to see more of Elizabeth. She raised the matter with Weston who said he needed your approval. Approve and I will send a message to Noakes Hall and Weston and Sir Robert can be here early evening.'

Luke warmed to the idea. In this environment his attentions to Elizabeth, or any of the other women, would be appropriate. The married men hunted and played cards while the bachelors and widowers dallied with potential partners. He had misgivings concerning Robert's presence but it might improve his demeanour if he spent time at Lidford House. 'Richard, thank you for your invitation which I accept. Robert can come if escorted by Hugh. Could your servant also bring back with him a change of clothes for me? I will list what I need. It might be somewhat provocative to your guests to appear before them in the full regalia of a Cromwellian Colonel.'

Luke spent the rest of the day diplomatically in his chamber awaiting the arrival of his civilian attire. He took the opportunity to assess the state of his investigation and of his personal circumstances. As far as the latter was concerned he wavered between believing the answer to Sir Anthony's murder lay in the Robert Noakes, Rutter and Lampard political and property nexus or with Nicholas Noakes and the high politics of the Royalists.

At the personal level the brief but clear comments of his host had reawakened his desire to do something about his feelings for Elizabeth. Yet he could not dismiss the horrible thought that she was using him. She had concealed the truth about Sir Anthony's physical and mental state and her interaction with him. She gave no hint of her role in the Sealed Knot and her relationship with Lidford still troubled him. The peer's behaviour on the previous evening, and his comments that morning might be to cover past intimacies with Elizabeth.

The pressure on Luke since his arrival in Somerset contributed to the ease in which he then dozed off despite his anguish over Elizabeth. He was awakened in the early evening by a loud knock. A servant left a moderate sized box on the floor containing Luke's change of clothes, and informed him that Hugh Weston had arrived. Now suitably attired Luke descended the great staircase into the magnificent hall where Elizabeth was welcoming the arrivals. She came across to him.

'Luke, walk with me in the garden?'

THE SPANISH RELATION

'Won't you be missed if you are not here to welcome the guests?' Luke somewhat peevishly replied.

'No, a few minutes will not matter and young Mary has to be trained in the role. I will speak to her for a minute and meet you on the steps of the entrance.'

Luke waited patiently at the bottom of the steps nodding to arriving guests. Elizabeth eventually swept down the portico steps arrayed magnificently in various shades of green all heavily embroidered with golden thread as befitted the daughter of a peer. As she led him through the rectangles and squares of Lidford's intricate formal garden Luke was about to declare his formal courtship when she anticipated his thoughts.

'Luke I know how you feel about me and I admit to similar feelings for you. I also know that Richard has spoken to you as he has to me. He enjoys the role of matchmaker. He treats me like a younger sister who having experienced difficult times deserves a new and better future with an ideal companion. To Richard that partner is you. He likes you. He sees in you the son he never had. In fact since the death of his favourite nephew, the Duke's youngest son, he has been considerably distraught. Your successful career as a cavalry commander has also raised your reputation in his eyes. Before you court me openly I have a proposition that will cool your ardour.'

Luke suddenly sensed an inexplicable chill. Elizabeth continued. 'Luke like most men you want a family, ideally a clutch of boys to continue the family name. Also as a younger son you need to enhance your estates, just as Richard has done, even to the point of outshining your older brother. The continuation of the family dynasty is basic for our class.'

'Elizabeth, I do not think of family or estates. I love you and want to be with you. Don't complicate matters.'

'Luke, if you marry me you will have no children. After Lydia was born the physician made it clear that my childbearing days were over. I could not bear to see your Tremayne line die out, and know that I was responsible. I know your brother has no children.'

'I have spent all my adult life without family. I just want you. You alone, if that is all that is possible.'

'Luke, put aside selfish personal desire and concentrate on the greater good of the Tremayne and Hanes families. I propose that you marry my daughter Lydia and produce a multitude of children. I will set you up immediately with considerable estates and on my death the total Hanes fortune will descend through my daughter and her husband to their children. Your eldest son by my daughter will be the wealthiest man in England. In this way the bloodline of our families as well as their material success will be ensured. Do not give me an answer now. Think about it. Take me back to the house it is starting to get cold.'

Luke was dumbfounded. He escorted Elizabeth back up the steps and then immediately retraced his path and walked off into the gathering gloom. What had promised to be a beautiful weekend in the vicinity, if not the company of his beloved Elizabeth had just exploded in his face. It did not help when he rounded one of the ornamental hedges and came face to face with Hugh and Lydia in a passionate embrace. His monosyllabic grunt to their warm greeting disconcerted them. Before Hugh could extend the conversation Luke disappeared in the darkness.

He must have walked for an hour or so and having reached a hill some distance from the house looking back he saw in its vicinity lighted tapers and lanterns, and in the cool crisp air he could make out sounds that reflected agitation and concern, if not disquiet and panic. He saw the lights fan out in every direction and noted that several were heading his way. He made his way through the trees to intersect with the nearest lantern-waving horseman.

'What's wrong?' Luke asked the mounted man when he came within earshot.

'One of my lord's household is missing. We are searching for her now.'

'Who is it?'

'Lady Mary's companion, Mistress Grace.'

'What happened?'

'While Lady Mary was receiving her father's guests Grace wandered off, some say with a gentleman, others that she was alone. No one thought anything of this until she failed to appear for supper. Searching and calling around the vicinity of the house brought no response so Lord Lidford has organized a thorough search—horsemen fanning out across the estate and then following this up with a detailed search on foot.'

While the horseman was explaining to Luke, an old forester had appeared out of the gloom and listened intently to the discussion.

'It's you old George. Perhaps you and this gentlemen can search the woods that cover this hill and I will ride on?'

Luke soon discovered that old George was Lord Lidford's head gamekeeper who had been looking for poachers who took advantage of Lidford's entertaining to hunt illegally. He too had seen the lanterns and tapers. He spoke, 'Zir, I been azearching below. Cannee vollow me five yards ta the right and circle the hill until we be at peak. Thataways the young lady be not missed. I lost my voice backalong, ee do the calling.'

Apart from finding a partly attired couple that were not husband and wife the search proved fruitless. Once they reached the pinnacle old George excused himself and melted back into the woods and Luke began his descent towards the house. There he met Richard who asked, 'Have you brought me any good news?'

'Your head gamekeeper and I searched the upper aspects of that nearest hill and found nothing but a couple of your wayward guests.'

'Do you think that Grace's disappearance is related to the other problems we're facing?'

'Are you suggesting she has been abducted to put pressure on you?'

'Maybe, but it could also be directed against Rutter.'

'It's a possibility and better than being raped and murdered by marauding villains. The gooseturds are very active in these parts from what you say.'

'I'm ending the search until dawn as it is very easy to miss someone on this estate especially if they are injured and unconscious.'

The search for Grace Rutter and the preceding long walk had made Luke exceedingly tired and he fell asleep immediately before the enormity of Elizabeth's proposition distracted him. When he awoke next morning he had no time for thought and joined one of the earliest group of searchers who headed off in the opposite direction to where he had gone the previous night. He had no time to see, let alone talk, to anyone else except a formal nod in the direction of Richard who continued to organize the search parties.

It was late in the afternoon that Luke and his group now soaked by the constant rain that had begun just after they set out heard three musket shots in quick succession—the signal that the search was over. It took almost an hour before Luke reached the house where he was met by a tearful Elizabeth and Lydia, and an even more distraught Lady Mary. Grace had been found amongst the reeds surrounding one of the lakes that comprised the lower levels of the estate. She was still alive—just. She had not been able to speak, and the doctor was still with her. Lidford appeared and asked Luke and Hugh to join him in an inner parlour.

'Gentlemen, I want your advice. Rutter to his credit has always kept out of his daughter's way and never wanted her reputation tarnished by association with him. But given the circumstances I think he should be informed and brought here.'

'How is Grace? What happened? Is she dying?' asked Hugh.

'We will know in a while when the doctor completes his examination,' replied Lidford.

Luke responded to Lidford's question.'Rutter should be told. I will ride to Charlton Noakes now and bring him back. Lidford nodded his approval.

Luke almost felt sorry for the little man. He was overwhelmed with grief and anxious to know exactly the situation of his daughter. When Luke with Rutter arrived back at Lidford House a servant immediately ushered them into Lord Lidford's private parlour. After the usual formalities and the expressions of grief and commiserations Lidford spoke. 'William, the news is both good and bad. The good news is that physically your daughter will recover. The bad news, and I cannot put it in any less direct way, she has been sodomized.'

William let out a long anguished half sigh, half muted scream and although unsteady on his feet managed to stumble into the nearest chair from where he broke into inconsolable sobbing.

29

ELIZABETH WANTED LYDIA REMOVED immediately from the atmosphere at Lidford House. Luke and Hugh who were about to return Robert to Noakes Hall readily agreed that Lydia could accompany them. After a couple of hours the travellers stopped for a rest and meal at the Cock and Fox. Given the constant drizzle the party was happy to dry out in front of a blazing fire and as the weather worsened they decided to remain there overnight.

There were few other guests in the inn but Luke began to feel apprehensive as several groups of horsemen suddenly descended upon the house around dusk. They took over the parlour and Luke's party reluctantly moved into a side chamber. Then without warning the door of that chamber was forced open and a stranger followed by several of his retinue burst into the room.

'Don't stop us Colonel. Our quarrel is not with you or the captain. It's the gentlefolk, the spawn of Sir Anthony Noakes, that must pay the price.'

Lydia and Robert were seized and taken out of the room, the door was closed and Luke could hear its large locking bar being put in place. Hugh was frantic. He beat on the door and shouted for assistance but over the heavy rain and the noise from the parlour he was not heard. The only possible avenue of escape from a room with no external openings and thick internal walls was upwards. Hugh stood on a bench and Luke balanced precariously on his shoulders hacked into the thin ceiling with his sword. Exiting through the roof Luke returned to the parlour and opened the door of the side chamber to release Hugh.

They immediately confronted the landlord who explained that the kidnappers had claimed they were friends of the Colonel and wanted to surprise him. When they left their leader slipped him a silver coin and suggested he not open the door for an hour. Luke could see no point in haranguing the landlord who clearly did not know the abductors and who had assumed the goings on were part of the bawdy give and take of tavern life. Hugh was anxious to follow the gang immediately but as Luke pointed out there would be no trace of their tracks in the pouring rain. He was almost hysterical. 'What do we do Luke, we must save Lydia?'

'Let's think. Who would want to abduct both Lydia and Robert? Are they being targeted because they are gentlefolk? If so the kidnappers might be Children of the New Dawn intent on wiping out the ruling elite. If, as their leader implied Lydia and Robert are victims because they are children of Sir Anthony then maybe the gooseturds are the culprits.'

Hugh appeared to have calmed himself and the thoughtful lawyer replaced the distraught lover. 'How did they know we would be here? We didn't know ourselves until the rain set in. How did they know who we were? We must have been followed from Lidford House which suggests the ever watchful gooseturds.'

'Hugh, ride onto Taunton and alert Tom Baxter. I will question a few of the customers here and then return to Lidford House and tell Elizabeth.'

After Hugh had left Luke decided against stopping the drinkers with a big announcement and explanation. He would do better to conceal his Cromwellian credentials and play the friend of kidnapped Royalist gentry. So he approached several groups of drinkers separately and won considerable confidence by supplying additional drinks. No one knew who the men were who stormed the side chamber and emerged with a man and a woman. In fact few admitted to noticing the event. Several claimed that given the way they talked they were not local but came from West Somerset or even Devon. Then one piece of trivia got Luke's attention. One drinker claimed that two of the men were wearing hatbands of yellow and orange—Children of the New Dawn?

It was well into the night and with the weather not improving Luke decided to stay until dawn. He hired a room and had almost dozed off when he heard a gentle knocking on his door. A woman's voice whispered softly, 'May I come in?' Luke was tired but time with one of the local wantons might at least release the tension that Lydia's kidnapping, or rather the thought of having to tell Elizabeth, had created. He opened the door and was pleasantly surprised to find a young well developed dark haired wench with a tiny waist and wide thighs. She wore nothing but a thin chemise which she had covered with a large shawl. Whether it was the cold night or the girl's sexual state but her nipples were long and taut and before either spoke Luke had them between his teeth and alternately nibbled and sucked them. The girl responded with one of the quickest orgasms that Luke had ever witnessed. She then began to caress him, he slipped inside her and after a deliberately prolonged period of vigorous thrusting she came again as Luke exploded.

After further caresses Luke was not sure whether he wanted to continue with this most satisfying encounter or to get some sleep. The actions of the girl determined that he would do neither. As he rolled over to mount her yet again he simultaneously saw and felt the point of a dagger against his throat. His first inappropriate thought was where had she hidden such a weapon. She spoke calmly, 'Sir, I mean you no harm and I act for a friend of yours. If you are to save the Lady Lydia you must come with me now.'

Luke confident that he could escape at any time decided he had nothing to lose. He followed the girl to her room where she dressed quickly and then led him quietly out of the inn and towards the stables. He was surprised to find his horse already saddled. Once out on the road Luke realized they were heading north towards Taunton. Some time later the weather became dangerous with a sudden and prolonged hailstorm. Luke and the girl sheltered in an outbuilding that faced the road and despite the difficulties he soon found his tongue and lips massaging her nipples while her hands stimulated his manhood. The sexual chemistry between them was incredible.

After both storms had passed they resumed their journey and just as they approached Taunton the girl led Luke into a forest and after riding for an hour with daylight increasing they reached a well built cottage in a small clearing. Smoke billowed from the chimney suggesting that the occupant had just risen and had refuelled the fire after it had been allowed to burn down over night.

As they approached the cottage the girl called out, 'Aunty Jane, Aunty its me Rebecca.' The girl dismounted and ran to the door of the cottage which was wide open. Before Luke had reached the door Rebecca had entered it and re-emerged looking distraught. 'She's gone, my aunt who was to meet you here is gone.'

'Calm yourself Rebecca. It's time to tell me what this is about. Who is your aunt and why did she want to see me?'

'My aunt belongs to that sisterhood which the Puritan parsons in Taunton are trying to destroy as diabolical witches. She is the daughter of Mother Sparrow, and I am a granddaughter of Mother Sparrow through another daughter who died when I was little. I lived with my Aunt Jane until I got work at various inns along the road to Dorset. My aunt received a message a few days ago from grandmother that she must get a message to you urgently that an attempt would be made to murder Robert and Lydia Noakes on their return from Lidford House. The would be murderers expected Robert and Lydia to return at different times and could hardly believe their luck when both took the road together. You all left earlier than expected so by the time I arrived at the Cock and Fox they had already been taken.'

'I'm sorry Rebecca I thought you worked there and visited me as part of your work.'

'You are partly right. I work the various inns up and down the Dorset road and have an arrangement with each of the landlords. Most of the time I also act for my aunt and her friends in selling potions and spells.'

'Why did your aunt want to meet me?'

'Grandmother was to send more details. I think she knew who the abductors were and what they planned. She hinted to Aunt Jane that she was taking steps to help the Noakes siblings but she insisted that you and you alone could save the day.'

'Do you think your aunt has gone to see your grandmother?'

'No, the fire has been freshly re-lit and the pot is simmering on the hob. Aunt Jane was about to have breakfast when she also was taken.'

'You're right. Look at the ground. It is very soft after the rain and at least five or six horses and one person walking have torn it up. Beside the footprints is a circular hole. Does your aunt walk with a stick?'

Rebecca nodded in the affirmative and began to sob gently. Luke was now much more optimistic. 'Taking your aunt might be the piece of luck we needed. We had no hope of following the kidnappers from the Cock and Fox but now with daylight and soft ground we have a better chance. I want you to ride on to Taunton and go straight to the military headquarters and say you are on the Protector's business and have an urgent message from Colonel Tremayne for Colonel Baxter. Tell him what has happened and ask that he send some men here to follow me, and others to Charlton Noakes to protect your grandmother. She might be the next victim.'

30

Luke soon overhauled the kidnappers. After an hour ambling through the forest they emerged into open fields. Luke recognised their leader from the Cock and Fox, Lydia, Robert and an older woman with a stick who he assumed was Aunt Jane. Beyond the first field was a home park and a ruined manor house. Luke suddenly recalled. He had been here before. Ten years earlier as Cromwell's army moved across Somerset the general ordered the manor house to be razed to the ground. In the decade since its owner had joined the King in France and the derelict buildings lay overgrown with vines and brambles.

The party disappeared into the ruins and by the time Luke had reached them he could not see anybody but heard what appeared to be very distant, entombed voices. The only part of the old house that remained usable was its underground cellars. One of the men stood guard at the entrance but Luke working his way among the broken masonry got close enough to hear what was being said. One voice ranted, 'Why are we waiting. Let's get it over and done with.' A calmer voice responded, 'He said to wait until he arrived and I am not going to cross him or we may be added to the list.'

Luke assumed that they were waiting for Amos Hogg. Perhaps these religious nutters were going to make a sacrifice—some ritual mumbo jumbo to help justify their cold blooded murder. Then the sentry shouted, 'The Captain is coming and he has the old hag with him.'

Luke could not believe his eyes. Coming across the field resplendent in a blue coat and with his red hair reflecting in the sunlight was Giles Yalden and the woman trailing alongside was Mother Sparrow. Before Luke had time to reconsider the situation he was hit from behind and passed out. When he came to he was in the cellar along with Mother Sparrow and her daughter Jane, and Robert and Lydia Noakes.

The Noakes half siblings were in a sorry state. It was difficult to ascertain who was sobbing the most. Robert alternated between bluster—he was a squire that no one dare touch, to pathetic attempts to buy his life—promising Yalden anything he wanted. Luke turned to Mother Sparrow, 'I thought the kidnappers were the Children of the New Dawn ridding the country of anti-Christian gentry. Why is Yalden involved?'

'That is what you were intended to believe. Some of Yalden's men wore the yellow and orange colours of Hogg's cult which they stole from their wives.'

'Does Yalden really intend to kill them?'

'Make no mistake about it. He will kill them, and because we know too much the rest of us as well.'

'But why? Is it getting revenge for old grudges?'

'No, it is highly political. The men who will soon kill us in cold blood believe they are doing the King's will. I'm surprised you haven't recognised them. Most are villagers from Charlton Noakes.'

'Why kill the Noakes siblings—Lydia at least is a committed royalist?'

'It's concern for the future of the Manor of Charlton Noakes and its lordship. It was bad enough for these obsessed Royalists that the previous lord and his wife was doing a deal with the Protector, but it was feared that Robert would sell out to Rutter, or if Robert died Lydia might marry Hugh Weston and the estate would eventually become his—an officer in Cromwell's army. It was all too much for Giles.'

'What happens to the manor if Robert and Lydia die without children?'

'It reverts to a man with impeccable Royalist credentials— that distant cousin Sir Toby Noakes.'

'Is Toby Noakes behind this plot?'

'No. This is a scheme concocted by an almost deranged Giles Yalden.'

'How do you know all this?'

'As you know the village is increasing divided. The murder of your men alienated many Royalists from Yalden's cause while Will Pyke has gradually won over most of the village to the compromise advocated by the late squire and Lady Elizabeth. Then I keep hearing about a gentleman in a golden cape who at times seems to control Yalden yet at others opposes him.'

'Why the delay? Why don't they kill us now?'

'I think a few of them are getting cold feet. The only one they would be happy to kill is Robert. Some of them fear my powers, and the retaliation that will come if they kill you has many of them worried.'

'I hope my men arrive before they complete the deed. Your granddaughter should have reached Baxter's headquarters and men sent to follow my track should not be far away.'

'That won't happen. Young Rebecca never made it to Baxter. Yalden's men who hover outside your army headquarters have detained her until Yalden finishes us off. He has promised me she will not be harmed.'

The conversation was interrupted by the arrival of Yalden.

'Sorry to keep you waiting but I have been busy organizing your deaths. Colonel, as befits an officer you will face a firing squad in front of this fine old manor house that you helped destroy. Mother Sparrow, her daughter and Lady Lydia will drink a potion that Mother Sparrow prepared so that you ladies will die a quick and painless death. Robert I shall enjoy what I will do to you. Remember my sister. That varlet Rutter told me everything.'

Robert let out a hideous scream protesting his innocence. Mother Sparrow took advantage of the noise to whisper to Luke. 'Delay as long as you can. Help is on the way. Do not despair.' Yalden sensed the communication and bellowed at the witch, 'Enough you old crone. Give the Lady Lydia and your daughter a draft of the potion.' Yalden presented Mother Sparrow with a filled goblet. As he did so Luke lunged forward knocking the goblet to the ground and its poisonous contents seeped away. Before he could cause any further damage Luke was restrained by two of Yalden's men while their leader left the cellar to refill the goblet. While he was gone Mother Sparrow took a chain from around her neck that held a small cross and swung it rhythmically in front of Lydia and spoke words of comfort to her. She visibly relaxed and her eyes appeared to glaze over. At the same time Jane seemed to induce a similar trance like state within herself.

When Yalden returned he did not attempt to give the goblet to Mother Sparrow. He demanded that first Lydia and then Jane take a mouthful of the potion. They did so without resistance. Yalden turned to Mother Sparrow, 'Now you interfering old baggage empty the goblet.' Before she had drained its contents Luke saw that the other women appeared dead. Yalden turned to his men. 'Stay here until you are sure that the women are dead, and then bring the cur Robert to me. Come Colonel we have business to complete.'

The two men emerged from the cellar and Yalden with a pistol to Luke's head forced him to stand before the destroyed portico of the house while three of his men at about twenty yards distance primed their muskets. 'I imagine Colonel that you have no wish to be blindfolded. On the count of three my men will fire. If you move before that I will discharge this pistol into your head.'

Luke threw himself suddenly at Yalden knocking the pistol from his hand. He had hoped to use Yalden's body to protect him from the musketeers who had downed their muskets and were running to their leader with swords drawn. Yalden waved them away. He was a big strong man well experienced in personal combat. Despite Luke's own strength and experience he sensed Yalden getting the better of him as they wrestled their way across the turf. In the end Yalden delivered a powerful blow to the head and then one to the stomach which left Luke disoriented and doubled up in pain. Yalden disengaged and ordered his men to tie Luke's hands and feet and then prop him against the remnant of the portico's column. They did so and resumed their position as a firing squad.

Luke's life did not rush before him, nor did tender thoughts of his beloved Elizabeth engulf him as he waited Yalden's order to fire. Instead he became focussed on his love making with the desirable Rebecca and her ever responsive nipples. He would die making love. As Yalden indicated he was about to give the order, Luke opened his eyes and looked at his executioners. He was still dazed but he thought he saw the fields come alive with yellow and orange flowers advancing ever closer. Before Yalden could give the order two horsemen appeared from behind the ruins waving scythes. Yalden's men became aware of hordes of brightly clothed people about to envelop them and two horsemen almost upon them. The musketeers ignored Yalden's order to shoot at Luke and turned their muskets on the advancing horsemen. They missed and quickly ran for their own horses followed by Yalden and galloped off into the nearest forest cover.

Luke could not believe his eyes. In front of him were hundreds of people, many of whom he recognized as womenfolk of Charlton Noakes. In the front of the crowd was a misshapen cripple waving a large staff and beside him was Mary Miller. She raced forward and covered him in kisses as she untied his ropes. 'Thank God we were in time,' she uttered. Luke replied, 'Unfortunately not in time to save the ladies.' Then he heard a voice behind him. 'It takes more than a self concocted poison to kill an old crone.' Emerging from the cellar were the three ladies followed by Robert who dragged the remaining two kidnappers after him. It looked as though both had had their heads crushed. Robert had jumped them and in one movement had crushed their heads together knocking them unconscious.

Amos Hogg mounted the steps of the portico and began to preach. While this was happening the former captives and Mary Miller sat on a small knoll while Mother Sparrow explained what had happened. 'A few days ago Giles Yalden came to me to enquire if I had a potion that would kill vermin quickly and with the minimum of pain. I was immediately suspicious because Giles was not a man upset by inflicting pain on humans let alone vermin. I was informed that Giles already knew that I was aware of his plans and that he might try to silence me. He made me test my potion on my own dog that immediately keeled over and appeared dead. Luckily Giles did not stay around long enough to see the dog recover. My potion caused symptoms that simulated death but the imbiber recovered after ten to fifteen minutes.'

'I'll never doubt the old arts again but how did the Children of the New Dawn get involved?'

Mary Miller took up the story. 'Mother Sparrow told me that Giles Yalden was to capture and murder the Noakes children and portray the attempt as the work of the Children. Two of the village women had wheedled out of their husbands that they were to meet at this ruined manor house around midday today. Amos, to protect the name of the Children, and several of the women to try and save their husbands from Yalden's influence, decided on a mass meeting today at twelve in the grounds of this ruined house. I kept a watch on Mother's house and when Yalden arrived and took her with him I followed them until I was sure that they were heading in this direction.'

After Amos had finished preaching and many of his flock had dispersed for what appeared to be random fornication he approached the Colonel. 'I am pleased to meet the powerful Colonel whom sister Mary says is a close friend of the Lord Protector himself. I wish you could convince Colonel

Baxter that we are not a threat to law and order but the only group in the county who support Oliver Cromwell.'

'Let me thank you for saving my life. I have already made my views clear to Tom Baxter that there are more important dangers to deal with than your group. Thanks again. While you are here can I ask you a few questions concerning the death of Sir Anthony Noakes?'

'Yes, I had expected to be arrested by your men and interrogated in Taunton Castle until I confessed, although Mary thought she had convinced you that I was not to blame. If someone had not got in first I would have killed Sir Anthony with my own hands. "Thou shalt break them with a rod of iron; thou shalt dash them in pieces like a potters vessel". We will destroy Satan's gentry and place the leadership of the county and nation into the hands of God-fearing people who will prepare the way for the Lord's return. I had planned the execution of Sir Anthony and that new satanic monster Lampard. The daughters of the New Dawn were to entice them into situations where they had little protection and then their brothers in Christ would dispatch then to Hell. "As smoke is driven away, so drive them away; as wax melteth before a fire, so let the wicked perish at the presence of God."'

'Be that as it may brother Hogg but can you tell me anything that might help determine who did kill Sir Anthony?'

'The Children of the New Dawn keep no secrets from me and I have followers among the servants at Noakes Hall and many of the women in the village. Two sightings on the night of the murder may help. One servant reported seeing Tom Hastings enter Noakes Hall by the Library door and another returning from the village saw a horseman emerge from the trees near the manor gate and head in direction of Taunton. In the moonlight she thought she saw the glint of a golden cape.'

'So what you're telling me is that around the time of the murder Hastings arrives and Golden Cape leaves?'

'Yes.'

'Can't you help me with more detail. Whom do your followers think responsible?'

'Golden Cape and Yalden. And it fits. Golden Cape has been seen with Yalden. He has visited Noakes Hall. You know that Yalden tried to assassinate Lady Elizabeth and now Yalden tries to execute Sir Robert and

Lady Lydia Noakes. I think the satanic agents of the late King Charles have fallen out amongst themselves. Perhaps it is the Lord's way. The ruling aristocracy is tearing itself apart.'

Luke thanked Amos once again for saving his life. Lydia, Robert, Mother Sparrow and her daughter accompanied Luke back to Taunton where Luke reported his adventures to Tom Baxter. The witches waited in Taunton until they heard that Rebecca had been found safe and well and all three returned to Jane's cottage to recover from their ordeal. Luke with Lydia and Robert continued on to Charlton Noakes. Several hours later Hugh Weston arrived. He with a troop of Baxter's men had doubled back and retraced Luke's steps and ultimately found a remnant of the Children of the New Dawn in the grounds of the ruined manor house. They told him what had happened and that Lydia was safe.

Luke returned to the Black Swan while Hugh remained at Noakes Hall to comfort Lydia after her frightening experience.

31

The rain set in, seriously disrupting the Midsummer festivities at Lidford House, already dampened by the assault on Grace Rutter. Elizabeth being informed that Lydia was none the worse for her adventures decided to stay to comfort Grace and Mary. The victim was traumatized. She had not spoken a word and could not provide any information as to her attacker.

Luke avoided thinking about Elizabeth's proposition by throwing himself obsessively into his investigation. He met Hugh and Will at the Black Swan on the Tuesday following Midsummer and immediately indicated his plan. 'Friends, I will arrest Cuthbert Mowle immediately but not in the way you might think. I learnt in Ireland the great advantage of wrong footing your opponent and keeping him totally, literally, in the dark. A band of hooded men will abduct Mowle, blindfold him, truss him up and carry him in absolute silence to a place of imprisonment where isolation and silence will prevail. This will give us two advantages. Nicholas Noakes alias Mowle alias the Count of Varga y Verganza will not know who has captured him or where he is. A week or so in isolation will make him more pliable to our eventual questioning and by removing him from the scene we will force his supporters to reveal themselves as they react to his mysterious disappearance.'

Will was impressed. 'Zooks, a great plan. Within days I will have Giles Yalden asking questions.'

'It sounds all right in theory but the details will make or break it,' responded Hugh.

'You are right, Hugh, the details are vital—as is absolute secrecy. Ride to Dunster Castle and inform the Governor to be ready for a high profile prisoner who must be kept in isolation and completely unaware as to where he is. Use my authority from the Lord Protector to overcome any qualms he might have. Let's borrow two wagons from Noakes Hall and leave them in Winslade Wood. After dark I with three others will meet in the woods where we will change into nondescript labouring clothes, and carry black masks ready to wear. We will remove any evidence of a military kind from our person and our horses, save for our weapons. Our discarded military gear will be taken in one of the wagons and concealed in Walter Weston's barn. The second wagon with a little hay or straw will progress up the High Street and be parked at the back of the Black Swan. Will, you will find some excuse to have Cuthbert leave the inn on his own. He will be seized, gagged and a hood placed over his head by masked men who will not talk in his presence. He will be bound and concealed in the wagon which will head for Dunster.'

Will spoke. 'Tomorrow night may be our chance. Mowle is always here on Wednesday and Thursday nights.'

'Tomorrow night, it is. Hugh, set off in the morning for Dunster and also let your father know that I will leave a wagon, with a covered load in his barn. Will, organize the disguises, and I will brief the men thoroughly on the enterprise.'

Next morning Will entered the parlour while Luke was eating his breakfast of bacon and eggs. 'God's mercy, Luke, you have a problem.'

'Will, we haven't begun yet, what could have gone wrong?'

'It's the rain. Charlton Mere has flooded the causeway. Pedestrians cannot use the Devon road or even reach Winslade Wood. It is still accessible to horsemen but the heavy wagon you had in mind would not make it through, and it would certainly get bogged between here and Dunster. This unseasonable rain is becoming dangerous. The Charlton could break its banks in a number of places. One of the common fields is under water already. Instead of the wagon you can use my light cart which is less likely to be bogged and which, if it is, three men could easily lift it out. I will leave it where you often see it—at the side of the inn.'

THE SPANISH RELATION

'Great, I will change the plan regarding the men. Someone might have noticed my troopers were missing from the Hall. I will second three of Baxter's men who can don their disguises in the anonymity of a large town and who will not be missed from their regiment. I will leave immediately because those men will need to be more thoroughly prepared.'

Luke left Charlton Noakes and headed towards Taunton when he saw not far behind him Hugh beginning his trip to Dunster. Luke waited for his friend, informed him of the changes, and ordered him to stay at Dunster until the prisoner was safely delivered.

'Luke, I have reservations. As a lawyer I protest against depriving a man of his liberty without just cause as determined by the courts.'

'Luckily Hugh, you are acting as a captain in the Protector's army to preserve the security of the state. Individual rights must give way to a higher interest. Individual rights are often the harbinger of anarchy and insecurity. When drums beat laws weep. It has always been so.'

'Nevertheless from a civilian point of view you are abducting a citizen. It smacks of the late King and his ministers when opponents to his illegal taxes found themselves whisked off to prison without any charges laid or defence counsel permitted.'

'Enough of the lawyer, you turn north here, Captain Weston, for Dunster. I will see you tomorrow.'

Luke spent the afternoon recruiting three suitable men and briefing them in detail on the mission and the code of silence expected. They would ride out towards Charlton Noakes separately and conceal themselves in the coppice just before the Gap. Luke would return to the Black Swan and when appropriate ride out and collect them.

It was dark when Cuthbert and Daniel returned to the inn from their customary early evening disappearance. Luke went for his men who rode quietly into town, at this stage unmasked. Luke re-entered the inn and signalled to Will to give Cuthbert a fictitious message that would provoke him to leave. Everything went according to plan. By the time Luke left the inn after ensuring that no one else left or followed Mowle the cart was well up the High Street with one of the troopers driving and his horse tethered behind. Luke overtook the cart and saw the trussed and hooded victim. As the rain continued to fall Luke covered the body with straw. At least Mowle would remain reasonably dry. Luke longed for his military leather jacket as the rain became heavier and heavier and penetrated his flimsy peasant clothing.

The group rode through the night with the incessant rain making the trip uncomfortable but the light cart managed to avoid getting stuck in mud. It was late morning when the group reached Dunster. Hugh appeared with a group of soldiers who immediately took the prisoner and lodged him in an isolated cell deep in the castle.

The Castle authorities issued the troop with a change of clothes and a meal of lentil potage. Luke presented himself to the Governor but told him little except that his prisoner posed a serious threat to the security of the nation and must under no circumstances have, or even hear, any conversation with another living soul.

Hugh burst into the room. 'Excuse me gentlemen I have bad news. I have just seen the prisoner without his hood. Luke, you abducted the wrong man. The man in the cell is Daniel Pyke.' Luke was dumbfounded. How could this have happened? Mowle went through the door. Luke ensured that no one followed. How did his men grab Pyke instead of Mowle? Luke explained to the Governor that a mistake had been made and the prisoner should be released without any explanation and allowed to find his own way home. He instructed his own troopers to make their own way back to Taunton at hourly intervals and report back to their unit first thing the following morning. Luke, Hugh and the Governor, an elderly infantry Colonel, who had seen service in Ireland, found words difficult.

'Colonel Tremayne I gather that I am participating in a disaster.'

'That you are Governor, we abducted the wrong man and I am at a loss to explain it.'

'Luke, this could backfire on you badly. Do you think we should try to placate young Pyke?' suggested Hugh.

'No, we had nothing to do with it. It was the gooseturds or Yalden's Royalist butchers or William Rutter's cutthroats. The army was not involved.'

Hugh tried again, 'A better approach is to come clean and pretend it was a joke organized by his father.' Before the officers could decide on a strategy they were disturbed by a commotion in the courtyard below. A lone horseman appeared at the gate leading a second horse, which had a large bag, slung across its back. Within minutes a soldier entered the room and addressed the Governor. 'Sir, there is a man at the gate who says he must see Colonel Tremayne urgently and that the parcel which he carries should be dispatched to the dungeon.'

Luke recognised that the horseman was Will and advised the Governor to assign the parcel to the dungeon and ask the horseman to join them. Will entered the room with an impish air of triumph. He could not conceal a broad grin and his largish ears appeared to be flapping as he addressed his friends.

'You dissembling ruffians have made a fine mess of the assignment. By Heaven I cannot understand how we Royalists lost the war.'

'Will, I can hardly believe it. You have actually delivered the designated traitor to us?'

'Yes, when you left I was amazed to see Mowle enter my back door. I knew something had gone wrong. I persuaded some of my girls to entice him into one of the rooms. When he entered I hit him forcefully on the back of the head and he crumpled to the floor. While the girls sat on him I tied his hands and legs and placed him in a large sack, which I draped over my horse, tightly securing my load, and went after you. Unfortunately the rain was so severe that I had to detour around several landsides that cost me a couple of hours. The only problem is that several of my girls saw me disable Mowle. Their silence may need to be bought quickly.'

Luke, obviously relieved, offered Will a warming mulled wine. 'Thanks Will. Our plan to confuse the network may be in jeopardy, but our plan to confuse Mowle has not been breached. How did we get your son instead of Mowle?'

'Daniel was standing in the entrance porch and when Mowle came through the door he sensed your men about to strike and pushed Daniel forward. As they efficiently removed their victim Mowle slid around the side of the inn before you came through the door. What are you going to do with Dan?' The Governor offered some advice. 'Why don't you return young Pyke the way he came, trussed, gagged and hooded in the back of the cart. His father can drive him home this evening and then find him in the cart outside the inn tomorrow morning. He would have no idea where he has been or why?'

'Governor, if you can find me lodgings for the rest of the day I will sleep until evening and accompany Will back to Charlton Noakes. This experience might actually frighten Daniel out of whatever he is doing for Mowle.'

That evening Will, Luke and young Daniel trussed up like a chicken ready for decapitation, began the journey home. During his silent ride Luke brooded over Elizabeth's proposal. He found it unpalatable in every regard. Lydia was a child who had not shown the slightest interest in him. His friend Hugh was enamoured of her and Luke thought that they would make a perfect couple, and Hugh, a worthy recipient of his mother-in-law's fortune. Elizabeth seemed to have missed the point. He was not concerned with property or status. He had led a disciplined life for almost two decades allowing nothing to intrude on his sense of duty. Now he was overwhelmed with a love for this one woman. Why did she make life so complicated?

32

Luke returned to the Black Swan well after noon and retired to his chamber and did not awaken until the next morning when Will knocked on his door. 'Luke, you have another problem. Sir Robert has disappeared again.'

Luke dressed quickly and rode to the Hall. Clark and one of the troopers designated to watch Robert met him. 'Mr Clark, what happened?'

'Sir Robert went for his usual early morning ride with one or two of your men keeping a discreet distance behind him. Apparently as he skirted the perimeter of Winslade Wood several horsemen appeared from nowhere and all of them including Sir Robert disappeared back into the woods. By the time your men reached the scene, delayed by the flooding stream and general bogginess of the landscape they found no one.'

Luke confirmed the details with his men and decided to return to the Black Swan having sent one of his troopers to ask Hugh to join him. Half an hour later Luke, Hugh and Will gathered in their usual parlour. Luke put the others in the picture. 'It looks as if Yalden has struck again. I must give him credit for persistence.' Will immediately added to the conversation.

'Sir Robert's been kidnapped and I know where they are headed.'

'How can you know such a thing?'

'There is nothing magical about it. My son Daniel has been up river visiting Yalden's cottage in search of Cuthbert Mowle. He has just returned and told me he had seen Sir Robert, William Rutter, his man Sampson Groom, the old notary Isaac Benjamin and a few others riding up the rain swept valley of the Charlton. They were probably heading for Sampson Groom's property in Upper Charlton which is Rutter's second home.'

'Is Daniel still here?'

'He is in the courtyard talking to the blacksmith.'

'Call him in, Will.'

Dan was somewhat surprised to be summoned into the inner circle of his father's powerful friends and addressed by Colonel Tremayne. 'Daniel, what can you tell us about Sampson Groom's property?'

'It is well up the valley. Giles Yalden is the only farmer beyond him before the peak. Beyond that there is only rocky terrain. You have to go down the other side of the hill to find any inhabitants.'

'Yalden is Groom's closest neighbour?'

'Yes, but there are vast expanses of woodland, wasteland and rocky outcrops between their cultivated areas.'

'If we were considering taking it by storm is there anything we should know about Groom's farmhouse?'

Such a question appealed to Daniel. 'The house is surrounded on two sides by dense woodland and on the third by the river. In front of the house lies his cultivated field.'

'Is there any other feature of relevance?'

'Yes, especially in this weather. Groom has raised the level of a dam across the river to the extent that he has flooded probably a third of his original arable. With this constant rain it has backed up further and now probably two thirds of his land is under water.'

'When you saw Rutter and Noakes how far up the road were they?'

'Two hours ago they were at the entry to Winslade Wood. Rutter had just joined them coming out of Goodman Weston's field.'

Dan left, and Hugh broke the silence. 'We cannot assume this is an abduction. Noakes probably went willingly with Rutter. They are partners of longstanding. They may not be heading to Groom's plot but escaping over the mountains into Devon. And what was Rutter doing coming out of our fields?'

'Whatever, I'll ask Baxter for an extra six troopers. That will give us fourteen men which should be enough to deal with Rutter and his allies if they refuse to deliver Noakes to us.'

THE SPANISH RELATION

By mid afternoon Luke's enhanced detachment was ready to progress up the valley against the continuing showers of rain. As they climbed out of the valley the rain became lighter, changing into an ever-thickening mist that reduced visibility. Suddenly Luke halted his men as he heard the thundering squelch of a horseman galloping down the dangerous road towards them. The horseman that emerged from the mist and nearly ran down the troop was Robert Noakes. Before Luke could reprimand him Noakes shouted frantically.

'I must warn the village. Rutter breached the dam and a great flood is heading towards Charlton Noakes.'

Luke ordered two of his troopers to join Sir Robert and encouraged the rest of his men to get to the dam as fast as they could. Within a few minutes they reached Groom's property. Groom with several of Rutter's men were labouring at the dam wall. To Luke's relief they were trying to stem the water and repair the breach. His men quickly dismounted and after a joint effort of an hour or more the wall was stabilised.

A fire was lit inside the house and while the company dried out Luke questioned Groom. 'Well done my man, but how was the wall breached?'

Sampson Groom would say as little as possible because what he knew could later be used to his own advantage. 'My master and Sir Robert had business to conclude. I made my house available for such a meeting as Sir Robert was under constant surveillance by your men. We met on the edge of Winslade Wood and came here.'

'How did the dam get breached?' Luke repeated angrily.

'I don't know. Mr Rutter and Sir Robert went outside and much later when I went after them I saw the dam breached and Sir Robert either trying to widen it or attempting some short-term repair. I shouted to him, and he replied that he must ride and warn the village.'

'And where was Mr Rutter?'

'Sir Robert said my master had fallen into the raging torrent. He was nowhere to be found although I searched below the wall while the rest of the men mended the breach. They have families in Charlton Noakes. Then you arrived.'

'Did Rutter slip or was he pushed by Sir Robert?'

Groom had been taught well by his late master. He could implicate Noakes now and claim he had murdered William, or he could be non-committal and blackmail Noakes in the future.

'Colonel, I did not see what happened.'

Luke spoke to the rest of Rutter's men, some of whom were genuinely upset by his demise. They had lost a generous employer, and given their past master it might be difficult to find a new job. Some of them went back outside and scrambled down the side of the dam in case the body of their master could be seen. After an hour of further searching without results they returned to Groom's house. Luke inspected the dam wall again, and then ordered his men back to the village. There could be much to do.

As they trotted back down the valley Hugh raised a question that had bothered him for the last hour or so. 'Luke, the breach in the wall was not accidental. Both Noakes and Rutter had a strong motive to flood the village. I told you of Sir Jasper's agreement with his tenants and the clause which stated if the village were destroyed the Lord of the Manor could re-establish it where he liked and reconstitute his tenancy agreements according to his own whim. If the village is flooded Sir Robert is in a position to impose the leases that he wants. If Rutter had lived he undoubtedly expected they would have been granted to him.'

'I know they are both undesirable characters but would they murder a whole village, including the relatives of their own men, for narrow financial gain?'

'Yes, since the horrible assault on his daughter you have been almost sympathetic to Rutter. Don't go soft on that vicious monster.'

'Well, Hugh if the village is destroyed let us hope the warning came in time to prevent any loss of life.'

As the group rounded the bend of the road near the entry to Winslade Wood they could see the village laid out before them. It was a sea of water. The entire valley was flooded but rising above it the houses were still there. If there had been a flooding wave it had failed to demolish the village. As they approached the Black Swan they heard singing and laughter. On entering the inn Luke was surprised to see most of the village, and many from Noakes Hall, celebrating their escape and toasting the health of their hero, Sir Robert.

It was the first time in his life that Sir Robert had received the thanks of anyone. He enjoyed his new status, and added to his popularity by providing drinks for the assembled group. Will sensed that in the drunken euphoria of the moment the villagers might start drinking healths to the King which would have led to rival healths by the soldiers to the Lord Protector. He foresaw a typical alehouse brawl developing. Will stepped forward. 'Villagers and friends of Charlton Noakes let us drink a health to Sir Robert, the saviour of the village, and to the memory of his late father Sir Anthony.'

Luke also picked up on potential conflict as the ale flowed and ordered his troops back to Noakes Hall to attend to their tired and wet horses. Hours later Will and Luke had a final drink for the night. Luke put Will in the picture concerning the events of the afternoon while Will described what had happened in the village.

'I was already worried with the rising level of the water and had only remarked to Daniel that a sudden surge in the water level could be dangerous to many of the village houses and might catch unawares many villagers who were out of doors. It was at that moment that Sir Robert appeared and told us that a dam had burst upstream and we should expect its impact within the hour. He sent one of your troopers to warn Weston and his household and the inhabitants of the wastelands, and the other to get the workers out of the lower fields of the manor. Walter Weston was here in no time and organized the members of the watch to get everybody to higher ground, which amounted to the Black Swan.'

'When the surge came was it a problem?'

'Yes and no. It was about four feet high close to the river. It demolished many outlying buildings. It would have swept away anyone in the fields to the east of the village. As it spread out across the valley it lost force and height. Only the more poorly built houses in High Street suffered any real damage although most of those in the southern half of the street had one to two feet of water covering the floor. If the whole dam wall had given way the village would have been demolished.'

33

The next morning was Sunday and the villagers gathered in the church for a special service of thanksgiving for the survival of their village. Luke ordered his troopers to attend, unarmed and wearing as close to civilian attire as they could muster. After the service Luke and Will accepted an invitation from Hugh to dine with him. Over dinner they assessed the progress of their enquiries.

Luke summed up: 'Mowle is securely under arrest and we will interrogate him towards the end of the week, Rutter is dead, and Noakes a hero. None of them is the murderer. Lampard is the one we should pursue. I am sure he ordered the killing. You were right Hugh. He is a very intelligent man who thinks many steps ahead of most of us. Lidford is convinced that Lampard is the high government official in contact with the Count.'

'Careful Luke, you have no evidence against Lampard. Varga's comments to Eglin could have referred to a number of people and that assumes that Varga was telling the truth and not simply promoting his cause. Politicians in England on all sides are positioning themselves should the King return. You and he simply dislike each other. If Lampard is to be pursued you need real evidence.'

Will added, 'I agree. Don't tangle with the most powerful man in the county without evidence. By George, something has just come to me. I hope I am wrong. A few days ago a man who I have seen a few times in the past called in at the Swan asking to leave a message for Tom Hastings. I said we had not seen him since a large number of men were killed attacking an army patrol but that I would leave the message with someone who would get it to his men. I passed it on to Mary Miller.'

'Interesting Will, but how does it relate to Lampard?'

'I asked around to see if any one knew the man. A waggoner from Taunton who had just delivered me a load of hops knew him well. He is a servant at the Four Bears and right hand man to its owner, Edward Lampard's younger brother.'

Hugh was equally cynical of Will's argument as he was of Luke, 'What are you suggesting Will? That because a servant of a relative of Lampard is looking for a villain such as Tom Hastings it implies that Sir Edward ordered, and the Green Glove executed, the murder of Sir Anthony?'

Luke retorted. 'Hugh, you are too much the lawyer. Any contact between the gooseturds and Lampard would support such an argument. The violence of the killing certainly fits the pattern of the Green Glove. This explains the problem we have had of relating what, on most of the evidence, is a political killing with the violence of the actual act. Lampard used the gooseturds to kill Sir Anthony. We know for certain that they followed him home through the village on the night of the murder.'

Walter Weston entered the room. 'Colonel, yesterday William Rutter arrived here unannounced and gave me this letter, which in the event of his death within a week was to be delivered to you. Should he survive that period he would reclaim the letter. Although his body has not been recovered, it seems he did not survive.'

Luke opened the letter and read it aloud.

Dear Colonel,

If you read this Edward Lampard or Robert Noakes have killed me for reasons which I outline. First to Noakes, he murdered his father, incensed by the discovery that given his step mother's marriage settlement he was virtually a pauper, and that his father had not bothered ter tell him even when he became heir. Noakes is a strong man especially above the waist and a rock held in his large hands delivered in a state of absolute fury is a lethal weapon. I was usin' this knowledge and his rape of Jane Clark several years ago to persuade him ter give me first option ter obtain the leases of as many properties as possible in Charlton Noakes. For more against Robert Noakes talk to Dr Basset.

Lampard had nothin' to do with the Noakes murder although it certainly 'elped him retain his dominance of the county. I fink Lampard wishes to conceal my links with him by 'aving me killed. There have been two attempts on my life. I think he panicked when he discovered your authority overrode his, and that a legal investigation of our joint activities by ya would have revealed what ya would call corruption, but which I still label good business. If this does not give ya what you need ter remove Lampard, and give me some revenge for his attempts on my life, try to establish his links with the King, and the cosy relationship he has with the gooseturds. Thank you for your kindness last week regardin' my daughter. I have left another letter with Walter Weston ter forward ter Lord Lidford on that matter. I trust that any investigation into my activities will not leave my daughter destitute.

Be careful. Lampard was furious after your recent meetin'. I have let him kna that I have made a full confession in writing of our joint sins and am forwarding it to ya. The gooseturds may already have ya name. I hope you are alive ter receive this letter.

Your 'umble servant

William Rutter.

Hugh spoke first. 'Lampard may have already employed the gooseturds to remove you.'

Will interjected. 'How does killing Luke save Lampard?'

'Lampard quite rightly believes that the authority I exercise is unusual and the Protector is not likely to give any successor such broad powers. Lampard could use his legal position and network to protect himself against a lesser authority. It would also buy him time to eliminate Rutter, if it still remained necessary, and to cover his tracks with the gooseturds and the King.'

'I have to play the lawyer again. Even if Rutter is telling us the truth, he does not provide any evidence that we can use against Sir Edward. Frankly all this letter does is to confirm a few suspicions. It proves nothing.'

Luke spoke quietly and intently, 'But Lampard doesn't know that. Rutter warned him of the existence of the letter but not its detail. We can turn this to our advantage. I will arrest Lampard.'

Luke arranged through Baxter to meet Lampard at army headquarters the following Tuesday morning. Baxter had addressed the request in terms of urgent matters of state but Luke was convinced that Lampard, in the light of Rutter's letter, would be prepared for the worst. Army headquarters was a large town house shaped as the letter H with two large courtyards and several long stables that housed many of the troopers as well as their horses. After Baxter had welcomed Lampard in the entrance hall the colonel showed the magistrate into a side parlour in which Luke was waiting.

'Good morning, Colonel Tremayne I am not surprised to see you're here. I imagine you and not matters of state are the reason for this summons.'

'Matters of state are very much to the fore. I have verifiable evidence that you are an enemy of the Commonwealth. On the basis of this evidence and by my authority from the Lord Protector I arrest you on the charges of treason, corruption and perversion of justice. You are held under the Protector's special authority, which the army will execute. You will be held at a place unknown to any but the army authorities until such time as the Protector will determine.

'You will not get way with this Tremayne. No one will give evidence against me.'

'Lampard we don't need others to lie for or against you, the facts of your malignancy will stand on their own. Captain, remove this man and deal with him as already explained to you by Colonel Baxter.'

Luke would have felt more comfortable if Lampard was enclosed in Dunster Castle. He could not expect to abduct the county's leading magistrate without some recriminations. He knew that already he had pushed his authority beyond that which the Protector intended by basically suspending Lampard's legal rights and imprisoning him until they had a stronger case. He hoped that the speed of the arrest without any preliminary warning had surprised Sir Edward. The official statement released by Baxter was that Sir Edward Lampard would be unavailable for several weeks as he was involved in matters reflecting on the security of the state. Baxter was placing him under house arrest in a bleak isolated manor house in the middle of Exmoor, with a host who was a cousin of Anthony Noakes. After the murder of Anthony, Toby Noakes had offered his services to Baxter to help in any way he could.

Luke left army headquarters just before noon. He noted that a group of horsemen left at precisely the same time and fell in a discreet distance behind him. Ahead he recognised another detachment of troopers which included some of the men that had been seconded to him on previous occasions. He galloped up to them and discovered they were heading out on patrol in the parishes on the near side of the Charlton. They rode together toward the Gap just before which they would part company. Prior to this Luke overheard a comment from one of the men that took some time to sink in.

'Cornet, what unit is that which has followed us from headquarters. At our briefing we were the only patrol today west of the town.'

Luke did not hear the reply but in turning his head he saw a group of six men, who as the patrol turned south, quickened their pace to catch up to him. As they got closer Luke realised they were not army. They lacked any regimental sash and other matters of detail that an experienced officer noticed.

Before he had time to think further he heard a shot fired in his direction. He saw the coppice in which he had waited on a number of occasions and pulled his horse's head in that direction. He reached the protection of the trees as musket after musket was fired at him. He dismounted but was painfully aware that as an officer he did not carry a carbine. He had a sword and a pistol.

He took cover behind a fallen tree as two men advanced towards him. His enemies had over whelming firepower. He had to make every shot count. He did. He managed to wound both of his attackers but one was still able to fire. He was more worried about the location of the other three men who had been following him. He did not have to wait long. He was surrounded. He drew his sword but this would be of little use if they chose to shoot him from afar. Fortunately for him their leader wanted the thrill of an execution.

'Throw down your pistol Colonel, and step forward into the clearing in front of you.'

Luke obliged. Approaching him unmasked were a number of faces he did not recognize but he knew their leader—Tom Hastings. 'Thomas Hastings, I thought you might have died murdering my men. You make a habit of killing soldiers.'

'This time it will be worth it, soldier boy. And you have a habit of murdering my men in this very coppice. You have upset a knavish fat purse so while I do something I really enjoy I am receiving a fortune for the act. Enjoy the thought as you speed to hell that you are worth one hundred times more than the last toad I executed. If there were more like you I would be a very wealthy man.'

'Hastings, name the fat purse and I will pardon you.'

'Colonel, I have all the legal protection I need so you offer me nothing. How do you think I have survived so long? Men, prepare your shot. Colonel, it will be quick. Five musket balls in the heart if my men perform to their best. Unfortunately we can't wait around to give you a slow lingering death.'

Before Hastings could give the order the coppice came alive with not five but ten to twelve musket shots followed by a charge of sword wielding men. Most of the shots had come from behind his assailants but two had come from behind him. He looked over his shoulder and saw two men hobbling towards him. One was Will and the other hardly recognizable with his bandages and scars, was Andrew. Andrew ignored him and strode to the writhing body of Tom Hastings. Andrew slowly prepared his musket, and shot Hastings through the neck. He quietly addressed the dying man.

'That butcher is for my comrades.'

The men approaching Luke were from the detachment that had just left him. Their leader reported. 'Sir, there are three dead and three badly wounded.'

'Save the civil administration any problems. You will take six dead bodies back to army headquarters, and inform Colonel Baxter that they all died in the skirmish.'

Luke turned to Will, 'It is lucky Hugh is not with us. He would have found some legal objections.'

Will had already seen this ruthless side of the Colonel. Once again he was glad he was on the Colonel's side. Will explained the rescue as they returned to the Black Swan. 'Thank Andrew and the young leader of that patrol. Andrew arrived just after you left this morning and I told him what had happened. We agreed that taking on Lampard was dangerous, and given the man's acumen and ability, he would probably strike before you could act against him. We discussed where along the road from Taunton provided the best place for an ambush and we agreed on the coppice. Just after coming through the Gap we heard shots. At the same time I could see a detachment of soldiers galloping from the south. We met on the edge of the coppice and established that it was you being attacked by the men who had followed you from Taunton. After you left the army patrol the troopers were suspicious of men that had followed you and when the shot was fired they instantly retraced their path at breakneck speed. You know the rest.'

Before they reached the Black Swan Andrew faltered in his saddle and slumped forward. Luke could see blood seeping through his clothes in a few places. 'Andrew, have you been shot?'

'No, old wounds have re-opened. I was to rest for at least another month.'

Will interceded, 'My friend you can stay at the Swan until you have fully recovered.' Luke was delighted that Andrew's return put further pressure on Yalden. Mowle had disappeared. Was Yalden the loyal agent of the King's man or was he a wild card acting on his own obsessions? If he was loyal to Nicholas why did he set out to murder his siblings? Perhaps Nicholas was behind that enterprise as well?

34

Hugh was frustrated and depressed. He worried about the delay in the interrogation of Mowle, and what Luke had done to Lampard. Hugh was still coming to terms with the attempted murder of his lover and now his friend. He could not believe that Lampard would resort to extra-legal means to achieve his ends. Perhaps the law was a façade and the politics of the nation operated outside of it. Luke had revealed his contempt of the law by his murder of old Jake's killer, his abduction of Mowle and now his killing of the wounded gooseturds. If the Protector's personal envoy, and the county's senior magistrate both ignored the law what hope had Hugh in cultivating respect for law and order among the masses. Those wild Levellers had been right. The law was there to contain the poor. The rich and powerful ignored it.

Luke was content. Things were falling into place. Mowle and Lampard were in custody. He would confront Robert Noakes with Rutter's assertions. But he would wait until Dr. Basset returned later in the week and follow up Rutter's hint that the cleric could provide more evidence against Robert. Robert got in first. He invited Luke and Hugh to lunch at the Hall two days hence. Elizabeth would return from Lidford House the day before and Robert made it clear that he wanted to make a statement in front of his family and the army investigators.

Given the occasion both soldiers dressed as cavalry officers strikingly defined by their red sashes and red hatbands, and the dull mustard colour of their cavalry jerkins and matching trousers. Robert had gained much confidence since his heroic deeds of the previous weekend. He dressed for the first time ever, according to Elizabeth, in a manner that befitted his station. Sir Robert wanted this occasion and the statement he was about to make to be symbolic of a new era. He wore a burgundy doublet, slashed both back and front revealing a daffodil yellow lining. Each slash was edged with silver thread. The separate doublet sleeves were reversed—yellow with a burgundy lining. His breeches were in matching burgundy and his stockings yellow. His lace collar was small but the lace at his cuffs was overdone. He wore a matching daffodil yellow sash around his waist. A wide brimmed burgundy hat with a small crown and a burgundy and yellow hatband accentuated his moonlike face. This was not the man that Luke had first encountered.

After a lavish meal, the family and leading members of the household withdrew into the large parlour next to the dining chamber. The women were seated and the men stood around the perimeter of the room.

'I have called you together because my behaviour in recent months requires explanation, and I have not told all about father's murder. Last week I was abducted by William Rutter who was determined to blackmail me into giving him the village of Charlton Noakes and all the lands associated with it. He was aware of great grandfather Jasper's agreement that should the village ever be destroyed the current squire could relocate the village and allocate houses and land rights according to his whim. Rutter had threatened in the past to burn the village and the attack on Matthew Clark's house was a warning to me that he was serious.

This unseasonable weather gave him a better idea. He was determined that as his other weapons against me, false allegations of rape and murder could not be proved that he would incriminate me by forcing me to breach the dam wall in the presence of witnesses. He would then have me sign a statement with a notary present that I would convert each lease as it became available into freehold, and give him the first option to purchase. He had a second paper already signed by his men that they had seen me breach the wall. It simply awaited the notary to endorse it. I was forced to the edge of the dam where part of the wall had been so constructed that one hard blow on a protruding wedge would have been sufficient to dislodge a critical section of it. Under coercion I smashed the wedge but the wall did not break away. Rutter edged his way along the wall to loosen it. He slipped and was swept away. His fall took much of the wall with it and a huge volume of water began pouring over the edge. I called to Rutter's men that he had fallen over the edge and that I was riding to warn the village. I hardly left the property when I ran into the Colonel. On a far more important matter—I was present at the murder of my father.'

Robert waited while the gathering indulged in an audible and mutual deep intake of breath. 'He summoned me home and when I arrived for the scheduled meeting in the library there were three men already there— William Rutter, a man who I have since discovered is a Cuthbert Mowle, and father. The discussion involved the disposal of the properties under my father's control. Rutter and Mowle insisted that father sign papers to transfer most of the estate to Rutter. Father demurred and Rutter hit him from behind with a large rock and while he lay slumped in his chair Mowle struck him several times with a dagger. Mowle is Rutter's new recruit in savage knavery. I was shocked. The two villains turned on me and demanded I sign the papers. If I refused they would testify that I murdered my father. I was in such a state at seeing father murdered before my eyes that I panicked. I feared for my life and escaped to London, returning briefly for my father's funeral and then again when Colonel Tremayne had me detained. It would have been sweet to avenge my father, but God in his wisdom has acted.

In terms of this household Lady Elizabeth and my half sister will soon move to another estate. Dr Basset has accepted a position with Lord Lidford as chaplain, and Mr Clark is seeking employment elsewhere. Those members of the household associated with them are released from their terms of employment.'

Sir Robert left the room before any of the group had a chance to question him. Luke mused that dead men have no friends but was jolted back into reality as Elizabeth asked him, Hugh, and Lydia to follow her into the parlour. 'Luke it looks as though your task here is finished and you will rejoin your regiment in London.'

'I don't think so. You surely do not believe your stepson?' Elizabeth ignored Luke's question. 'Luke, have you considered my proposal?'

Luke could play the same game. He sidestepped the question. 'Elizabeth, my task is only finished if I can prove Robert told the truth, and I cannot believe that you want to discuss the other matter in front of Hugh and Lydia.'

'Craven coward. It concerns them, and the matter must be resolved.'

Luke who a few days earlier had ordered the execution of a number of wounded brigands without a twinge of conscience was anxious not to hurt Hugh. Elizabeth was determined to make him confront the issue. 'Luke, you have avoided me from the moment I put the proposition to you. This way you will give me an answer.'

'Giving you an answer was never a problem. I reject your proposal completely, and I recommend Hugh Weston as a most able provider of sons that will do credit to your father.'

Hugh interposed, 'What's this about?'

'Elizabeth proposed that I should marry Lydia to satisfy my need to be a father and to sire a large dynasty that would ultimately in the person of our eldest son inherit the Hanes fortune. Forgive me, Mistress Lydia, but I have no desire to marry you. I desire your mother. Having aired these issues I am sure that you two want a quiet word with Elizabeth. I have made my position very clear.'

Luke left the room and the Hall, and returned to the Black Swan. He wanted to discuss Sir Robert's statement with Will and Andrew. Back in the parlour Lydia who had not said a word attacked her mother. 'How could you propose such a thing when you know how much I love Hugh?'

'Lydia, love does not make a marriage. A marriage based on love rarely lasts. I am responsible for the disposal of much property and you are the major vehicle of such disposition. It would be most appropriate that in the end my father's estates fell into the hands of his great grandson who would also be the son of the young boy he treated almost as another son. I also had a very personal reason for trying to find Luke a wife other than myself. Luke deserves to have children. As I am unable to have any more children my proposition is a reasonable solution.'

'Maybe reasonable to you mother but it completely ignores the wishes of Hugh and myself, and from what he has just said, of Luke as well.'

Hugh spoke. 'This is probably not a good time but as Luke has already intimated my intentions, I wish to formalise them. Lady Elizabeth, I seek permission to court your daughter with the intention of marriage sooner rather than later.'

'Hugh, forgive me. My concern for Luke coloured my judgment. Although you are not from Cornwall, and your father is not a gentleman, you have conducted yourself in a manner that would make Lydia a good husband, and yourself an efficient administrator of much property. I can see that I will have to do much to be forgiven by my daughter. Agreeing to your proposal would be the first step.'

'No mother, agreeing to the proposal will completely wipe out my crossness over your silly proposal.'

Mother and daughter hugged and kissed, while Hugh had a grin of the proverbial Cheshire cat as he followed after Luke.

Later, back at the inn Luke and Hugh told the others of Robert's statement. None of them were satisfied. Hugh expressed the general view.

'It's too neat and there is no one to corroborate the new squire's interpretation of events. He blames it on a dead man and a stranger. If Mowle is the legitimate squire then Robert is left with nothing. Fate removed one of Robert's major problems, Rutter. This pack of lies might get rid of another, Mowle.'

The group discussed their next moves. Luke would go to Dunster and question Mowle with Robert's evidence as a focus of their discussion. Hugh would talk to the notary and any of the men who may have witnessed Rutter's accident, especially Sampson Groom. Will and Andrew would follow up alehouse gossip. They were just about to disperse for the evening when they heard a considerable disturbance in the hall and Daniel Pyke entered the parlour. 'Father, there are two bodies in the far ditch. With the flood receding Goodman Napp went to inspect the drainage ditches between the common fields and the manor. He sent his man to tell you and the Constable.'

Will, Andrew, Luke, Daniel and several drinkers picked their way around the muddy fields heading for the far ditch and the lonely figure of Goodman Napp. Both bodies were face down in the water. Napp had not attempted to touch them. Luke climbed into the ditch and reeled back in surprise. Martha Rodd and a girl identified by Will as her sister, Emma, had had their throats cut. Before the onlookers could comment Andrew who had wandered some distance from the others called out. 'There is another body over here. It's Willie Calf.'

Luke, Andrew and Will concluded that Martha had been murdered by Tom Hastings in revenge for helping to identify him and speculated that the others may have been unfortunate witnesses to the event. The Constable at that very moment was uncovering another two bodies that had been washed up under one of his own hedges. They had been in water for some time and were later identified as former servants at the Hall.

35

GILES YALDEN WAS CONFUSED yet determined. He could not openly enter Charlton Noakes since his attempt on the Noakes siblings. Luke and Andrew's survival had put a price on his head. His murder of several troopers gave any soldier authority to take him dead or alive. He had betrayed his best friend, Will, in the service of the King, and now the King's man had disappeared. In addition the claim of that detestable little man Rutter that Robert Noakes raped his sister filled his head with conflicting priorities.

His duty was clear. He must find the Count and failing that complete the mission by removing the rest of the Royalist traitors. When that was done he would avenge his sister. Most of this he must do alone as Will had now convinced most of his men to rally around Lady Elizabeth, and Luke had procured a pardon for them for their role in the massacre of his unit.

Where was the Count? Lady Elizabeth, Tremayne, or Pyke must know. He suddenly thought of a plan which with the help of his brother-in-law James Clark might force them to reveal what they knew. He would abduct the Pyke siblings—Tamsin and Daniel. Daniel was an ally of the Count and would tell Giles all he wanted to know without recourse to abduction but it would protect the boy from the wrath of his father. His sister probably knew what Lady Elizabeth knew. Giles simply waited outside the Black Swan until Daniel came outside to empty some swill for the pigs. Giles placed a large bag over his head tied it round the neck and placed the confused lad on the horse.

THE SPANISH RELATION

'Don't worry Dan, it's Giles. I am doing this to help you.' Once they were out of the village Giles released the bag and Daniel took a long breath of fresh air. 'Well now I know. At least this time it was a short trip and not hours bundled up in a wagon'

'What do you mean, Dan?'

'This is the second time I have been abducted from the Inn and hooded. The last time when the hood was removed I was in a castle dungeon in which the guards seemed to be military although I could not be sure because not a word was uttered from the moment I left the inn until I returned a day or two later.'

Giles laughed at the chances of two abductions in as many weeks for young Daniel and probed him for every detail of his previous abduction. Giles was certain it was military. During the war the absolute silence approach had been a technique his Irish allies had used. Tremayne had served in Ireland for years. Tremayne was the abductor and Daniel was taken to a castle. There were several in the area but the army's main strongholds were at Exeter and Dunster. Further questioning as to the terrain the wagon encountered convinced Giles that Daniel had been taken to Dunster.

'No body asked you any questions?' Giles double-checked.

'Absolute silence, all the time.'

'Why do you think you were kidnapped?'

'Mistaken identity. As soon as they discovered who I was I was brought back.'

'Tell me again exactly how you were kidnapped?'

'I went out of the front door of the Swan and waited a second or two as it was raining when the door burst open and someone shoved me forward. As I fell forward I was scooped up by the black masked kidnappers and bundled into a wagon.'

'The army has the Count at Dunster. Has your father mentioned anything that may indicate if and when they will try to move him?'

'Giles, you are my friend as is the Count but I will not betray father.'

'Son, you must choose between your father and the King. You saw the letters that the Count had—the signatures of the King and of the King of Spain. Sadly that evil Lady Elizabeth has led your father astray. I had orders from the King to execute her.'

'She's not an evil woman. My sister works for her and says she is honourable and kind.'

Giles could only smile to himself as to the naivety of youth. There would be no need to kidnap Tamsin or involve the lad further in his plans. He would rescue the Count and deal with those who had helped mislead the villagers. Amos Hogg had been preaching for months that the traditional leadership of King and gentry had to be destroyed and still advocated that God's representative was Oliver Cromwell and the army. His convert Mary Miller had used her influence in the village to support the Cromwellian Colonel and the treacherous landlord. Then they had interfered to rescue his captives. This could wait. The first priority was to rescue the count.

Tremayne was a ruthless and efficient operator. He would not leave the interrogation of the Count to underlings. All Giles had to do was to wait and follow the Colonel and if he headed north the die was cast.

It was. Next day Luke left the inn before dawn and Giles was close behind him. Giles knew the area well and began to assess where it would be best to ambush the Colonel. Then he completely changed his mind. The death of the Colonel was not a major aspect of his plan. Rescue of the Count must take priority. When the count was safe then he could deal with Tremayne. The investigation of the murder of the squire was also peripheral and his brother-in-law had made it clear that the perpetrator was known and would be dealt with in due course. Unfortunately Tremayne's investigation was getting in the way of the Count's mission to keep English royalists loyal to the King's cause.

Just after Luke had left the Black Swan one of Giles's former militiamen roused the sleeping Will Pyke. Giles had approached him to accompany him to Dunster and let him know that Dan Pyke was aware of the situation. Owing Will a favour and concerned by the split in the Royalist ranks the former bluecoat in the end gave his loyalty to a long term local rather than a relative new comer. Will awoke Daniel and through a combination of cajoling and gentle reasoning Will elicited the whole story.

He quickly informed Andrew and together they decided that Andrew would ride ahead and warn Luke while Will would ask Hugh Weston with a couple of troopers to ride after Giles. Andrew was careful and as he came close to anybody on the road he cut across the fields. It was not long before he saw ahead of him a red haired horseman—the man who had shot his cornet and left him and his men for dead. Hatred and revenge welled up inside of him. He could solve this problem once and for all. There would be no need to warn Luke if Giles Yalden was killed. As Andrew came to the top of a small rise he saw Yalden half way down the slope about to be obscured by the mists that were arising from a small stream further down the road. This was it. Andrew spurred his horse and charged down the slope shouting wildly with sabre swishing into the wind. Giles turned and just managed to get his sword out of its scabbard to parry the slicing blow of the veteran soldier. 'This time we are on even terms you murdering rogue. This is for young Roger.'

The point of Andrew's sword had penetrated the upper arm of his opponent and blood became to pump vigorously over Giles's jerkin. The two men thrusted and parried for several minutes and while Giles's loss of blood made him feel a little faint he recognized that his opponent had slowed considerably and appeared to have difficulty raising his sword above his head. Andrew had overestimated the extent of his recovery from the near fatal shooting by Giles and his men and he momentarily sensed his end as his sword failed to parry a slicing blow from the red haired Royalist that severed his neck and throat. Andrew slumped to the ground already dead.

As Giles dismounted to make sure that his attacker had been dispatched he had little time to enjoy his victory. He vaguely heard a shot. The carbine bullet hit him behind the ear and as he fell to the ground Luke emerged from the mist, primed the carbine again and shot the dying Giles between the eyes. 'That is for Roger and Andrew and the rest of my troopers.'

Luke had sensed that he was being followed and had stopped in the mist to see if his senses had been accurate. He heard a scuffle not knowing who was involved until he emerged from the mist and discharged his carbine at the notorious red head he saw standing over Andrew.

The ruthless Cromwellian colonel knelt over the body of his sergeant and wept. They had been together for over a decade and at least twice in Ireland Andrew had saved his commanding officer. Luke had been too late to return the favour. He dragged Yalden's body to the edge of the stream and threw it under a large bramble bush that covered the water's edge. He carefully placed Andrew on his own horse and led the faithful steed and its lifeless rider back to the nearest village. He was explaining to the local constable his version of events when a troop of horse led by Hugh Weston arrived and appraised of the situation agreed to return with Andrew's body to Charlton Noakes and allow Luke to continue his journey to Dunster alone.

36

Luke reached Dunster and met the prisoner. Luke's hope that incarceration and silence had weakened Mowle's resolve was soon quashed.

'I assumed it was you. The operation was too disciplined to have been the gooseturds, the Sealed Knot, or any local agents of the government. Where am I?'

'You are in Dunster Castle—held for two reasons, the murder of Sir Anthony Noakes, and as a Royalist agent in the pay of the King of Spain dividing the local community as a precursor to a Spanish invasion. On the first charge I will eventually hand you over to the civil authorities, on the second you may be summarily executed under my military authority.'

'Evidence against me, Colonel?'

'On the second charge substantial. I can confirm your use of documents from the would-be Charles II and from the King of Spain, your attempt to subvert the Royalist network and the use of the Yalden unit to massacre my men and attempt to execute Lady Elizabeth Noakes and probably the abduction of Sir Robert and Lady Lydia Noakes. Your involvement in the murder of Odams and the attempt to blow up Lord Lidford can also be established. It is the murder of Sir Anthony that worries me. I have nothing more than charge and counter charge.'

'If I am guilty of all you have just listed why do you doubt that I killed Sir Anthony?'

'Because my dear Count you are Nicholas Noakes and while you might execute your father for political reasons you would not crush his head with a massive rock.'

The Count considered carefully what he might say as a tear rolled down his cheek as he thought of his father. 'How long have you known my real identity?'

'A few weeks. You were followed on a number of occasions but linking Varga with Nicholas Noakes was largely surmise.'

'Colonel you have considerable evidence against me on the big political issues but do not waste your time on them. Send me to London and within weeks the Spanish Ambassador will have secured my release. Inform the Lord Protector of my capture and await further orders.'

'Sir Nicholas before we leave these political issues what did you hope to achieve?'

'I will not reveal the details of my mission but in general terms your surmise is close, but it misses the key point. I was not sent to England to disrupt the county community, nor to undermine the government of Oliver Cromwell. The Spanish Government recognises Cromwell's regime and His Catholic Majesty King Philip is seeking an alliance with England against France.'

'Well, why are you here?'

'I was in Paris representing King Philip and was requested by the foreigners around King Charles who knew my Somerset background to undertake this mission. I was to destroy a network of Royalist traitors in the West Country disloyal to their English King. By their own admission these traitors agreed to recognize Cromwell's regime for the next few years. One day you will discover their treachery goes much deeper. You will be sickened. My mission is simple, destroy the leadership of the Sealed Knot and restore the Royalist gentry to their traditional loyalty to the King. I have failed. Odams is dead but Lidford and Lady Elizabeth survive—and I did not recover those damnable lists.'

'You went further. You tried to subvert members of the current government.'

'No, I had no mandate to effect any change in the loyalty of the existing administration. It is difficult to trust friends, what real gain is there in trusting former enemies? I don't deny that some government supporters in the county sought my help to communicate with King Charles. I will deny that I told you this, but documents relevant to these farsighted trimmers was sent back to the court in Paris—deliberately by a very insecure network. The Protector's agents should by now have these incriminating documents. If you have any officials under surveillance or arrest on these matters I guarantee they will be taken out of your jurisdiction within the month.'

'That tidies up a few loose ends. My mission in Somerset as you know was to uncover the murderer of your father. Yesterday your brother accused you and William Rutter of the deed. What have you to say?'

Nicholas Noakes was for a moment struck dumb. 'My evil brother, his perfidy knows no limits. One person and one person alone murdered father. It was Robert.'

'What exactly happened?'

'My father and I wrote to each other regularly, but it was too much of an embarrassment for him to acknowledge my Spanish nationality and Catholic faith in public so he pretended that contact had been lost. Five years ago he put it abroad that I had disappeared believed killed in an assault on a Dutch town. I also communicated with James Clark who after his wife's murder became a fellow papist. Stephen Basset also was aware of these developments. When I was sent on this mission I thought it would be an opportunity to put things right at two levels. I would persuade my father to cease his treacherous activities and we would put Noakes Hall back on an even footing, and the future roles of Robert and Lydia could be clarified. Although Robert was pretending to be heir his succession could be challenged without the formal renunciation of my rights. To be safe Robert needed my letter, or my death. It seems that he is aiming for the latter.'

'If Robert had not killed Sir Anthony would you have executed him?'

'Come, Colonel I do not have to tell you that duty in a just cause overrides all personal considerations. Father, with Odam, Lidford and others were tried in absentia by the King and found guilty of treason. My mandate was to carry out these executions with an option that I could in the case of my own father seek reconciliation. And as I discovered father was far from being a willing participant. He was led and dominated by his wife. Thus my orders to execute her.'

'What happened on the night of your father's murder?'

'We met in the library. I was there first and sat behind my father's desk. Robert at first stood in the dark behind the open door to the garden. I had taken the precaution to have Clark hidden behind a secret panel in the library and one of his men hidden in the shrubbery near the library door. The man was to prevent anyone entering the library after my father arrived—which he did most effectively. Father entered and after a warm paternal greeting he sat down opposite me with Robert now sitting in a chair just behind him. I raised the issues of treachery but was interrupted by a loud thump as the body of an intruder hit the floor. Clark's man dragged him outside. Robert intervened at this stage and sought to have the family issues discussed first. He somewhat tersely asked if I had brought my letter of renunciation. Father exploded. He told Robert he was a disgrace and that when the nation was in turmoil and his own father about to be executed by his eldest son all he could think about was his unwarranted inheritance. Father then went on to say that on his death Robert would in fact be a pauper. All the lands of his stepmother that he had counted on would revert to her, or if she died to Lydia, not to him. And if Robert continued to cause trouble he would allow the authorities to investigate a stream of sexual assaults and murders which for decades he had covered up.'

'What did your father mean?'

'I thought you might have uncovered this yourself. Robert is sick as far as women are concerned. He is involved in every form of sexual deviance. He sodomizes women and pigs. Father had to remove many female servants, and at great cost to conceal Robert's behaviour. He was certain that Robert had raped and murdered James Clark's wife.'

'Jesu,' exclaimed Luke as he placed his head in his hands.

'What's wrong, Colonel?'

Luke briefly described the events at Lord Lidford's and the assault on Grace Rutter. His mind raced irrationally forward. Perhaps they too readily assumed that Hastings had killed Willie Calf, Martha Rodd and her sister. Perhaps the girls had been unnaturally raped and murdered by Robert.

'Continue, Sir Nicholas.'

'Robert was in a fury. His whole future, which was potentially so bright if I executed father and gave Robert my letter of renunciation, was suddenly in tatters. He would die a common criminal and young Lydia would inherit the Lordship of the Manor until she married. Father changed from a frail, sad old man into a fiery demon and provoked Robert even further. He revealed he would marry Lydia to our distant cousin Sir Toby Noakes. With my renunciation of the position and Robert disinherited through his criminality Lydia would inherit the estates which would become those of her husband. She would eventually inherit her mother's fortune. Sir Toby Noakes would not only be squire of Charlton Noakes but one of the wealthiest men in England.

Robert exploded. He rose from his chair picked up the rock or statue that Clark's man had let fall to the floor and swung his arm with incredible power and smashed the rock into father's head. He lent over him and sensing he was still breathing drew father's dagger and stabbed him repeatedly. He grabbed a bundle of papers from the table and swept the remainder onto the floor. I was transfixed and before I could say anything Robert ran back into the night.

I was distracted beyond belief. I thought the least I could do was to give this brutal murder the veneer of a political assassination. Father at least deserved that. I took his sword and broke it into two and placed it on the desk in front of him. James Clark came though the concealed door in the panel and told me to leave immediately. He would tidy up and inform the authorities. I told him not to give any details, or admit that he had seen and heard the murder through an eyehole in the panel. I would deal with my brother in due course but I did not want the episode to undermine my mission. To this end I had to execute Clark's man who had seen Robert murder father, and Robert's personal groom whom I knew was a spy for Sir Edward Lampard.

Clark later had second thoughts about directing attention towards a political motive. It might backfire. After I left he removed the broken sword and replaced it with another that he placed in father's scabbard. Since the murder I have kept in touch with the household by meeting Clark in the library or sending messages through Daniel Pyke to his sister Tamsin to forward to Clark. There, Colonel, are the answers to your questions.'

'Sir Nicholas, I do not believe every word of your statement. But I do accept your version of the murder rather than your brother's. Rutter is a small man and physically weak. He could not wield a rock with the force you describe. On the other hand your brother is a very powerful man with excessively large hands. I saw what he did to two of Yalden's men. We must bring him to justice. If I release you, can I have your word as a Spanish nobleman and an English gentlemen that you will accompany me back to Noakes Hall, and make no attempt to escape until we have an admission from your brother.'

'You have my word. I promised myself that I would not leave England until father was avenged.'

'I asked you earlier if Robert had not run amok would you have executed your father?'

'No, I had come to realise that father was not in control of his faculties. He had become repetitive and forgetful, probably a general decline due to drink and age. Sir Anthony was not the real traitor. He was a puppet of the organizing genius behind the transfer of the Royalist faithful into supporters of Cromwell—Lady Elizabeth. She is able, powerful, and dangerous. Do not trust her. She has used her relatives at the King's Court to orchestrate my recall and she could probably do the same to you through her influence at Whitehall. The Hanes family network is wealthy, widespread and powerful. They have determined that the Royalist cause is best served by supporting the Protector than the King in exile.'

Luke released Nicholas and the two men had a long relaxed though often silent supper. Luke found a great empathy with Nicholas. Luke could understand the nobility of purpose and the sense of honour and duty that drove Nicholas to carry out his mission, even if it meant executing his father as a traitor to the King. The vicious animalistic assault on his father by his brother Robert on the other hand was a dishonourable act of savagery that had to be avenged.

'Sir Nicholas, I think that I owe you my life.'

'The golden cape?'

'Was it you? Why would a Spanish catholic count save a Cromwellian colonel?'

'We were both following the messenger to uncover the source and destination of the letters, and I thought your arrival in Charlton Noakes would bring my enemies out in the open. I hoped to take advantage of your investigation to wipe out the enemies of the King.'

Next morning they set out for Charlton Noakes. They laughed about the accidental snatching of Daniel, and Luke took the opportunity on Will's behalf to ascertain the role of Daniel in the Count's activities.

'I showed the lad my letter from the King and asked him to run errands on the King's behalf. He knew his father was an active agent for the cause so he did not suspect that his actions would conflict with his father's.'

Nicholas found Luke's tale of his adventures while following Cuthbert Mowle most amusing. He confessed that he was not aware that he was being followed on any of the nights, but on his visits to the Papist households during the day he admitted to some feelings of ill ease. Luke also told Nicholas a heavily slanted tale of the death of his hench man. 'My sergeant caught up with your man Yalden as he followed me to Dunster. They fought a duel and both are dead.'

'I am sure Giles Yalden died with honour in the name of the King. He was a loyal and faithful servant determined to do his duty. But I am surprised that he attempted to kill my siblings. That was not any plan of mine.'

Luke did not tell Nicholas the whole truth. He felt a modicum of guilt in killing in such a dishonourable fashion the agent of the man who had saved his life. They stopped at the Four Bears where Nicholas gathered a change of clothes. Luke decided to stay there as well while he arranged to smuggle Nicholas into the village undetected, and to send an updated report from Baxter's headquarters to the Protector. Next morning while most of the village was at church Nicholas was smuggled into the Black Swan and would share a room with Daniel until confrontation with Robert was appropriate.

In part Nicholas wished he had not given his word to Luke. He could utilize the secret passages and panels of his ancestral home, appear in Robert's bedchamber, dispatch him and return without being missed. Nor would he tell Luke that from the coppice just beyond the Gap there was an old mining tunnel that cut through the ridge and came out within the manor grounds. A thicket of brambles and boulders obscured its entrance. If Luke did not deal with his brother quickly Nicholas would break his word in the greater cause of justice.

37

Sir Robert wasted no time in exerting his authority as squire. He was free of his father and soon Clark, Basset and Lady Elizabeth would be gone. He ordered Clark to call a meeting of all servants. Some were dismissed and others promoted. Sir Robert would be served by people loyal to him, and not to the memory of his father and stepmother.

He summoned Henry Gibbs and demanded the return of half the glebe land to the manor, and a significant portion of the tithes that his father had permitted to the use of the church. Gibbs was told to announce at the next church service that any lease becoming vacant would no longer be renewed on a black feather rent and Sir Robert would allot the tenancy as a ten-year lease to the highest bidder. He informed Gibbs that he had dispensed with the services of Dr Basset as private chaplain, and would be attending the parish church, and expected the family pew to be available forthwith. The rector would limit his sermons to a half an hour, or the squire would walk out and expect the congregation to follow him.

Sir Robert had given up prospects of marriage with Katherine Basset due to her father's opposition. He was impressed with Lady Mary Lidford and he had to act before Basset poisoned Lidford's mind. Rutter's death had been a financial bonus. That death had cancelled many of Robert's debts and voided his promise to cede assets. Noakes Hall was on the path to financial recovery.

The next day, Sunday, Robert was sitting in the library while the household on his orders were crammed into the chapel to hear Dr Basset's last sermon. It was the last service in the chapel as Robert had plans to utilize the space more effectively. It was another symbol of his power. He had forced dozens of people to listen to boring old Stephen while he, alone of the entire household, did not attend.

He was therefore taken aback when James Clark knocked on the door. The steward did not wait on formalities. 'Sir, that was an excellent performance the other day but it was a pack of lies. You murdered your father, and Cuthbert Mowle is your brother, as you very well know. I can prove both points. My man was outside the door dealing with intruders and heard everything that happened.'

Clark thought it best not to reveal the existence of a hidden panel in the library. Despite over thirty years of living in the house Robert was unaware of most of the hidden passages, secret doorways, and concealed rooms that his great grandfather had built. Clark had informed Nicholas of their location. Robert went a ghastly greenish white and his eyes became mere slits.

'I don't believe you Clark. Your man outside the door disappeared with my personal groom. So why are you telling me this?'

'I can prove it. Make no mistake.'

Clark proceeded to outline the details of the conversation between the father and his two sons. 'I want a deal. Sir Nicholas has disappeared and nothing can bring your father back. I am leaving. I cannot get out of this house fast enough now you are the master. I do not want the cost and agony of formally having you charged with murder as I could not rely on the system to find you guilty.'

'What is it that you want?'

'For my silence I want very little. Although you can never put right what you did to my wife all those years ago, you can make some slight recompense. I kept my peace for the sake of the family, and the generous increase in my income which your father provided. I want you to appoint my son as your new steward and to lease him two additional properties in the village at nominal rent; renew the leases of the families whose daughters you have mistreated at a similar rent: and write to Lord Eglin recommending me for the position of deputy steward. You lose little by this. I am also no fool. I have left a written account of what I know.'

James Clark departed. Robert seethed. This upstart would not ruin him. But for the moment there were more immediate tasks. Colonel Tremayne must remove his troops from Noakes Hall. He would send a bill for their upkeep and that of their horses to army headquarters. He would appoint a new lawyer in place of Hugh Weston and takes steps to sue Tremayne for abduction and wrongful arrest. He had tried to contact Lampard for days without success. He needed this powerful man as a friend. He would hasten the departure of Basset, Clark, Elizabeth, Lydia and their servants. He could not wait to be rid of his unhappy past. He could revert to the days, before his father forbade it, of visiting the girls in Taunton, or inviting them to the Hall, and he would continue to disappear to London with the more willing village wenches—an outlet of which his father was never aware. Now he could do as he liked. That maxim spouting colonel should remember—new lords, new laws.

As Clark was confronting Robert, Nicholas was safely smuggled into Charlton Noakes by Will,—and Luke went to church. He struggled to keep awake as Henry Gibbs announced the new squire's agenda and took his disconcerted flock through obscure passages of Isaiah. Instead of dozing off, Luke planned his next move. He had to act quickly. He wanted to validate what Nicholas had told him regarding his brother's sexual perversion. He would follow up Rutter's suggestion to talk to Dr Basset. After church he would see Basset, and then visit Walter Weston.

He arrived at the Hall in the early afternoon and immediately felt the chill. He asked to see Dr Basset and the servant disappeared leaving him unattended at the door. After much waiting the servant returned without speaking pointed across the hall to a door fronting onto the chapel. Luke fumed at this deliberate insult. He crossed the hall and knocked. Dr Basset immediately answered. He was unaware that the Colonel had been kept waiting at the entrance. No doubt the lackey acted under instructions.

Dr Basset looked his age. He was in his seventies. The strain of his last service in the chapel that had been his spiritual home for the last decade, his anticipated move into Dorset after thirty years in Charlton Noakes and the events of the last three months were evident. Basset was a short man whose baldhead was covered by a tight fitting burgundy coif. He was dressed in a burgundy long coat and his broad white beard had been slightly trimmed.

Luke could not resist the thought that if the beard was all, a goat might preach.

'Colonel, we never had our long talk and now your mission appears to have been accomplished.'

Luke was not sympathetic. He believed that if Basset had told him the full story early in the investigation a lot of time could have been saved. 'Dr Basset do not play games with me. You know full well that my investigation is not over. A bit of information from you and I might be in a position to make an arrest.'

'You don't accept Robert's fairytale? How can I help?'

'Was it true that Sir Anthony, due to a combination of drink, depression and senility was incapable of sustained political activity?'

'Yes, sadly Anthony's health seriously declined in recent years but I think the re-involvement in political activity over the past three months brought back snatches of the old Anthony. In bad periods Elizabeth and I covered for him very well and he still had enough physical strength and political acumen to carry off the part.'

'Was Lady Elizabeth the real leader of the Sealed Knot?'

'I am not privy to the inner workings of the Sealed Knot but Elizabeth, Lord Lidford, and Sir Thomas Odams spent a lot of time together while Anthony drank alone or chatted with me.'

'Did you know that Sir Anthony planned to keep the estate in the Noakes family and ultimately get control of Lady Elizabeth's fortune by marrying his daughter Lydia to his cousin Sir Toby?'

'Yes, a brilliant scheme. Anthony at his best although the idea infuriated Elizabeth. I must admit that just after the murder I suspected that she might have been responsible. She would do anything to protect her daughter and her fortune. If Anthony's plan had progressed there was no way that she could stop her fortune and estates falling under the control of Sir Toby, whom she disliked.'

'Is there anything else you can tell me about Anthony and Elizabeth before I ask you about Robert?'

'Yes, I could not answer your earlier question about Elizabeth and the Sealed Knot in any detail but Elizabeth is a very powerful women in her own right.'

'What do you mean?'

'She has an extensive political network across England including Whitehall, and at the King's Court in Paris. Her father Lord Hanes had four sisters, all of whom married into the highest aristocracy. The many sons of these marriages, Elizabeth's cousins, are now in powerful positions. One is on Cromwell's Council of State. When I first went to Whitehall on behalf of the Sealed Knot I delivered the first letter for the Protector to Elizabeth's cousin.'

Luke was amazed. He pondered on the full implications of this revelation. Nicholas's comment about being recalled, and the links between Charlton Noakes and Whitehall began to make sense. He nearly forgot his line of questioning. 'Robert has problems with women. It was suggested that you could confirm a multitude of cover-ups to conceal his abominations. I need your help now because it happened again a few days ago at Lidford House. Grace Rutter was assaulted in the manner favoured by Robert. There may be two further victims in the village.'

'God forgive me, I wrestled for years with my conscience when this began. Anthony through careful monitoring and effective coercion removed from Robert the opportunity to transgress. Since the old squire's death Robert has obviously fallen back into his old ways. You can see why I was distraught over his infatuation with my Katherine. He was a real nuisance in London and I was grateful when your troopers arrived and brought him back here. I must send Katherine on to Lidford House immediately.'

Before their conversation was completed there was a loud knock on the door and without waiting for an answer Sir Robert strode in. 'Good afternoon Colonel, as your enquiries are at an end I would like you to remove your troops and their horses immediately from my stables. I shall expect compensation for the cost of their upkeep over the past few weeks and after I take advice I may take legal action against you for unlawfully depriving me of my liberty.'

'Sir Robert, you may be the puffed up, toad-like squire of Charlton Noakes with his enemies dead, his income ensured and his name cleared, but my troops are still here under the authority of the Protector who would expect a grateful citizen to willingly assist his men in the exercise of their duty by the free provision of food and services. And I still have a number of unanswered questions. For example, why should I believe your story of what happened at the dam? Also I may wish to take action regarding the lies that you told us initially. I will remove my men when I have tidied up all the loose ends. And I would warn your servants not to snub your visitors or they might retaliate and take out their fury on the master.'

Luke turned toward Stephen Basset. 'Good evening, Dr Basset, and I wish you well at Lidford House. For you, Sir Robert, if I hear that my men are in any way hindered in their duty or deprived of appropriate rations I will place Noakes Hall under direct military control and its petulant squire under arrest. Wait until we have left the county before you behave like a peevish cur. Good day.'

Robert Noakes almost convulsed. He had not been sure whom he hated most—Clark, Basset, or his stepmother. For the moment Tremayne went to the top of his list.

Luke had lost his temper and was concerned that he may have forewarned Robert of impending action. Luke was anxious to see Walter Weston. To calm down he galloped through the manorial grounds, into Winslade Wood, crossed the Devon road, cleared a hedge bordering the Weston farm and rode frenetically across the field to the house. The Constable had noted the unusual mode and speed of entry, and was waiting for him at the barn. 'Colonel, you seem distressed.'

'I have just come from an odious confrontation with that perverted knave, Robert Noakes. Sadly, I took out my fury on my horse. But I am here on a very sensitive matter.'

'How can I help?'

'You know of the unnatural assault on Grace Rutter at Lidford House a week or so ago. Did the Rodd sisters suffer the same indignity?'

'The bodies are with relatives in preparation for tomorrow's burials. The only way to get any information, although I doubt it would be useful as the bodies were immersed in water for some time, and they have been dead for several days, would be to get a doctor in from Taunton. I am loath to upset the relatives. Is this evidence vital to your case?'

'No, it would simply confirm evidence from other quarters.'

'I could ask Mother Sparrow to try to establish any penetration but I think this is way outside her experience. Given the activities of these girls they may have acted willingly in this way from time to time so the evidence would not be conclusive against any rapist. No, Luke I cannot allow the bodies to be examined.'

'Has your investigation of the several village deaths brought up any information that is unexpected?'

'No, the doctor who examined the bodies found by Napp confirmed that they had been dead for some time from their wounds before they were put in, or fell in the water. I suspect they were buried under the hedges at the back of the village plots and the surging water washed them into the ditch where they were found.'

'Has Rutter's body been found?'

'No, I interviewed the old notary who was at Groom's place that day, and a couple of Rutter's men. Their answers are vague, confusing and in part contradictory. No one admits seeing William fall but several imply that Sir Robert pushed him. The two bodies washed up under my hedge raise some issues. Both had their throats cut in an identical manner. They were both senior servants at the Hall who were last seen on the night of the murder. I talked to several of the household and there is no doubt that they were killed on the night of the murder. Why and by whom remains a mystery.'

Luke did not enlighten the Constable regarding Nicholas's confession. He allowed Walter to continue.

'If you accept servant gossip at the Hall it is because they knew too much. Perhaps they witnessed the murder and the murderer had them killed. Yet the manner of their execution is so different from the blunt instrument that killed Sir Anthony I do not think this is the case. I have discovered from a source outside the village that Robert's groom was an agent of Sir Edward Lampard. Seeing that Noakes Hall was a hotbed of Royalist plots it would be reasonable to suspect that the Royalists may have discovered the spy and executed him accordingly. This would be plausible except that the deputy steward was Clark's right hand man and devoted to the Royalist cause. Yet I believe they were killed by the same man.'

'Goodman Weston, I will be frank. I have gathered most of the evidence I need, and when I am ready I will convene a meeting up at the Hall. I would like you as the representative of the law to be present.'

'Would not Sir Edward Lampard be a better choice?'

'Sir, it would not surprise me if within a week or so Sir Edward will be in the Tower of London.'

'You have been a busy man, Colonel. No doubt all will be revealed.'

'I have not told Hugh but I have recommended to the Protector that he appoint your son as High Constable in place of Rutter until a new bench of magistrates can choose a permanent replacement.'

'It may help him decide whether he wants to be a lawyer or a soldier.'

'If all goes well with my enquiry and in his love life Hugh will have time for neither. He will through his marriage to Lydia become squire of Charlton Noakes.'

'We must wait on God, my son.'

38

Tamsin Pyke was given one evening a week break from her role as Elizabeth's personal maid. Every Sunday evening she returned to the Black Swan and ate with her parents and brother. It was a little later than usual when she returned to the Hall and she was anxious to beat Mr Clark's curfew. The servants' door would be locked at midnight. It was nearly that now. As she skirted around the west wing of the house to beat the deadline she noticed that the library's external door was slightly ajar. This would save her from embarrassment should the servants' door be locked. She would slip inside and make it to her room without being seen. She was just about to slip through the door when she became aware of muffled voices. There were at least two persons in the darkened library. She retreated.

Tamsin reached the unlocked servants' door but as she entered the house curiosity overcame her. She moved silently through the kitchen, across the great hall and into the parlour that led into the library. She could still hear the voices. All of a sudden they stopped and Tamsin panicked. She threw herself behind a chest and waited, and waited. No one came out of the room. After several minutes she plucked up enough courage to gently ease the door open. She was surprised to find the room empty but initially assumed the talkers had left through the external door. But that door was shut fast from the inside.

Somewhat amazed at the disappearance of her phantom speakers she headed for the great staircase and her room. Just as she reached the bottom of the stairs adjacent to the kitchen door she heard what appeared to be a muffled scream. She ran through the kitchen door and was hit from behind. Some hours later but before dawn she was found by the kitchen maid whose duty it was to light the fires. The maid informed the deputy steward who was responsible for the household from midnight to sunrise. He decided it was far too early to inform anyone. He helped the maid get Tamsin upstairs and into bed.

Well after the sun was up the deputy went to inform his superior and to his surprise Mr Clark was not in his room. He informed Lady Elizabeth of Tamsin's situation and noted in passing that Mr Clark could not be found. Elizabeth told him to send a servant to the Black Swan to inform Tamsin's parents and to let Colonel Tremayne know that Clark was missing.

Nicholas, Luke and Will were having breakfast together when a servant arrived from the Hall. Will immediately informed his wife who headed for the Hall with her basket of ointments and herbs. Nicholas groaned.

'Luke I have a confession to make. After Daniel fell asleep last night I made my way to the Hall and entered it by one of the secret tunnels. I met with James Clark whom I put in the picture about my own situation. I have been missing for over a week and my men no doubt were frantic and I did not want their activity to cut across ours. He told me that he had just confronted Robert with an ultimatum. Robert would employ his son as the new steward, grant numerous village families new leases at nominal rent, and write James a reference for Lord Eglin or he would reveal what he knew about the deaths of his wife and my father. He was not worried about any violent reaction from Robert because he said he made it quite clear to him that others had this information, and would reveal it if anything happened to him. I think he underestimated Robert's new found arrogance and foolhardiness.'

'I also underestimated you, Nicholas. But you have kept your word and are still here and your unauthorized visitation may be of value.'

Luke and Will headed for the Hall. As they approached the manorial boundary they could see a group of labourers standing around on the edge of the ditch. When they recognised the Colonel they waved wildly and one of then pointed into the ditch and with his other hand gave the impression that he was cutting his throat. 'Will, I think we may have found James Clark.'

The body was Clark's, and Luke instructed the onlookers to inform the Constable and take the body to the inn. Will appeared livid. 'Robert is a sick scurvy knave. Jane Clark was found in exactly the same place years ago.'

As they approached the front door of Noakes Hall Sir Robert strode out and began a tirade in their direction.

'Goodman Pyke, I am sorry to hear about your daughter but you will visit her through the servants' entrance. As for you Colonel you have no further business here and I ask you to leave.'

Luke dismounted. He silently walked up to Noakes and put his face, in breach of accepted good manners within inches of Robert and his blue eyes bored into the new squire's head.

'Stand out of my way. Until I hand over to the Constable, I am here to investigate the murder of James Clark, and I expect the full co-operation of you and your household. William Pyke is here as my acting Sergeant and will enter the Hall at my side, and through this door.'

Robert backed off. Luke and Will headed for Tamsin's bedchamber. When they arrived the room was already crowded with Elizabeth, Nell Pyke, and a couple of fellow servants. Luke ascertained that Tamsin was ready to be questioned. She recounted her story. The voices she heard were Clark and Nicholas. Clark left by the external door which Nicholas closed before disappearing through the panel.

'Tamsin, Mr Clark was a man who kept to a regular routine. What exactly did he do each night before retiring?'

'Mr Clark began his rounds at half past eleven and would first check on the upstairs rooms and finally those on the ground floor. He would then walk around the outside of the house and at midnight he would lock the servants' door, walk through the kitchen to check that the fires were out and then across the hall to his room.'

'Everybody in the household knew these movements?' Tamsin nodded in agreement. Luke turned to Will. 'I think we can reasonably assume that Clark was murdered in the kitchen and that Tamsin was assaulted to enable the murderer to remove the body.'

Will looked elated. 'More than that Colonel. The weapon used on Tamsin was the same one that killed Clark. Clark's wound included in its centre a second indentation where part of the object penetrated further than the rest. Tamsin had the same sort of indentation. The blow that killed Clark was delivered with great ferocity, that on Tamsin's skull was a gentle nudge.'

'Great work, Will. Stay with your daughter. I will inspect the kitchen.'

As Luke left Elizabeth slipped her hand into his and squeezed it very tightly. Luke unsettled by recent information withdrew his, and ignoring her surprised glance, went downstairs to the kitchen. The slate floor of the kitchen had been washed and scrubbed and then covered with a layer of new straw, as it was every morning. The kitchen maid who found the body of the comatose Tamsin said that in washing the floor she was surprised how far across the room Tamsin's blood had spread. Luke was sure that the blood furthest from Tamsin belonged to Clark. It was time to talk to Robert.

Robert had second thoughts on how he treated Tremayne. While the Colonel exercised power it would be wise to discontinue the aggressive stance, although Robert felt good that he had established his position. Vengeance against Colonel Tremayne could wait. Robert never forgot an insult or humiliation.

'I hope Colonel that my household has been co-operative.' Robert simpered.

'Exceedingly so, to the point that I already have a suspect.'

'And who might that be?'

'You Sir Robert.'

'Don't be ridiculous. Why should I murder a man, I admit I detested, at the very time that he is about to leave me. If I murdered him ten years ago my life would have been a lot happier.'

'Unfortunately for you Robert. You did have a motive.' Luke had decided that shock tactics might just work. He would endeavour to throw Robert off balance. 'Yesterday afternoon James Clark presented you with an ultimatum. If you did not give his son employment and land, and give some village families leases under very favourable terms and write a glowing reference for himself he would reveal to the authorities information to your detriment.'

For a moment the colour drained from Robert's face. How did Tremayne know of the conversation? Concern with this issue nearly led him to admit the interview had taken place. Then he saw the answer. Tamsin Pyke had passed the information on to Tremayne when she went home the previous evening. Clark claimed he had informed others. The colour returned to his face.

'Tremayne, everybody knows that you hate me and because of this you are being set up to believe this nonsense. Lady Elizabeth is out to damage my reputation. No such meeting took place. It is the word of the informant against mine. Clark was out to damage me at every opportunity. To tell Tamsin a pack of lies just prior to his departure would have been a clever parting shot. And you fell for it.'

'Robert, wherever the truth lies there remains two simple facts—your steward has been murdered and a servant assaulted. Both, I believe in your kitchen. There have been four murders in this house in recent weeks.'

Robert walked out.

Luke left a message with the obnoxious servant who had obstructed his visit to Basset the previous day. The household would gather in the great hall tomorrow at ten. Luke visited his men before leaving the manor and gave them detailed instructions for the following day. As Luke cantered around the front of the house he could see the tall Elizabeth waving to him from the windows of the long gallery. He ignored her and stared intently ahead. Tomorrow would end the investigation.

Luke returned to the Black Swan and with Hugh and Nicholas planned their operation of the next day with the precision that one would expect from three experienced soldiers. Robert in his quirky way would have puffed up with pride if he had known how much experience and ability was being devoted to his destruction. Late in the afternoon Will returned from the Hall and joined them.

Will sat quietly smiling while the others brought him up to date with their plans. He could not contain himself any longer.

'Gentlemen, I have found the murder weapon. After I left Tamsin I looked around outside the kitchen to see if the murderer had discarded his weapon. I found nothing. I then remembered that two persons had been struck on the head in the vicinity of the library. I went around to that side of the house. Again there was nothing in the garden. Then I looked up. Above the door of the library there is a carved figure of a Greek god holding in one hand a book and in the other an orb. At first I thought it was all carved from one piece of rock. I fiddled with the orb and it came away—a perfect sphere with a shaft like attachment by which it is fitted into the hand of the god.'

'Will, this is your day. First you discover that the same weapon is used on Tamsin as on Clark and now you locate the weapon itself?'

'Luke, I have not finished. It also proves that Sir Robert was the murderer of Sir Anthony.'

'How so?'

'The orb is large. I have reasonably large hands but I had to hold the orb by the shaft. The injuries inflicted on Sir Anthony and Mr Clark indicated that the killer held the orb in his hand and hit the victim first of all with the shaft. The cutting edges of the shaft and the massive weight of the orb itself account for the wounds that the victims suffered. Only someone with gigantic hands could hold the orb itself and use it as a controlled weapon. And who has the largest hands in the county?'

'At last, the evidence we needed. Great work Will.'

The group settled down to a few drinks. Some time later Nell Pyke returned from the Hall and approached Luke.

'Colonel, there was a minor accident at the Hall after Will left. Mother Sparrow who had come up to the Hall to help after she returned from her daughters late this afternoon. She slipped on the stairs and knocked herself out. When she came to she insisted on getting a message to you. She now remembered the events of the day her house was fired. She wrote a name on this note.'

Luke read the note and smiled. He did not quite believe in Mother Sparrow's powers but her confirmation of what Will had decisively proved, was nevertheless surprisingly comforting. Yet when he retired he was not comforted. His mind and his body were wracked by thoughts of Elizabeth and when he dozed off his dreams became nightmares.

39

Luke slept in and had a late breakfast. He had just finished when a detachment of some twelve troopers arrived under the leadership of the young officer who had helped save his life a few days earlier. Luke thanked him again and asked him his name.

'Cornet John Martin, sir. I am Colonel Baxter's nephew.'

'I hope I didn't make life difficult for you with your uncle regarding the execution of the wounded gooseturds?'

'You don't remember, sir, but I was in command of the escort that failed to save your men. I was pleased to make some amends.'

Luke gave young Martin his instructions. His troopers were to surround the house, remain mounted and prevent any one entering or leaving the building once Luke had started proceedings.

In the half hour leading up to ten o'clock the household gathered in the great hall and were joined by the Westons and Lord Lidford. Luke arrived with Will just before the hour. Nicholas would find his own clandestine path to the Hall. The gathering was surprised that Luke was followed into the hall by his troopers in full military apparel and in addition to their swords, daggers and carbines they held sharpened short pikes. They placed themselves at each of the doors leading from the hall. Luke had marched them in the way he remembered Oliver Cromwell had done when he dismissed his parliaments. Luke Tremayne had a sense of the dramatic.

Robert was uneasy. Why had Luke brought so many troops and why bring them into the house? Perhaps his constant provocation of the soldier had brought a dangerous over reaction. Luke raised his hand and the noise of conversation subsided.

'I was sent here by the Lord Protector to uncover the murderer of Sir Anthony Noakes. Today I bring this enquiry to an end. It is generally believed that Sir Anthony was murdered by William Rutter to improve his chances of obtaining power and property in the village. I was not convinced by that explanation. Recently another witness who was present at the murder has come forward and we have evidence that only a specific person with certain characteristics could have delivered the fatal blow.'

Luke's steel blue eyes bored into Robert trying to seize upon any discernible reaction. The absolute quiet of the room was shattered by the sound of musket fire and the shattering of one of the panes of glass in the window. Intermittent fire continued. Luke ordered his men in the room not to move while Hugh went to investigate. There was much shouting, but the gunfire ceased.

Hugh returned and reported. 'The manor house is under siege by a body of armed horsemen who refuse to leave until they have a member of this household in their hands. However the leader of the attackers was persuaded to cease firing by a gentlemen who seems to exercise control over them and whom I have invited to join us.'

Hugh signalled to the soldier at the main door and a man entered the room—Cuthbert Mowle. It was clear to Luke that Nicholas would keep his word—just. He would see his brother go down, but despite Yalden's demise he had put together a small body of his own men ready to effect his rescue. No doubt if he explained to some of the family's old retainers that he was Sir Nicholas they would have rallied to his support.

Luke turned to the new arrival, 'Welcome, many here would know our visitor as Cuthbert Mowle, a recent arrival in the village. In another environment he is the Count of Varga y Verganza, the special envoy of the would be King of England, and of the King of Spain. However in the context of this enquiry and this house he is the rightful squire, Sir Nicholas Noakes.'

After an initial communal intake of air the room lapsed into absolute quietness. Robert was the first to break the silence and his words were spluttered out in a tirade of simple denial and rebuttal. 'This man is not my brother. He is an impostor.'

'Let us hear his story,' retorted Luke.

Nicholas recounted his role in England and the events of the night of the murder and concluded. 'I accuse my brother and demand justice.'

Luke took control.

'I formally indict you Robert Noakes for the murder of Sir Anthony Noakes, and of James and Jane Clark. Further charges involving the murder of William Rutter and the unnatural rape of several women will be forthcoming. Take him away.'

Robert Noakes jumped to his feet and before a trooper could reach him grabbed his half sister Lydia in his powerful arms and put his dagger to her throat. 'One step closer and I will slit her throat.' Luke could see the terrified expression on Elizabeth's face, and knowing Robert's character the Colonel could not risk any false moves. For Robert it would be the final victory over Elizabeth if he cut Lydia's throat even though the act would bring his own death. Robert held Lydia off the ground with the arm that did not hold the dagger and backed along the wall of the great hall. He suddenly lunged his back against a panel, which sprung open, and in a flash he and Lydia were gone. The hidden door, when reached by the soldiers was shut firmly from the inside.

Lidford comforted Elizabeth while Luke began to break down the door. The rest of his men and those from Baxter's detachment fanned out across the estate. The secret passage would most likely exit within the manorial boundaries. Nicholas would know where it led. He turned to where Nicholas had been standing. Nicholas was gone. The door was finally opened and Luke and Hugh armed with a lighted taper quickly entered the passage. Luke as a child had been brought up on stories of secret passages in which wicked priests and Spanish agents were able to escape as Cornish patriots invested their hideaways. There were always hidden treasures and unexpected turns, cobwebs and vipers, and the constant drip of water. Apart from the sharp descent down a carefully constructed set of stairs made of the same honey limestone of which the house was constructed the rest of the trek was on a slightly upward path. Luke and Hugh did not have to crouch as the tunnel was high and wide.

The floor was of slate and the walls were of basalt. The roof retained the original clay of the area supported by crossbeams at close regular intervals. Hugh believed that they were heading due north under the house and he expected to come out somewhere in the barn or the stable. He was probably right because after a few minutes the tunnel came to an intersection. There were tunnels to the left, probably the stable and to the right, probably the barn, but the main path lay straight ahead. Luke picked up the trail. Although footprints on the floor were hard to see in the tapered light Lydia's farthingale expanded dresses left clear traces along the wall. The marks indicated that the quarry had moved straight on. The tunnel was less maintained beyond the intersection. The floor was no longer slate but clay and the walls appeared more like the dry walling popular in some areas of the county. In parts of the floor they had to go around large boulders that the tunnellers had clearly not been able to remove. Hugh suddenly stopped and yelped. Ahead in the flickering flame they both saw what appeared to be a body. Racing madly towards the prone figure Hugh to his relief discovered it was a bundled up set of skirts. Lydia who normally wore up to seven skirts or petticoats was obviously impeding Robert's escape. Hugh recognised them as the outer skirt and the top underskirt. Both men ran on. Although their assumption that the skirts had been removed for ease of progress seemed reasonable, darker interpretations flashed through their minds. They were dealing with a sexual deviant.

Eventually they saw daylight in the distance. The tunnel came to an abrupt end and a rather poorly constructed looking ladder led them up to a platform hewn out of the rock and a fairly narrow tunnel along which they crawled. At the end of this tunnel there was a small boulder that had hastily been placed over the entrance. Luke pushed it aside and found himself at the back of a cave the entrance to which was some way in the distance. He waited for Hugh and both men worked their way around this boulder-strewn cave. On moving out into the sunlight they found they were almost at the pinnacle of the ridge that ran along the edge of the wasteland. A few paces more they could look down into the neighbouring valley. While heavily forested along the top of the ridge the rest of this valley had been cleared into large farms. There were no villages. Once below the trees Robert would be in open farmland.

They turned around and looked back on Charlton Noakes. Luke saw his men searching various parts of the estate. He waved for some time until one of them recognized him and after a few minutes a trooper reached them. Luke instructed him to send Baxter's men to the entrance of the next valley to block off Noakes's exit, and for his own men, with horses for Hugh and himself, to meet them where they were as soon as possible.

Luke was impressed as the troopers below quickly formed into two groups and followed the paths designated for them. Young John Martin was a capable young officer. After this was over Luke would offer him a commission in his own regiment. Luke's current troop was soon with him and they began the descent into the next valley. Luke assumed that Robert would head further down the valley and escape in the direction of Taunton. Martin's men would deny his exit from the valley and his men would force Robert into their arms. He would not get far and Lydia would soon be safe. This rather self satisfied assumption was immediately destroyed. Hugh pointed out two horsemen going up the valley and not down. Flashes of bright orange, which Hugh blushingly admitted were Lydia's favourite colours for her under layers of petticoat, left no doubt that they were the fugitives.

'They have made good ground. They've stolen horses from that farmhouse halfway up the next hill,' commented Luke. In due course they reached the farmhouse and were met by a distraught young woman. She was relieved to find that these horsemen were in pursuit of her earlier visitor. She was the daughter of the household and her parents and servants were working in distant fields or on their way back from the Taunton market.

The girl explained, 'The man threatened to kill me unless I gave him food. He took my brother's musket and a sword of my father. He made the girl remove most of her clothing and forced me to help remove her farthingale. She was left with a smock and two petticoats.'

The girl thought to herself that two petticoats were still excessive. 'He also made the girl remove her fancy shoes and stole my only other pair which he made her wear. He took a heavy woollen cape and after he left the house I saw him take two of father's horses.' Hugh took the liberty of telling the girl she could keep Lydia's discards as recompense for her trouble. He turned to Luke. 'Where do you think he is heading?'

'There is nothing up this valley except the wastes of Exmoor and the estates of his cousin, Sir Toby. I have no idea where that estate is although some of Martin's men may have been this way to deliver a prisoner. It will be hard to track Robert in such an area although the recent rains may help us. As a boy I spent much time with my father hunting on Dartmoor, but I have no experience of Exmoor.'

40

Luke had to assume that Robert was heading for his cousin Toby's sprawling but infertile estate. Ironically it was the house in which Sir Edward Lampard had been imprisoned until orders from Whitehall had seen him returned to army headquarters in Taunton. Luke was unaware of this relocation. He progressively prised out of reluctant locals the whereabouts of Black Top Manor. Cromwell's cavalry was not popular in these parts.

The Noakes boys, when they visited this estate as youngsters, stayed in one of the deserted farmhouses on the very edge of habitable country. Nicholas had the advantage and when his men reported that Luke and his troopers were heading west and not east he concluded that the farmhouse of their childhood was his brother's destination. With luck and good riding he could beat his brother and Luke to this isolated spot. He wanted to say a final farewell to Noakes Hall and the village but that would have to wait. When Luke's troop finally reached Black Top Manor, after much misdirection by the locals, he was pleasantly surprised by his reception. Sir Toby may live in an isolated area but he was well versed in the political machinations of his fellow gentry. The local squire knew a lot more than he let on.

Why did Colonel Baxter choose this maverick to guard Sir Edward? Was the impressive man who stood before him the mastermind of a major smuggling operation? Was marriage to Lydia a viable possibility or did Sir Toby placate a sick old man? This was not the time for such speculation and

Luke quickly put Toby in the picture, and in his turn Toby apprised Luke of the removal of Sir Edward on the direct orders of the Protector.

'How sad that my cousin should be murdered by his own son and that Nicholas is out there determined to track his brother down before you do. I will come with you. This is a family matter. The Noakes of Black Top Manor for decades have put up with the taunt that we brought disgrace upon the senior branch of the Noakes dynasty. Whatever we did was trivial compared to cousin Robbie. I must try to limit the damage that he has wrought. I can even pretend to play the gallant, and rescue my might have been wife.'

Toby beamed at the thought but returned quickly to the task at hand.

'When Nicholas and Robert were boys my father let the two brothers stay in the furthest farmhouse from the manor in the middle of the moor. They didn't know at the time but they were protected by several of father's shepherds who during the day taught them much about Exmoor. This happened nearly thirty years ago so I doubt that either brother can cope with the vagaries of the moor. Both would still remember their farmhouse. I am sure that is where both brothers are heading.'

Toby, although of the same generation as Sir Anthony, was a decade or more younger. He bore some resemblance to Robert with broad shoulders and rather short build. He had a mass of shoulder length black curly hair and a bushy black beard. He revealed immediate organizing ability and rapport with his servants as he assembled them to assist the Colonel. The group now numbering some twenty or more men followed Toby through his cultivated fields onto the moor itself. Luke, looking down the valley, could just make out young Martin's men who were now following perhaps two hours behind him. The longer evening enabled Luke and Toby to come within sight of the farmhouse before it became dark. Luke halted his men, and with Toby he quietly traversed the open moor land, crawling for the last part up sodden ditches, which since the recent rains were in places full of water.

When they reached the perimeter of the farmhouse Luke recognised the man who was organizing a group of men stationed some distance from, but in front of the farm. It was Nicholas. Toby was right. Cousin Nicholas had got there first and was laying an ambush for his brother. Luke decided that their men would stay some distance from the house and follow Robert and his captive when they arrived toward the house thereby surrounding him. As it was now dark Luke and Toby decided to do nothing until morning.

This did not satisfy Hugh. He could not wait. His beloved was in danger and without consulting Luke or Toby he slipped away. Hugh had noticed that the farm was surrounded by moor land, criss-crossed with ditches on three sides and it would be difficult for Robert dragging an unwilling Lydia to stay hidden in such terrain. On the far side of the farm there were outcrops of rock. Hugh, trying desperately to think like Robert, decided that the fugitive would check out whether the farmhouse was occupied from a vantage point amongst the rocks. Hugh took up a position between two of the largest rocks and waited. He was not surprised that Nicholas's rapidly raised group of Royalist amateurs were so sloppy in their attempts to remain hidden. A cough rang out in the cold air, as did the sound of someone urinating into a water filled ditch. If Robert were already in the area he would have been alerted.

He was, and he had. Robert entered the rocky outcrop well before Hugh and was immediately aware that the farmhouse was occupied, and of Hugh's precise location. It was now too dark for any of the parties to act and they settled down for the night to watch and wait. Even Robert thought this was the safest approach although he moved through the stony hillock and preceded someway up a sunken path, partly water filled and surrounded on both sides by tall sedges that would lead him across the moor. When Lydia was asleep he would return and deal with Hugh.

In the half-light of early dawn Luke awoke and immediately noticed that Hugh was missing. He adjudged correctly that the Captain had gone after his lover. Assuming that Robert and consequently Hugh would have continued north, deeper into Exmoor rather than double back and face oncoming surges of pursuers, he skirted around the eastern side of the farm house and headed towards the rocky hillock to its rear. Just as he made the first cluster of rocks he heard a cry of alarm and pain. He clambered over the first little rise and there on the ground he saw Hugh. Luke was just in time to see another figure disappear between two upstanding rocks. The figure was Robert, who clearly annoyed that he had been disturbed before he had finished his business, aimed a small boulder at the pursuing Colonel. The pursuit had to take second place to helping Hugh. A large gash undoubtedly caused by a rock had opened up Hugh's head. There was blood splattered over the rocks.

Luke stood on the hillock and called out. 'Sir Toby, send some men over here. I have found Captain Weston badly wounded. Our fugitive has just run off further into the Moor. I will follow.'

Luke half ran and half walked along this sodden, often water covered, path and when it straightened out for brief periods Luke saw Robert some distance ahead. Robert appeared to be half carrying and half dragging Lydia. As the path twisted and turned Luke was not sure where his quarry was until he suddenly turned a corner and the path opened out into a broad clearing with a pond on the right hand side and a tall almost perpendicular rocky cliff face on the left. There in the middle of the clearing was Robert. Lydia was seriously impeding his progress and he had decided to kill her. With so many people chasing him her bargaining value was over.

As Luke challenged him he drew his sword, but not to fight. Robert intended to slice Lydia's throat. He knew how Luke would react. While Luke stopped to tend the dying Lydia he would escape. As he tried to manoeuvre his victim into the right position for the deadly deed Lydia found some superhuman power that enabled her to jump away from him with such force that with horror Luke saw her fly through the air and fall with a deep throaty splash into the pond.

He was about to clash swords with Robert when Lydia began struggling and screaming that she was sinking and being dragged down. Luke suddenly realised it was a watery bog. He knew nothing of such phenomena except that he should drag Lydia out before she sank further into the mire. Robert also assessed the situation and saw that this provided him with the opportunity to escape. Killing Tremayne was a lesser priority than escape and now without Lydia he would outpace his pursuers. As Luke moved to the edge of the bog Robert disappeared further up the track. Luke in his ignorance mistook a heavily algae covered part of the pond for its firm edge and as he moved to reach Lydia he slipped and fell in himself. He tried to calm Lydia but he was at a loss as to what to do. As he moved closer to Lydia he was drawn deeper into the mire. Before panic set in he heard the canter of a sole horseman sloshing up the path. Round the corner came Nicholas.

'Stop moving Luke. As a boy I discovered the secrets of these bogs from one of the local shepherds. If you don't move you are safe. Lydia you are so light you will almost float. Just stay still. I will throw you some large branches to hold onto until our men reach you and drag you out. I will get my brother and avenge the family honour. I will see you both again before I leave England but at a time and place of my choosing.'

'No you won't my dear brother,' echoed a voice from high on the rocks.

There on top of the pinnacle stood Robert his musket pointed directly at Nicholas. All three sensed their vulnerability. Robert would shoot Nicholas and then with plenty of time to reload he would pick Luke and Lydia off as they stood hopelessly inert in the quagmire. Robert directed his musket at the heart of his brother who stood as befitted a Somerset gentleman and Spanish count rigidly at attention with his eyes focused on his brother. As Robert was about to fire a creature emerged from behind Robert and threw itself upon him sending both of them hurtling down the steep cliff face and landing with sickening thuds on the jagged rocks at its base.

Nicholas raced across to the body of his brother. Ironically his head had been caved in by the force of the fall but he was still alive. Nicholas drew his dagger and cut the throat of his brother intoning several times, 'For family and father'. He then turned towards his friends.

'Sweet sister, until you marry you have all the rights of the squire of Charlton Noakes. I will bring my letter of renunciation when we meet again.'

Luke interjected, 'What or who was it that saved our lives?'

Nicholas picked his way through the rocks at the base of the cliff to the second crumpled body. It was lifeless. Nicholas rolled it over and was transfixed with surprise, 'Jesu, Luke, we have been saved by a dead man. It is Rutter. However I must go, as I am now once more a fugitive from your justice but I will see you again soon.'

Nicholas raised his sword and saluted Luke and his half sister and rode back the way he had come. After a period of almost an hour Luke and Lydia heard the squelch of many horses coming up the path. It was a mixed group of Toby's men and his own. Toby spoke. 'I am sorry Colonel that we have taken so long. My cousin's men blocked the path until Nicholas returned. He apprised us of what has happened here so let us get you out and the bodies back to the manor house. Mistress Lydia you will be pleased to know that Captain Weston has a very sore head but has regained consciousness and appears to be alright.'

On the way back to Black Top manor Lydia spoke to Luke.

'I cannot believe that I was saved by that horrible man. How did he come to be here?'

'I do not know, Lydia. He probably heard that Robert had raped his daughter and with so many groups in pursuit—my men, Nicholas's group, Sir Toby's retainers and Martin's troopers—he mingled in and was accepted as a fellow pursuer. He may have followed me and left the path earlier and circled around to the other side of the cliff face when he heard Robert speaking with us. Sometimes I think God's justice is more appropriate than man's. In the end it was what Robert did to Grace that caused his death, not the murder of his father.'

41

A WEEK LATER AT NOAKES Hall Luke met with Elizabeth, Lydia, Hugh and Walter Weston and Will Pyke. He did this with some urgency as he had orders to return immediately to London. Colonel Baxter and the civil authorities would handle any outstanding matters.

Before meeting with the others Elizabeth spoke to Luke.

'Given what has happened over the last three or four months neither of us have had time to really talk about our situation. I know that Richard is convinced that you and I should marry and live happily ever after. I am torn between two strong emotions. At times I believe that I need time to adjust to the changes—moving out of a house where I have lived for twenty years, relocating in a strange area and creating a new household. All this sometimes appears overwhelming. On the other hand I know how I feel when I am with you. It is not only physical but also deeply emotional. You make me feel young and beautiful with the whole world in front of us. I can hardly bear to be without you.'

'Elizabeth, we are similar. Part of me wants to be with you forever, yet I have serious doubts. I am not sure that my military upbringing and attitudes could cope with being the penniless husband of the wealthiest woman in England. Could our love survive the day to day routine of such an existence There is a lot of truth in the maxim "Go down the ladder when you marry a wife; go up when you chose a friend." We are good friends. Let's keep it that way.'

'Luke, if that is all that worries you our marriage settlement will not be like the one with Anthony. All that I have on our marriage will, according to the common law of England, become yours. You will inherit father's fortune and I know that he would be proud that the boy he was so fond of should have the care of his dynastic inheritance. You would be one of the wealthiest men in England and surely in that position you would not feel inferior to your wife.'

Luke ignored Elizabeth's response. 'There is a second reason. All I have done for more than twenty years is to soldier. I know nothing else. All my energies and thoughts have been concentrated on the particular military assignment before me. I fear that I would miss such activity and it might provide a negative in our relationship. I have seen how it has cut across my feelings for you during this investigation.'

'Luke, given your activities in recent months I am sure you could adapt to the political life and intrigue of county politics in which as a great landowner you would exert a powerful influence. You could become the new Anthony Noakes or Edward Lampard, or if you prefer we could make Cornwall our base instead of Somerset.'

'Elizabeth, I am not being honest. So far I have let my heart dominate. There is a deeper reason that cools my love for you. Trust. It is said "Half the truth is often the whole lie." Throughout my investigation you have not told me the truth either regarding your relationship with Sir Anthony, your role in the Sealed Knot or your vast network that penetrates to Whitehall itself. You were probably responsible for the attack on me before I left Whitehall.'

'I did not know that it was you who would be sent. Yes, I admit that our friends were concerned that if Cromwell sent an army man to Somerset he might get in the way of the delicate negotiations that were proceeding here. After all you admit that you do not like your Lord Protector getting cosy with Royalists. Whatever else you think I have done it has been for the cause. You of all people cannot belittle me for putting greater interests above my own.'

'Elizabeth, give ourselves more time. If after I return to London and you settle into your new home, and Hugh and Lydia are happily married, we still feel like we do now, then we can reconsider the situation.'

'Luke, we do not have much time. Neither of us is young and I know how Richard regrets that he never remarried after his wife's death. I do not want to make the same mistake. I will remarry, but I prefer my new partner to be you.'

Luke was trying to avoid an embrace when Tamsin entered to announce that the others were in the parlour waiting for them. The group informed each other of recent and projected developments. Luke's final order from the Protector under his current assignment was to combine his return to Whitehall with escorting Sir Edward Lampard to the Tower of London. Lampard would stay there pending the outcome of his trial for treason. As Government agents had intercepted letters from Lampard to the King Luke felt that Nodding Ned would get his just deserts. Luke was happy that his suggestions to the Protector that Hugh be made High Constable were ignored. The Protector announced that Walter Weston would be the new High Constable and with that elevation, the property whose owner would provide the next village Constable was the Black Swan. William Pyke would be the new law in Charlton Noakes.

Elizabeth had organised for the banns for the wedding of her daughter Lydia and Captain Hugh Weston to be read for the next three Sundays and the marriage to take place within five weeks. From that time Hugh would be the new squire of Charlton Noakes and had already indicated that he would renew the leases of the villagers, not at a token black feather but at a rate about a third of that intended by Robert. Grace Rutter had been left the freehold properties of her father in the parish but sold them to Elizabeth who leased them to a number of locals. Elizabeth would move out of Noakes Hall and make one of her Dorset properties her home as she did not wish to be too far from her daughter, or as Luke could not help thinking, from Lord Lidford. Hugh acted to reconcile local Royalists and Parliamentarians. He appointed Matthew Clark as his steward.

Luke revealed that when he returned to the Black Swan after the Exmoor adventure there was a letter from William Rutter awaiting him.

> *'Dear Colonel, I am still alive. However if I do not survive much longer I want ter put the record straight. I kidnapped Robert Noakes ter force him ter change 'is leases into freehold and ter give me the first option. Earlier I tried to coerce young Clark out of his tenancy so Noakes could begin the process. I intended ter make Robert break the dam wall, (and my men*

would have confirmed that they saw him do it) in order to rebuild the village and grant leases on my terms. Unfortunately my careful structure did not break away at Noakes's pathetic attempt ter dislodge the wedge. I went a little too close ter him endeavourin' ter free it up. He twisted suddenly and pushed me over the edge. My fall took away a significant part of the wall. By sheer good fortune the ragin' torrent threw me away from the rocks and lodged me in a deep side channel where I was stuck for a day amid logs and reeds. Sampson Groom found me and I have been staying with him. Today my men discovered that Robert Noakes was accused of murdering his father and raping my daughter and that you were chasin' 'im inter Exmoor. I suspected he was going for Black Top Manor. I am headin' there now.

I will avenge my daughter. Your servant William Rutter

Lydia remarked quietly, 'He was an evil man, but he loved his daughter, and he did save our lives.' The silence that followed the reading of Rutter's letter and Lydia's comment was suddenly shattered by much noise in the wall of the parlour and one of the panels swung aside. Nicholas emerged.

'Do not try to arrest me Luke. The few men I have left are in the various tunnels of the house and will emerge to protect me. Matthew Clark knows the layout of these and as your new steward, Hugh, he will give you an interesting tour. Robert was not aware of most of them. Sister, here is the letter renouncing my rights as squire of Noakes Manor, and of my allegiance to the government of England. From the moment I leave here Nicholas Noakes is truly dead, and I become forever the Count of Varga y Verganza, faithful servant of his most Catholic Majesty.'

He handed Lydia a sealed letter. 'It is one of my regrets that I never knew you as a sister, and you may never forgive me for ordering the execution of your mother, but I am sure that you and your children will be a blessing to the family, and although the Noakes name will disappear the Noakes blood will continue in the new Weston dynasty. I am glad to see Hugh that you appear fully recovered. It looks like a happy ending all round except for you and I, Luke.'

'What do you mean Nicholas?'

'I failed to remove the leadership of the Sealed Knot, and you have been seriously misled by Lady Elizabeth, Lord Lidford, Sir Edward Lampard and even by my fellow Papists. You have been told that the political events in this county are related to attempts of the Royalist gentry led by Lady Elizabeth and Lord Lidford to reach a temporary agreement to support the Protector's administration for the time being and that given this there should be reconciliation at the local level between former Royalists and Parliamentarians in support of the Protectorate.'

'And is that a lie?'

'Yes, my dear Colonel. It is a lie. The truth should put you and I on the same side. The agreement is far more fundamental than the fairytale concocted by my stepmother and her friends. You will see why I was willing to execute her in the name of King Charles. Her escape was the biggest failure of my mission.

Luke, the gentry of this county are planning to make Cromwell king. They want a Cromwellian dynasty. They want to give you King Oliver. I am in England to defend the rights of the legitimate house of Stuart because in English law once a ruler is recognised by Parliament as King, and can exert monarchical powers he is the King. If stepmother and her cohorts succeed Charles will never return. I know you and the army oppose the return of monarchy in any form. Your comrades have died in their thousands to protect that principle. Neither of us wants to see Oliver Cromwell as King. You and I should drink to that. To General Cromwell, and King Charles.'

He lifted an imaginary goblet to Luke and pulling his golden cape around him stepped back through the panelling, and was gone. Luke turned his cold blue eyes on Elizabeth and left the room without speaking.

Nineteen months later a newly assembled parliament dominated by the gentry offered the Crown to Oliver Cromwell.

Lightning Source UK Ltd.
Milton Keynes UK
UKHW041835041222
413394UK00010B/32/J